AN ANGELIC OFFER

Rhea was determined she would not find him charming; she would not smile back at him. But if Deacon wanted to work at her store, she'd darn well work his hide off. "You can organize the stock back here, but you will not, under any circumstances, come out front."

"Believe me, I'd rather sit down to dinner with Gabriel and his cronies than set foot on the other side of that curtain."

Rhea frowned. "Gabriel?"

That crooked little smile got bigger. "You know— big wings, shiny halo, that whole 'guess what, Mary?' thing."

Rhea sputtered and gaped, and when she couldn't contain it anymore, she laughed right out loud at the absurdity of it all. Angel Gabriel indeed.

"Can I open up now?" She pushed out of her chair again, but he still wouldn't let her pass.

"Not yet." His eyes, still sparkling, held her gaze steady. "Let me be nice to you…"

Other *Leisure* books by Laura Drewry:

THE DEVIL'S DAUGHTER

LAURA DREWRY

DANCING *with the* DEVIL

LEISURE BOOKS NEW YORK CITY

A LEISURE BOOK®

December 2008

Published by

Dorchester Publishing Co., Inc.
200 Madison Avenue
New York, NY 10016

ISBN 10: 0-8439-6049-3
ISBN 13: 978-0-8439-6049-5

Printed in the United States of America.

10 9 8 7 6 5 4 3 2 1

Visit us on the web at www.dorchesterpub.com.

ACKNOWLEDGMENTS

This book is dedicated to my three amazing sisters:

Soo, my one-woman entourage
Don, who continues to pray for my sorry arse
and Annie, with love and prayers.

As always, enormous thanks to Ron, Thomas, Michael & John, my editor Leah Hultenschmidt, my agent Holly Root, and a very special thank-you to Sean, who went back in after the fire to bring out my laptop and manuscript.

CHAPTER ONE

Penance, TX
Spring 1882

"Hell hath no fury . . ." Deacon paused at the bottom of the steps and eyed the ramshackle cabin. The last time he'd seen it, he'd all but expected it to collapse under a great sigh of aged wood and chipped paint.

He should have known better.

Much like its tenant, the house remained standing, determined to survive, daring something—or someone—to try and knock it over.

Sparse patches of weeds and brilliant yellow dandelions dotted the narrow yard, all fenced in by rickety wooden rails that looked like they'd blow over with the first big gust. From around back came the constant clucking of chickens and a faint waft of cow dung.

Ah, to be back among the mortals again.

Deacon had no sooner lifted his freshly polished boot to the bottom step when the front door banged open, and out she blew with twenty-four inches of Winchester leveled at his forehead. Even *she* couldn't miss at this range.

Gazing down the length of the sleek black barrel, he dared to climb the first step.

"Hello, Rhea." He moved up one more, eyeing that twitchy trigger finger of hers.

"Go to hell."

He stopped, chuckled softly. "Just got back, actually."

Rhea's coffee-colored eyes narrowed; her heart-shaped face seemed thinner than usual and her lips, usually full and smiling, were drawn together in a tight line. Much of her long brown hair had fallen from its loose braid and now hung in chaotic waves over her shoulders and across her forehead. Her dress, an abominably ugly black rag, draped from her frame as though she were nothing more than a post it had been tossed over.

Deacon frowned. To look at her now, one would never believe she had a waist, let alone curves that could send a man over the edge of sanity.

Shifting the rifle a little, she adjusted her grip and steadied her stance. "What d'you want?"

Best start with something small. He tipped his face up to hers and smiled slowly. "I suppose it would be too much to expect dinner?"

A loud snort ripped from her delicate throat. "The only meal you'll get from me is a mouthful of lead."

Deacon fought back a laugh. She'd never been overly concerned about the powers he wielded or what he could do to a little spit of a thing like her. No, that had never been Rhea's way.

He twirled his black bowler hat casually in his hands, but never took his gaze away from her or her rifle. "That's not very hospitable of you."

"If it's hospitality you want," she spat, "you best go see your friend Salma."

"Salma . . . ?" Deacon grimaced slightly. "Oh, *her*."

"Yes, *her*."

He lifted his right shoulder in the barest of shrugs. "She never meant anything to me."

Another snort. "She meant enough that you took her to bed."

"Pfft. That's how it would seem, yes." He considered moving up a step, but the look in her eyes kept him still. "But I can explain about that and how things have changed. *I've* changed."

"So have I. Now get."

"Rhea—"

The sound of her cocking the rifle echoed across the dry, deserted yard. Deacon backed down the steps slowly, his palms up.

"How about a cup of coffee? That's not asking too much, is it?"

The first shot sprayed loose gravel across the toes of his shiny black boots. All that time he'd spent buffing and polishing them . . . What a waste.

"Now, Rhea—"

The second bullet hit the dirt between his feet. Damn, she could cock that thing fast.

"You've been practicing."

The third shot would have hit him directly in the groin if he hadn't anticipated it and leapt out of the way.

He almost laughed at the absurdity of the situation, but choked it back when she stopped to reload.

"Let me explain—"

She lifted the rifle and set the sight directly at his chest. "No."

"Rhea—"

She squeezed her right eye closed and focused her left on the gun sight. "One . . ."

"I'm sorry."

"Two . . ." Her fingers curled tighter around the barrel.

"Be reasonable."

"Thr—" The word died behind the blast of her next shot.

Burning pain ripped through his right shoulder and

sent him staggering back into the fence, the echo of the last shot taunting him as it repeated across the dry land.

Blinking, he frowned at his shoulder, then back at Rhea. Eyes wide with shock stared back at him in disbelief. Her mouth opened in a small O, but she didn't lower the rifle.

"You shot me."

After a second, she blinked hard and gave her head a quick shake. "You should've moved." Another blink, this one followed by a stiff swallow.

"I tried!" He pulled a neatly folded handkerchief from his breast pocket and pressed it against the open wound, never taking his eyes off Rhea.

She shook the hair back from her face. "No you didn't. You could have just . . . you know . . . *appeared* . . . over there."

"In case you weren't listening," he snarled, "things have changed."

She didn't look convinced, but her death-grip on the gun loosened slightly. "How?"

His boots were filthy, his jacket was ruined, and *now* she wanted to talk. Women!

"He took my powers . . ." Good thing the fence was there to lean on.

"Why?"

Deacon dared look away from her, knowing full well she could easily take him down with one more shot and probably would. Damn, his shoulder burned.

"I was supposed to . . ." His now-scarlet handkerchief seeped blood over his hand and down the sleeve of his ruined jacket. A body only had so much blood, and there seemed to be an awful lot of it flowing down his arm in warm red rivers. That couldn't be good. "I, um . . ."

All this blood was enough to make a mortal man queasy. Good thing he wasn't . . . Oooh, what was that?

His stomach dipped and shifted, causing an even odder reaction in his knees. He lifted his head to look back at Rhea—and instantly regretted it. The ground beneath him began to spin in slow, lazy circles. Daylight faded to shadows until he could see nothing except a tiny dot of light directly in front of him. And in that dot stood Rhea, the rifle still cocked and ready.

He shook his head to clear it, but that made everything worse. The ground spun faster, the shadows grew darker and tighter, and his stomach threatened to revolt any second. If he didn't find his balance soon, he'd end up on his backside in the dirt.

"Maybe you should sit down." Rhea's voice, guarded, but concerned, seemed a hundred miles away. "You don't look so good."

"Don't . . . be . . ." He gripped the fence rail tighter. Each breath was more difficult than the last. "I'm f—"

Rhea didn't move for a long time. She'd shot him; she'd really shot him.

Deacon.

The son of Satan.

But how . . . and why hadn't he moved? He'd always loved to do that disappearing and reappearing thing on her, but he hadn't done it this time.

And now he lay completely motionless in her yard. *Was he dead?*

She blinked hard, shook her head.

"Think."

There was no way the shots had gone unnoticed, so it would only be a matter of time before someone came to investigate.

That was the problem in a town this small; a person couldn't burp without everyone knowing about it.

One step at a time, she made her way down the stairs,

barely blinking, keeping the rifle cocked and at the ready. The Deacon she knew would never allow dirt on his clothes, so he was either really hurt or she was in a heap load of trouble.

His bowler hat lay a few feet away, covered in dry Texas dust; his boots were scuffed and dirty from her bullets and from scraping against the ground when he fell. And his jacket . . .

Oh no, Deacon would never allow blood—especially his own—to stain his precious suit. She pushed the toe of her boot against his hip and then jumped back, braced for his attack.

Nothing.

She did it a second time, but still he didn't move. Finally she lowered the rifle and nudged the barrel right up against his ribs. Not so much as a flinch.

After another long moment, she crouched beside him, torn between what he deserved, what would make her life infinitely easier, and what she knew must be done.

There had been a time when she was convinced she loved the lying cur and that he loved her. She'd been so stupid back then. Stupid and blind. He'd seduced her with such finesse, she hadn't even realized it was happening until it was too late.

Rhea shook the memory free and swiped her sleeve across her eyes. If she had any sense, she'd let him bleed to death right there in her yard.

But she'd never been terribly sensible when it came to Deacon.

She crouched over him, frowning at the changes she hadn't noticed before she'd shot him. His golden brown hair, always kept short and neat, tickled the tops of his ears and curled slightly against his neck. His usually smooth complexion now creased slightly across his forehead and around the corners of his eyes. Rhea's fingers twitched against the urge to touch his square jaw, to caress the bone structure she'd memorized so thoroughly and ease each one of those lines from his perfect face.

Scratches on his precious boots were too deep and worn to have been made today, even with the bullets flying. His fancy black suit—usually crisp, clean and pressed—seemed oddly faded—just slightly, mind you, but faded nonetheless. Even his shirt, always brilliantly white and starched stiff, appeared a shade duller.

On anyone else, it wouldn't have seemed odd, but on Deacon . . .

Rhea frowned. Come to think of it, his eyes hadn't been right, either. Normally a soft and laughing blue, they'd seemed a bit tired and darker when she'd stared into them down the barrel of her rifle.

Damn it.

With great reluctance, she set the safety on the rifle, laid it on the ground and moved around to Deacon's head. She grabbed him under the arms and began to drag him toward the steps, cursing every time she tripped on the hem of her skirt.

Good grief, he was heavy! Inch by inch, she managed to heave him up the steps and in through the front door. A thick, dark streak of blood trailed down his arm, across the porch and over the floor behind him.

She straightened, took a deep breath and hoisted him, one end at a time, up onto her straw tick in the corner. If she had any strength left, she would have hauled him through to her brother's room and up onto his bed, but her muscles screamed at the mere idea.

No, Deacon would be fine on her bed for now.

When she was certain he wouldn't roll off, she darted back outside, retrieved the rifle and set it beside the door.

How on earth was she going to explain this? Women

just didn't go about shooting their "husbands," especially when those husbands were supposed to be dead already.

Once Mr. Worth caught wind of this, he'd no doubt print it on the front page of his cursed paper.

SHERIFF'S SISTER SHOOTS DEAD HUSBAND.

Newspaper or not, she was in a heap of trouble.

Rhea dug around the kitchen area, gathering the sharpest of all the dull knives, the pot of lukewarm water from the stove and a clean sheet. After dumping the supplies on the floor next to the bed, she went back for one more thing: the last of Colin's whiskey.

She gulped a large swallow, gagged against the burn and threw a silent curse at Deacon. Just seeing him again was enough to make her chug the rest of the bottle, but he needed it more than she did.

With fumbling fingers, she reached beneath his jacket, yanked his shirt from his waistband and began the arduous task of releasing the perfectly aligned buttons. It was bad enough she'd shot a hole through his precious silk sleeve; there'd be no telling what he'd do if she actually went so far as to cut the shirt away from his body or rip off a single one of those mother-of-pearl buttons.

Rhea rolled her eyes. *Vanity, thy name is Deacon.*

When the shirt was finally opened, she took the jacket and shirt cuffs of his good sleeve and tried to drag them down his arm.

"This would be a whole lot easier if you would just bend your elbow a little," she muttered.

She tugged, wiggled, heaved and jerked until his good arm finally pulled free of its sleeve. After another small pull from the whiskey bottle, she climbed up on the bed and positioned herself at his head. She lifted him by the shoulders, mindful of his wound, then used her own shoulder to keep him up as she pulled his jacket and shirt from around his body. When they were free, she eased him back down and slipped the sleeves from his wounded arm.

She threw the shirt and jacket over the back of a chair, then turned back to her patient. A dusting of dark hair covered his bronzed chest, and for a startling moment, she wondered what it felt like. Would it be coarse like a beard, or soft and silky like the hair on his head?

"Ninny." She scrubbed her hands over her face before turning her full attention to the wound itself. Fortunately, the bullet had missed the bone and sliced straight through the fleshy part of his upper arm, saving her the nasty job of trying to dig it out.

Unfortunately, it also meant the ragged wound was open and seeping blood onto the quilt.

Where was that hanky he'd used?

"Never mind," she muttered as she shoved him, none too gently, until he lay half on his side, half on his stomach. The sight of his bare back froze the breath in her lungs.

From shoulder blade to hip, scars zigzagged across his skin in countless shapes and lengths. A few looked as though they'd been left by open cuts, while others— like the large one above his right hip—were unmistakably burn marks.

"What on earth . . . ?" She ran her finger along the ragged edge of the large burn, where it puckered slightly, and then across the patch of skin that appeared stretched and thin. It looked as though . . . It couldn't be . . . but it looked as though many of the marks were new scars over top of old ones.

"Sweet Mother of God." Rhea exhaled slowly. What

could he have possibly done to deserve such punishment? The agony he must have suffered . . .

No. She wouldn't feel sorry for him. He didn't deserve her pity, and he wouldn't want it anyway. After a quick mental shake, she reached for the sheet, cut it in long even strips, then set them across his hip for easy access. While she'd been worrying over his other wounds, his newest one continued to bleed.

She tied a strip above the wound, then pressed a few others against both sides. When the bleeding slowed, she eased the pressure from the back of his shoulder and tipped the whiskey bottle over the wound.

She wet an end of one strip in the tepid water and did her best to clean the blood from around both sides of the wound before dousing the area with more whiskey and wrapping his shoulder with the remaining strips of sheet.

Curse her bad aim. And double-curse his poor reflexes. She hadn't meant to actually hit him; but then again, she hadn't expected him to move so slowly either.

She sat back on her haunches and let out an enormous gush of air. Now what?

Wait for him to recover? Or die? No, she wasn't that lucky. If he'd been telling the truth, he had no powers, so where did that leave him?

It left him on her bed, that's where. And not just lying there either, but *bleeding* there; one more mess for Rhea to clean up.

Typical Deacon. He always—

Ernest Miller burst in through the door, breathless, his hat askew and a huge stick in his hand. Rhea jumped back, knocking the empty whiskey bottle sideways, but she managed to grab it up before it smashed on the floor.

Ernest stumbled toward her, his gaze darting all around

until he noticed Deacon's motionless form on the tick. "Are you okay?"

"I'm fine." Rhea shook her head at the boy and set about gathering up the remaining supplies. "Who's minding the store?"

"I locked it up," he said, gasping over every word. "Folks said they heard shots . . . The sheriff's out at the Dietrich place . . ." With shaky hands, he dropped the stick, adjusted his hat and gripped the back of a chair for support. "Who's that?"

"He's, um, he used to be a friend of Colin's." It wasn't a lie—Deacon really had known her brother—but it wasn't exactly the whole truth either. Any friendship they might have had was destroyed the last time Deacon had come to town.

Ernest bent at the waist, breathing hard. "And you shot him?"

Shooting Deacon obviously wasn't the smartest thing she'd ever done; in fact, she'd just doubled the problems she already had. "He took me by surprise."

Ernest slumped into a chair across from Deacon and eyed the bottle in Rhea's hand. "Can I get something to drink?"

"There's water out in the barrel."

Without a second glance, Rhea set to cleaning up the blood trail on the floor. Ernest had no doubt run the two miles from the store, but she didn't need his protection, she didn't want his protection, and she thought she'd made that perfectly clear the last time he came to her rescue waving a makeshift weapon.

She watched out the small window as he walked toward the rain barrel and swallowed a dipper-full of water. A second later, it came shooting back out his nose and mouth, toppling him to his knees in a fit of choking gasps.

He caught her eye through the window and held up a hand to wave off her concern. She snorted softly. Oh, she was concerned alright—concerned he'd really hurt himself and she'd be forced to put him up in the bed next to Deacon.

Rhea sighed. It was going to be a helluva long day.

CHAPTER TWO

Deacon pried his eyes open, then squeezed them shut against the pain that shot up his shoulder. What the—?

Rhea.

She'd shot him. Took her four shots, if he recalled correctly; but she'd finally hit him, and he'd gone down hard, without the least bit of style or finesse.

Damn it. Living without powers was going to be more difficult than he'd anticipated.

Voices outside, muffled by the squawking chickens, prodded him to sit up. One of the voices was Rhea's, but he couldn't make out the other. With a long inhale, he eased his body off the lump of porcupine quills Rhea called a bed and stood in the middle of the room, steadying himself against a chair back until he gained his balance.

Tight, even strips of cloth wrapped his shoulder and upper arm, but the rest of his upper body was bare. Deacon ground his teeth against a rising curse and set to finding his shirt.

If Rhea had been the one to tend him, she would have seen . . . everything. A sick feeling pitted his stomach. Being shot was one thing, the physical agony his father had repeatedly laced across his back was yet another; both were manageable.

But if Rhea looked at him with so much as an ounce of pity . . .

Where the hell was his shirt?

He lifted blankets, stooped to look under the table and on the seat of both chairs, each movement shooting new pain up and down his arm. The cabin was too small to hide anything, so where had she put it?

"You need to go back to the store." Rhea's voice, low and tight, floated through the crack under the door. "We can't afford to be closed in the middle of the day."

He strained to hear the rest of the conversation outside, but their voices were too low. If he could just find his—

"To hell with it." Pushing open the door to Colin's room, he grabbed the first shirt he could find. It was a horrible scrap of plain blue cotton, worn at the elbows and missing the first two buttons, but at least it would cover him. He eased his injured arm in first, then the other, buttoning it as he walked toward the door.

The cotton scraped against his skin like gravel. How did humans wear such fabric every day?

"You can't stay here alone with him," the second voice said. "It ain't right."

"What do you think is going to happen?" Rhea snapped. "In case you hadn't noticed, I shot him—"

"Hell of a shot, too." Deacon grinned over a wince as he stepped out onto the small porch.

Rhea blanched as she stood up from the bucket she'd been bent over and flicked out a twisted piece of laundry. His white silk shirt.

"You're fine." She rolled her eyes, but not before he saw the flash of concern she tried to hide. "The bullet barely nicked you."

His shoulder throbbed, his head began to spin slowly and his stomach pitched, but still he laughed right out loud. She could pretend she wasn't worried about his arm as much as she wanted. He'd seen the truth in her eyes.

Her false bravado was exactly the kind of thing that made Deacon enjoy her all the more. Beneath his horrible cotton shirt, each of his scars prickled sharply, forcing him to remember how much each small enjoyment had cost him.

The young man Rhea employed at her store stood nearby, his hat clutched between his hands, his wheat-blond hair matted with sweat. Though they'd never been formally introduced, Deacon knew who he was from Rhea's past descriptions.

Deacon made his way down the first step just as the boy stepped toward him, his hand extended. "Ernest Miller."

Deacon frowned at the boy's hand and moved down the remaining steps with a steadiness he didn't feel. Humans—they always had to touch each other for some reason. He, on the other hand, had no inclination to touch any of them—except Rhea, of course. Her, he couldn't touch enough.

With a sigh of resignation, he shook the boy's hand quickly, then let it drop. "I'm Deacon."

Rhea's entire body stiffened. Her jaw tightened and her chest heaved in three deep breaths.

"*Deacon*?" A flicker of confused disbelief passed over the boy's face. "You mean . . . but you're dead."

"Dead?" Deacon repeated, staring him down. "Clearly you can see that is not the case."

Rhea cleared her throat loudly, keeping her gaze as far away from Deacon as she could. "Please, Ernest. Go back to the store. Now."

"But he's your *husband* . . . he's been dead for months."
He blinked faster than anyone Deacon had ever seen.
"And now he's alive again . . . and you *shot* him?"

"Ernest!" Rhea barked. "Just go back to the store.
And if you see Colin, please tell him to come home."

From somewhere inside the pathetic excuse of a building they used as a barn, a cow bawled loud and long
while the chickens continued to squawk inside their pen.

Ernest opened his mouth to protest Rhea's orders,
seemed to reconsider a moment, then closed it. It was a
decision Deacon almost applauded. Rhea wasn't one to
lose an argument, and the poor young Ernest looked as
though he'd learned that lesson the hard way.

Mumbling beneath his breath, Ernest smoothed his
hair back, clapped on his hat and walked away. The afternoon sun chased after him in long waves of dry heat,
making his image shimmer as he marched down the
road, out of sight.

Deacon waited until Rhea's shaky hands had hung
his shirt on the line.

"So," he said, chuckling at her discomfort. "Would
you care to explain how I came to miss my own wed-
ding? And my funeral."

"I don't—" she blustered, then stopped. Color spread
up her throat and over her cheeks. "You're such a . . .
a . . ."

"Devil?" Deacon grinned back at her, fueling her
anger.

Notwithstanding the horrendous black rag she wore,
Rhea was prettier than any woman he'd ever seen, especially when she was angry or flustered. Her eyes were
the color of creamed coffee, she curved in all the most
important places, and while she looked every bit the
lady, her tongue could curse him out like nobody's business, even while her soft full lips begged to be kissed.

Her brown hair was pulled back in its usual unimaginative loose braid, but even so, she couldn't hide the streaks of caramel and gold the sun shot through it, hinting at its rich and silky soft strands.

If she'd only let it down so he could . . .

Deacon gave himself a hard mental shake. She'd gotten a whole lot faster with that Winchester, and if this afternoon was any indication, she'd be happy to take aim at him again. No point in making her a widow twice.

She returned his gaze, taking in the length of him, as he'd done to her. If she was pleased with what she saw, she kept it well hidden. A heartbeat later, she backed away and returned to her washing. Deacon lowered himself to the bottom step, watching as her arms swooshed around the wash bucket. She moved with a fluid grace, even as she dropped another shirt into the water and began the monotonous task of scrubbing it clean.

Still, her hands trembled.

"I'm waiting, Rhea."

She completely ignored him, focusing instead on that blasted shirt. She wrung it out, gave it a quick flick and hung it next to his on the line. "Colin won't be terribly eager to put you up tonight, but given the circumstances, I'm sure he will. I'll go stay at the store."

"You can't leave—you shot me!"

"And I'm sorry about that." She did sound a little bit sorry, but not so much that she wouldn't shoot him again if the need arose. "But I gave you enough warning."

He pulled himself up to stand, wincing more than was necessary. Her gaze barely flickered his way. Damn.

"I haven't two cents to my name," he said slowly. "And considering what you've done to me, the least you can do is stay until I've recovered."

"The least I can do?" Rhea turned from the wash and advanced on him.

"Rhea—"

"Don't 'Rhea' me." She stretched onto the tips of her toes, bringing her eye-level with him. "It's not my fault you don't know when to stay away. Everything would have been just fine if you hadn't come back."

Deacon frowned. He'd forgotten how good Rhea smelled. She had a soft, clean scent that always caught him unaware.

"Yet here I am." He reached to tuck a strand of hair back from her face, but she slapped his hand away.

"Don't touch me."

Perhaps it was the way her bottom lip trembled slightly when she said it, or maybe it was the rip of pain that flashed across her eyes, but something belied her tightly spoken words.

He leaned closer and breathed his words against her cheek. "That's not what you said the last time I was here."

She shoved away from him. "A weak moment on my part, one that won't be repeated."

He made to follow her, but one step away from the railing, his knees threatened to buckle, so he eased back to its safety as casually as possible. Out where she stood, there was no railing for support, and while his body could withstand a great deal of abuse, his pride had had enough for one day.

Instead, he flashed the most charming smile he could muster, given the constant throbbing in his shoulder. "But you made me your husband, and while you still haven't explained how that happened, I believe it's common practice with you humans for husbands to touch their wives." He opened his eyes wide in feigned shock. "In fact, if I understand it correctly, some wives actually enjoy it."

She gave a sad little laugh and shook her head as she bent to empty the washtub. "Yes, well, this wife is warning you—touch me again, and the next bullet'll go right between your eyes." She might have been more threatening if her voice hadn't wavered so much.

"But I've changed."

"What's changed, Deacon? Are you no longer the son of the devil? Are you capable of even the slightest human emotion?"

"You know—"

"Yes," she interrupted. "I do know. Try, just for a moment, to imagine what it's like to have your heart—" She stopped abruptly, swallowed and shook her head. "How could you imagine it? You don't have a heart."

The strained expression on her face and the hitch in her voice froze Deacon's retort before it could slip off his tongue.

He'd hurt her. It couldn't have been helped at the time, but that didn't mean a whole lot now.

"Of course I have a heart," he finally replied. "It's just never been as soft as yours, is all."

Rhea's shoulders sagged a little, and her voice quivered with resignation. "What do you want, Deacon?"

Seeing her this way shouldn't have bothered him as much as it did, and now all he wanted was to make her smile again, just once.

"I came back to make things right between us," he said. "Of course, if I had any idea we'd been married in my absence, I would have been back a lot sooner."

She clenched her jaw and exhaled loudly. "I didn't think I'd ever see you again . . ."

"Ah, sweetheart." His grin came easier this time. "I just can't seem to stay away from you."

She didn't smile. Her lips didn't even twitch. Deacon returned to his spot on the bottom step, wincing against Colin's shirt. His shoulder throbbed, and Rhea's scent was making him dizzy.

"You should go lie down," she muttered, "before I have to haul your sorry hide back up those stairs."

Damn Deacon.

Rhea pushed her braid back over her shoulder and slumped down on the short wooden stool beside the cow. With a calm brought from a lifetime of practice, she eased the milk from the animal's full udder in an even rhythm.

Why did Deacon have to come back? She'd spent the last eight months trying to put him out of her mind, of trying to forget what he looked like, how he smelled, the way her bones melted when his fingers danced against her skin . . .

Damn him! And damn her own stupid self.

Why couldn't she have fallen in love with a normal man? Or at least one who was human? But no, once she'd let Deacon into her heart, she was lost to anyone else, and no matter how hard she tried to reason it out, it stuck. She was in love with the devil's own son, a man utterly infuriating yet altogether charming at the same time.

That crooked smile and those ridiculous fancy clothes . . .

With a sigh, Rhea surrendered to both the smile that tugged at her lips and the tear that quivered, then slid down her cheek. Such was the way with Deacon.

He provoked her, pushed her and made her mad enough to spit. Then he'd look at her with so much tenderness, confusion and raw desire, she didn't know if she was coming or going most of the time.

No other man made her feel that way. And no other man smelled of warm sandalwood mixed with sunshine.

Deacon did.

The constant zinging of milk against the side of the

bucket echoed through the barn. Rhea slowed her rhythm a little before she sent the flow right over the edge.

"Don't do this." She swiped a hot tear away and blinked back another. "Don't."

Instead of crying, she should be figuring a way out of the mess she was now in. How on earth was she going to explain the miraculous return of her dead husband—especially when he wasn't legally her husband?

For a little while, last summer, she'd thought he wanted to be her husband, but she'd been horribly, horribly wrong.

She licked her suddenly dry lips and tried to swallow. Even after all this time, she could still taste his kiss; more than just a flash of passion, it melded them together in a way Rhea found impossible to explain because, like so many other things about Deacon, it made absolutely no sense.

Rhea sighed. It didn't matter how charming he was or how he tempted her in ways no other man could—the truth could no longer be ignored.

He would never love her the way she wanted him to, the way she needed him to. It just wasn't in him. And even though she'd forged his name on the marriage certificate, making him her husband, he could never give her what she wanted most: his love, a home and children.

Rhea pressed her fist against the deep ache in her chest. God help her, she wanted children. She could have had them, too, if she hadn't been so hasty in her decision to "marry" last year. But she'd done what she'd done, and there was nothing to do now but move forward.

At least it had secured the store for her, and that was something no one could take away. Maybe in time, once Deacon was out of her life again, she'd be able to push him completely out of her heart and find another man to love; one who would share her life, her store and her desire for children.

"Rhea?" Colin's voiced bounced through the open barn door.

"In here!"

She released the cow, lifted the pail of milk into her arms and went to face her brother.

"What the hell's going on?"

"Deacon's back," she said.

"I heard." Troubled brown eyes stared back at her. "Heard you tried to kill him, too."

Two days of stubble covered Colin's chin, his too-long hair lay in dark chaos around his ears, and by the lingering odor, it was anyone's guess if he'd swallowed any of the whiskey or simply bathed in it. Even the star pinned to his chest had lost its shine.

"Hardly." She shrugged past him and the horse he'd left tied to the rail and climbed the stairs to the porch. "He got in the way of my warning shots."

"Warning shots?" He clomped up the stairs behind her, his voice a rumbling growl. "You just tried to kill a walking, talking dead man."

Rhea rested her hands flat against the door, wishing she didn't have to inhale when he stood so close. "How can anyone try to kill someone who's already dead?"

"I ain't got time for bullshit, Rhea. You knew he wasn't dead, didn't ya?"

"Yes." She could sure use another swig of that whiskey, but of course she'd used the last of it on Deacon's wound. Drat, drat, drat.

Teeth ground tight, she set the milk pail on the small kitchen table and waited while Colin struck a match to the lamp, sending pale light flickering through the dim room.

Deacon struggled to sit up on the bed, obviously hampered by his weakened arm, but Rhea made no move to help him. If he needed assistance, he'd have to get it from Colin. She needed to avoid physical contact with him as much as possible.

His eyes squinted tight, then blinked open against the light. "Colin, is that you?"

Her brother clicked his tongue. "Wish I could say it's good to see you, but we both know I'd be lying. You all right?"

Deacon laughed, groaned, then laughed again. "Despite your sister's best efforts, I think I'll live."

"It was *not* my best effort," Rhea snapped. "And he's fine."

Colin didn't so much as acknowledge she'd spoken, keeping his hard angry stare focused on Deacon instead. "Do you want to press charges?"

Rhea and Deacon both choked at the same time. "What?"

"She tried to kill you," he said. His voice held absolutely no emotion, but his left eye twitched, his jaw muscles clenched and his back tightened.

"I did not! I simply tried to warn him off." Rhea could hardly breathe. Colin wouldn't . . . oh, no. Colin wouldn't want to, but Deacon . . . He had every right to send her to jail, and there would be no defense if he did. She was guilty as sin.

"Relax, Sheriff." Deacon's shocked expression gave way to something Rhea could only attribute to irritation. "It was an accident."

Colin's shoulders relaxed, and his jaw unclenched. He dragged one of the crooked chairs closer, indicated for Rhea to sit, then straddled the other chair himself.

"Miller can mind the store for a while longer." As usual, he spoke Ernest's name as though spitting poison off his tongue.

Rhea dug through the pile of rags on the table until she found one to cover the milk. "I don't think—"

"That much is obvious." Colin's anger hung between them. "I'm not expectin' you to think right now; just answer a few questions. Surely you can manage that."

She should have known this moment would come, should have prepared for it. But she hadn't, and now here it was. Her life depended on what these two men would do next.

"Fine." She flopped down in the chair and folded her hands in her lap. "What do you want to know?"

"How I became your husband, to start with," Deacon answered.

Rhea cringed as Colin's eyes nearly popped out of their sockets.

"*What?*" For a second, she thought he might fall right off his chair. "He didn't know?"

She pursed her lips, blinked, then slowly shook her head.

"How the hell does a man not know he's married?"

"Colin, please." She squeezed her knuckles tight enough to turn them white. "Calm down."

"Don't tell me to calm down, Rhea," he growled. "What the hell have you done? And what's his part in all of it?"

"He had nothing to do with any of it," she answered grudgingly. Oh, how she'd love to blame Deacon for this mess; one more thing to hate him for. Unfortunately, there was no one to blame but herself. "It's not as bad as it sounds. Just listen."

"Oh, I'm listenin' all right," Colin muttered. "You just haven't said anything."

Rhea drew in a long slow breath. "Our store meant everything to Ma and Pa. They worked their whole lives to earn the reputation for being honest and fair. It meant everything to them."

Colin rolled his eyes. "Yeah, I know exactly how *important* it was to them. Get to the point, Rhea."

She lifted her chin slightly and shrugged. "You didn't want it."

"So what?"

"I did. More than anything else, I wanted that store and you knew it." She glanced at Deacon, who'd pulled himself up to sit a little straighter.

"I knew, all right. I also knew because of him"— Colin jerked his thumb toward Deacon—"you were driving your reputation into the ground and taking the store with you. I saw the ledgers, Rhea. Business was down to almost nothing, and our only hope was to sell the damned thing."

"So you sent me to stay with Cousin Margaret in Houston with the mind to sell the store out from under me."

Colin's jaw tightened, but he didn't deny her accusation.

"It's all right, Colin," she said. "Our parents took a lifetime to build their good name, and I almost destroyed it overnight. I know you were just trying to protect me, and while I appreciate it, it didn't help. It was my responsibility to make things right, not yours."

"And you thought the best way to do that was to get married?"

She exhaled slowly. "Yes."

Deacon and Colin spoke at the same time.

"To me."

"To him."

"Of course." Honestly. This wasn't nearly as complicated as these two were making it seem. "It only stood to reason that marrying him would take some of the tarnish off our name."

The two men glanced at each other, frowned, then turned back to Rhea as Deacon asked the dreaded question. "How, exactly, did we get married if I wasn't there?"

"W-well," she began. "It was easier than you'd think, actually. Cousin Margaret kept her parents' marriage certificate in their family Bible. I simply copied it on to a new sheet of paper, changed the names and came home married."

"To him."

"Correct."

"But he wasn't there."

"Correct."

Colin's frown deepened. "And the business you said he was finishing up in Houston?"

"There was no business," she admitted. "I lied."

"You lied."

Fear gripped Rhea's stomach and twisted it into a giant knot. "I needed to do something—and fast—or you were going to sell my store. Marriage seemed like the quickest way to save the store and our name."

"But why not marry for real?" Colin asked tersely. "What were you thinking?"

Rhea clicked her tongue. How could men be so stupid? "For goodness sake, Colin, you were days away from selling the store to the Dietrichs! Do you honestly think I had time to go through a courtship?"

"That doesn't answer my question," he snarled. "There's plenty of fellas here in Penance—surely to God you could have found *someone* crazy enough to marry you."

A stifled snort came from Deacon's direction, but Rhea ignored him. Despite what Colin insinuated, she could have found plenty of men to marry if she had the time or inclination.

Heat crept up her neck and butterflies twitched in her stomach. "All my life, I watched Ma and Pa. They loved each other, Colin. Really and truly loved each other."

Her brother's jaw tightened 'til she thought the muscles would snap.

"I wanted that, too, and everyone in town knew it."

Colin's grunt left little room for doubt on what he thought of her romantic side. "You only saw what you wanted to see," Colin ground out. "Their marriage wasn't everything you think it was."

"They loved each other, and that's what's important." Rhea nodded. "I wasn't about to marry a man I didn't love, and after what happened with Deacon, the only way to salvage our name was to marry him."

"So what are you saying? You love Deacon?"

She blinked rapidly, cursed the tightness in her throat and tried to forget Deacon was sitting right there. If her mouth was any dryer, she wouldn't be able to swallow at all.

"After he left last summer," she said, hoping neither man would notice she'd sidestepped the question, "Mrs. Foster made sure I knew everything people were saying about us, about how 'scandalous' our relationship was. I never expected him to set foot in this town again, so he was a safe risk."

"A safe risk?" Colin came out of his chair like he'd been shot. "Do you hear what you're saying?"

"It made perfect sense," she retorted, then added more softly, "at the time."

Why did Deacon keep grinning like that? Surely he didn't want to be married to her any more than she wanted to be married to him—not for real, anyway. In her pretend world, it was the perfect arrangement.

"At the time," Colin grunted, his fingers gripping the back of his chair tight enough to snap the spindles. "Let me get this straight," he muttered. "You're not legally married, yet you have a piece of paper that says you are."

God help her. "Correct."

"And you did this just so you could keep that stupid store?" Colin's growl became increasingly louder with each word.

"You make it sound like I robbed a bank or something."

"For God's sake, Rhea—it's forgery!" The vein in his neck pulsed dangerously fast.

"No, it's not," she said, wishing she didn't sound so pathetically desperate. "No one got hurt from it, and it's not as if I stole anything from anyone."

"Except my freedom," Deacon threw in.

"Forgery is forgery." Colin reached for the shelf that usually housed his whiskey and found it wanting. "Dammit."

"Deacon doesn't care, do you?" She twisted in her chair to face him.

"Well . . ."

Colin didn't let him finish. "And it wasn't enough that you falsified a marriage, but then you went and falsified his death, too!"

"I had to. People kept asking where he was, and why he didn't come to live here in Penance." She shrugged. "I couldn't very well tell them he'd been dragged back to H—"

"Houston," Deacon interjected.

"Right," she muttered. "Houston." It was one thing for her to know who he truly was or where he'd been, but it was something else entirely for others to learn the truth.

"Dammit." Colin slammed his hands down on the

tabletop and glared pointedly at Deacon. "You swear you didn't know any of this?"

Deacon offered a half shrug. "Not a thing."

Oooh, she'd like to slap that righteous smirk off his face.

"Colin, please." She shot Deacon a warning look before turning to face her brother. "Nobody has to know."

"*I* know!" The force of his yell rattled inside Rhea's skull. "Damn it, Rhea, *I* know!"

Silence followed. The realization of what she'd done began to sink into Rhea's brain. She hadn't even thought about Colin when she'd jumped into this plan; all she'd been thinking about was keeping the store.

It was all she had left of her parents. It was all that mattered.

When the silence nearly swallowed her, Rhea stood and pushed her chair beneath the table.

"So what do we do?" she asked.

Colin shook his head in utter disbelief. "I have no idea."

"It seems to me"—Deacon cleared his throat—"the easiest thing would be for us to marry for real."

If she hadn't been holding the back of her chair, Rhea would have fallen straight on her face.

"I . . ." She stopped, took a breath and kept her eyes fixed on Colin. "No."

"Why not?" Both spoke in unison, each sounding just as affronted.

"Colin, please." She lowered her voice, but there was no way to prevent Deacon from hearing. "There are things you don't know about him."

"Like what?"

She couldn't tell him! For goodness sake, it was still unbelievable to her most of the time; she certainly couldn't try to explain it to her brother. It only took the briefest of glances at Deacon to know he was thinking the same thing.

Rhea cleared her throat and forced her voice into an impatient sigh. "He doesn't love me, and after what he did . . . there's no possible way I could ever trust him again."

"Excuse me," Deacon said, "but noth—"

Rhea spoke over him before Colin could pay him any mind. "There must be another way," she said, desperation clawing its way out on every word.

"Like what?" he snipped.

"Why can't we simply . . . continue this way?" she asked tentatively. "Nobody has to know any of this, and if Deacon leaves right away . . ."

"I'm not leaving."

Colin cast a quick glance in Deacon's direction. "You're *staying*?"

"For a short while," he said cautiously.

Rhea clicked her tongue. "How long is a 'short while'?"

"Doesn't matter," Colin said. "Thanks to Ernest, half the town knows you're back and that Rhea tried to blow your head off. The other half'll know by sundown. So for the time being, until we can find a way out of this, you two are going to have to keep up the impression you're married. And you're going to have to come up with one helluva good story about how he came back from the dead."

"Wait just a minute," Deacon said, his hand raised. "Don't I get any say in this?"

Colin's expression turned hard as granite. "By all means," he quipped. "Have your say. You can choose to spend the next little while doing right by my sister—the same woman you compromised and then humiliated by taking up with a whore at the saloon—or you can choose to humiliate her further, and ruin any chance she has of living a normal life. Which will it be?"

Deacon didn't answer right away, and it took every ounce of self-control Rhea could muster not to throttle him. What was there to think about? It wasn't like she was asking him to love her for real—all she needed was for him to pretend.

They both knew he'd done it before, so surely it wouldn't be too much work for him to do it again.

After a horribly long moment, Deacon pushed up slowly from the bed, took a second to find his balance and grinned.

"I'm happy to pretend if she is." He tipped his head a little to the right. "What do you say, Rhea? Can you pretend to love me?"

Rhea's fingers itched for the Winchester. One more shot—that was all she'd need.

CHAPTER THREE

Deacon sat in the gloom of the tiny cabin, staring at the closed door. It had been hours since Rhea had shut it behind her and walked back to town, yet her presence lingered all around him. And just when his mind started accepting the fact she wasn't even thinking about him the same way, Ernest arrived with a bottle of laudanum from her.

So why didn't he sleep? He'd downed enough of the damned tincture to set an elephant on its rear, yet here he was, wide awake, trying his damnedest *not* to think about being married to Rhea.

He cursed aloud and banged his head back against the wall. What the hell was wrong with him? His life had been ticking along just fine until that blasted day when he'd met Colin and his firecracker of a sister. Next thing he knew, Rhea had kicked his whole world sideways.

Nothing had been right since.

A slow smile spread across his mouth. Rhea had done more than kick things sideways; she'd given him a reason to keep coming back. She wasn't afraid of anything, least of all him, and she'd just as soon shoot him than cower or bend to his will. His throbbing shoulder was ample proof of that.

He squeezed his eyes shut, listening to the sounds of early morning creeping between the cracks in the cabin walls.

The air in the room shifted slightly, and Deacon heaved a long sigh. He should have expected her.

Not Rhea.

Kit.

"I hate when you do that," he grumbled, opening one eye at a time to find his younger sister standing over him.

"Yet you didn't think twice about doing the same thing to Lucille."

The mere mention of their other sister made Deacon groan and chuckle at the same time. He couldn't deny what Kit said; he used to pop in on Lucille all the time, and she'd hated it just as much as he did now.

"Where's this 'Colin'?"

"In the other room."

"And the woman?"

"She's spending the night in town."

With a quick snap of her fingers, Kit sent a flame dancing against the lamp's wick. Deacon squinted through the light, then stared openmouthed at his sister.

"What are you wearing?" he gaped.

His sister's whole face lit up. "Wonderful, isn't it? I wish I'd done this years ago."

Kit's red hair grew wild around her head, her cat-green eyes took in everything around her and her mouth was set in its usual smirk. The lower half of her body was clothed not in a skirt or dress—as it certainly should have been—but in men's trousers.

Denim trousers!

And to make it worse, she was wearing a faded flannel shirt, every bit as ugly as the ones Colin had hanging on the nail in his room.

Her feet were stuffed into brown leather boots, and a red-checked bandana hung half out of her front pocket. If Deacon didn't know better, he'd swear she was a regular old cowhand.

"You can't be serious," he said. It was bad enough he'd been forced to borrow one of Colin's shirts, but to wear such things willingly . . . ugh.

"Oh yes, I am." She lifted her hands in the air and turned in a slow pirouette. "I'm never wearing a corset again."

Deacon shook his head slowly. Typical Kit—she did what she wanted, when she wanted, and to hell with everyone else.

He swung his legs over the side of the bed and stretched out the kinks. "I suppose it shouldn't surprise me that you're here."

"No," she said, "I suppose it shouldn't."

A slow breath seeped out of Deacon's lungs. Even though his father had kicked him out of Hell, Deacon knew better than to think he was actually free.

"Here." Kit reached into the pocket of her denim pants, pulled out a huge wad of paper bills and dumped it on the table. "You look like you could use a trip to the nearest clothier, Mr. Vanity."

"Honestly, Kit, if I didn't know better," he said, "I might think you were being charitable."

"And if I didn't know better," she retorted, "I might think you were planning on staying here with the humans."

"That's why he sent you?" Deacon eyed his sister carefully. "To make sure I don't get too comfortable here?"

Kit shrugged indifferently.

"I'm not Lucille," he grumbled. "I have absolutely no hope or expectation of ever being free, so you're wasting your time."

"That's all right." Kit tipped her head to the right a little and smiled brightly. "It would seem I have plenty of time to waste."

She twisted one of the chairs away from the table and plunked herself down. "Besides, I had to see for myself what all the fuss was about. Did you really let that woman shoot you?"

"I didn't *let* her do anything," he groused. "But without any powers . . ."

"Ah, yes." Kit nodded. "Not easy living as the mortals do, is it? Especially when they start shooting."

Her grin should have irritated him, but instead he found himself grinning back.

"In my defense, she did miss the first three times." He glanced down at his arm and smiled ruefully. "But that fourth shot . . ."

After a lengthy silence, Kit shifted in her chair and shrugged. If she meant it to look nonchalant, she failed miserably. "You can get your powers back anytime you like," she said. "All you have to do is ask."

"Ha!" Deacon nearly choked on his laughter. "He'd like that, wouldn't he?" The words had barely left his tongue when a sharp wave of prickles swept over the scars on his back. Guess his father didn't appreciate being spoken about this way.

Not one to miss such things, Kit lifted her brow, twisted her mouth to the side and asked, "How bad was it?"

"Getting shot?" Deacon pushed up from the bed under his sister's watchful gaze and moved toward the window. Damn her scrutiny; it made it that much tougher to hide each twitch and every wince. "Not as much fun as you'd think, actually."

"That's not what I meant," she said, "and you know it."

Of course he knew it, but he wasn't about to discuss

the details of his torment with anyone. He'd learned to push each haunting memory into the deepest darkest part of his being, so if he tried hard enough, he could almost convince himself the suffering hadn't actually happened.

Just another nightmare.

"How bad?" she repeated.

He leaned his right hip against the window ledge and exhaled slowly. "Bad."

Outside, light teased the edges of the horizon, whispering its promise across the sky; the promise of another day, another opportunity to make things better.

Or to make them horribly worse.

"I don't understand." Kit pushed her hands through her hair, shaking the chaos loose around her head. "Of all the places you could have gone, you chose to come back here, even though you know he's going to make you suffer for it. Why?"

Small as it was, Deacon couldn't help his smile. "You know what these God-fearing humans say: that which does not kill us . . ."

"That's not funny." Her mouth turned down in a deep frown.

Kit watched him for a long time, her green eyes narrowing in close inspection, as though she expected to find some deep dark secret written across his face. Finally she gave up and shook her head.

"That time you spent with Lucille and her human did something to you," Kit said quietly. "You've changed."

Deacon blinked at her words. She was right; he had changed, and he had Lucille to blame—or thank—for that. He hadn't yet determined which was more appropriate.

Lucille had somehow found it within herself to endanger her own soul for the sake of a human. It didn't make sense.

Then again, few things about humans made sense.

"If Lucille had any comprehension of Father's true wrath or the tremendous chance she was taking, she never would have let herself fall in love."

"But you understand, don't you?" Kit leaned over so her elbows rested on her knees.

Oh, he understood, all right. It was a lesson he'd never forget, and one he'd never survive learning again.

They stared at each other for a long moment, neither voicing what they knew the other was thinking. Best to keep fears and past pains buried inside. Talking about them only weakened a body.

"You're not trying to break free, but you don't want your powers back." After a long moment, Kit threw her hands up. "Then why are you here?"

Deacon held his facial muscles completely still, refusing even the slightest twitch. "I need to make things right with Rhea."

"You *what*?" Kit's eyes nearly bulged out of their sockets. "But we don't make things right!" she cried. "That's the other side's job."

"Do you think I *wanted* to come back?" he ground out. "That I *enjoy* these infuriating feelings of light that plague me day and night? Believe me, Kit, my life would be significantly easier if I'd never met this woman."

Easier, yes; meaningful, no.

"Then leave! You don't owe her anything."

"You misunderstand." He chewed the inside of his cheek before continuing. "I'm not here for her. I'm here for myself. Ever since I left last summer, I can feel her pain as though it's my own."

"What do you mean?"

"It's difficult to explain," he answered. "It's as though the pain in her heart runs so deep that she has somehow pushed it on to me."

"Humans don't possess powers like that," Kit scoffed.

"I never thought so, either, until I met Rhea," Deacon countered. "I don't know how she's doing it, but I've never had that feeling with another human."

"So what are you going to do about it?"

"End it, of course." If he could end Rhea's pain, he could end his own, and they would both be free. "I'll tell her the truth, apologize, she'll forgive me, and that will be that."

"You're insane." Kit blinked past her disbelief and shook her head slowly. "This woman isn't about to forgive you just because you . . . ugh . . . apologize." Her face puckered over the word. "You made her think you had sex with a whore. Human women don't forgive or forget things like that." Kit's face smoothed into a wry grin. "It's no wonder she tried to kill you."

Deacon forced a smile back. He knew the truth. Rhea may have tried to kill him, but she hadn't tried very hard. And no matter what she said, or how many shots she fired, the truth blazed from her eyes like a raging inferno.

She was mad and she was hurt, but she still loved him and he didn't need his powers to see it.

"While we're on the subject," Kit said, "why *didn't* you sleep with that whore? You paid her well enough."

"I didn't want to," he answered at length. "I just wanted to make Rhea think I had."

"Why?"

Regret swirled through him like a hurricane.

"Things had become complicated between us. It was like part of her was becoming part of me, and the longer we were together, the harder she was to resist." Deacon chewed the inside of his cheek. "When it was time for me to leave and deal with Lucille, I never thought I'd come back to Rhea. But no matter where I was or what

I was doing, I could feel her pain. I knew if I didn't do something drastic, she'd waste the rest of her life waiting for me."

If Kit's eyes rolled any higher, they'd probably roll right out of her head. "With talk like that, you'll never be accused of being humble, will you?"

"Regardless," he went on, "it didn't work. She wants to hate me, and she's tried very hard to do it, but she can't."

"You're unbelievable." Kit's chuckle was not directed at the situation, but at him. "I bet if she heard you now, she'd hate you plenty."

"No, she wouldn't." If only his voice sounded as confident as he wished it would. "And since it's my fault she can't hate me, I need to ease the pain in her heart so that she'll stop pushing it on me."

Deep creases puckered Kit's forehead. "First you go out of your way to break this woman's heart, and now you've come back to fix it. There is something seriously wrong with you."

Undoubtedly.

"Humans call it affection." A small flicker of light bubbled across his heart before he could do anything to stop it. "It's a power unlike any we have."

Something akin to horror fell across Kit's face. "And you have this . . . *affection* . . . for her?"

"I think I do." The light pushed toward the surface, but he forced it back. Kit didn't need to know the depth of his affection; it was bad enough he knew about it himself.

The horror on her face turned to shock. "You're not thinking about doing the same thing Lucille did?"

"Of course not." He shifted his hip a little on the window ledge. "Rhea has made it quite clear she will never want me the way Lucille's human wanted her."

"Strange, then, that she chose to 'marry' you."

"You know about that?"

"Of course. Word spreads fast as lightning in this town, especially around the poker tables." Kit crossed her left leg over her right and set to swinging her booted foot back and forth. "So how are you going to 'end it'?"

"Rhea's smart," he said with a shrug. "Once I tell her the truth, she'll understand why I did what I did, her pain will subside, and then everything will be as it should."

"The truth." Kit grunted in utter disgust. "Need I remind you what happened the last time you told her the truth?"

"Need *I* remind *you* that I bear the constant remembrance across my back?" The mere mention of his scars made them tingle again, but he didn't move, didn't give Kit the slightest indication their father could still cause him discomfort, even from such a distance.

If it killed him, he'd never give evidence of the fear that iced his veins. The punishment for what he was trying to do would surpass anything he'd been through so far. Yet for some incomprehensible reason, it paled in comparison to Rhea's pain, pain *he'd* caused her.

It wasn't as if he'd never caused another human pain before, but this was different. Rhea's pain ate at him constantly, gnawing and grinding until he thought he'd go stark raving mad.

Kit's voice continued to buzz in his head.

"And you think by telling her the truth, she will instantly forget all that you've done to her and you can both go on and live happily ever after?"

The bubble inside him popped, leaving nothing but a dim flicker of light in its place. "I'm the devil's son, Kit. There is no happily ever after for me."

"But you still want *her* to have one."

Deacon ground his teeth together until his jaw ached.

The thought of Rhea finding happiness with any other man made the bile in his stomach boil. But given the choice of that or living the rest of his life feeling every twitch of pain in her heart . . .

There simply was no choice.

Though he hadn't shaved in days, Colin at least had washed this morning. He'd even gone so far as to shed the filthy sweat-stained shirt he'd worn for the last three days in lieu of a clean one. He hadn't actually tucked it in, but Rhea wasn't going to hound him about that.

It was enough for now that he didn't smell like the bottom of an overflowing spittoon anymore.

As she tended the eggs and ham frying on the stove, Rhea tried to make herself as small as possible. Cramped at the best of times, the cabin was worse now with Deacon there. His presence overwhelmed the room, his scent filled Rhea's every breath and his eyes followed her every move. Even with her back turned, she felt him watching.

She filled plates for both men, set them on the table, then poured herself a cup of coffee.

"I trust the laudanum helped you sleep."

"A bit." Deacon settled into one of the crooked chairs and grinned sheepishly. "You didn't have to stay at the store last night."

"I couldn't very well stay here," she said over the rim of her mug. "Unless, of course, I wanted to sleep in the barn—which I didn't."

"Most *married* people sleep together," Colin grunted as he slumped into his own chair.

"Oh, honestly!" Even in the privacy of their own home, it was improper of him to say such things. Deacon's smirk widened.

Colin stuffed a fork full of eggs into his mouth, then spun the utensil around to point it at her. "You're the one who dragged me into this mess, Rhea, so don't go and get all righteous on me now."

"I did nothing to you."

"No?" He choked on his next swallow, then beat the tines of his fork against the star pinned to his shirt. "You broke the law—how does that *not* involve me?"

Deacon leaned lower over his plate, as though ducking from Colin's shouts. Or maybe it was the chunks of egg flying from Colin's mouth.

"You act as though I killed someone." She took a sip of her coffee, then set the cup of bitter brew on the table. "It's a piece of paper, for goodness sake."

Colin threw his fork down on his plate and shoved back from the table. "That piece of paper is a lie, Rhea."

"A lie that has no effect on you or anyone else."

"Except me," Deacon mumbled over his eggs.

"Dammit, Rhea, if anyone finds out what you've done, neither of us will ever be able to hold our heads up in this town again." He scrubbed his hands over his face. "And while that might not mean anything to you, it means something to me."

Her heart stuttered, as did the retort that sprang to her tongue. "That's not fair, Colin. I only did all this to help restore our family name. You've never . . . I mean, I didn't think . . ."

"No, you didn't. That's the problem."

"Whoa." Deacon set his fork down, raised both hands and slowly got to his feet. "I thought we decided last night to just carry on with this charade until we can come up with a better idea."

"Right." Rhea nodded nervously. Her throat burned with tears, but she swallowed them back. It was too late for regrets. She'd acted in haste, and now she'd have to do whatever it took to make things right.

"Surely," Deacon continued, "there must be a way we can rectify this without forging any more documents or causing any more trouble."

"Yes," Rhea said, desperate for a solution, "there must be something we . . . I . . . can do."

Colin blew out a long breath and gripped the back of his chair until his knuckles whitened.

"I don't know," he finally said. "All I know is that you've caused enough trouble by claiming you were married and then putting on the devastated widow act."

Rhea could feel Deacon grinning at her. "Devastated by my death, were you?"

"Shut up."

Colin's pointed straight at Deacon. "If you were any kinda man to start with, you woulda married her the last time you were here instead of doin' what you did."

Rhea and Deacon spoke at the same time.

"I don't think—"

"He couldn't—"

Colin ignored Deacon and set his sights on Rhea. "And you." He pursed his lips tight, shook his head and cursed quietly. "It don't matter what he did or didn't do. You created this mess, so now you're going to do whatever it takes to fix things."

Panic sparked in Rhea's veins. "Like what?"

"To start with, you're going to stop wearing widow's black. You wanted to play a married woman, so that's what you're going to play. You're a woman in love with her husband—more so now that he's miraculously come back from the dead. You'll be seen together in town, and you'll damn well live under the same roof."

"Don't be ridiculous, Colin. The three of us can't possibly live here—it's too small."

"You got that right. The two of you can go set up house above that blasted store."

"What?" Rhea's throat instantly constricted. "I can't live with him by myself—it's not proper."

"What's not proper?" Colin roared. "You're married!"

"But people will think—"

"You're damn right that's what they're going to think, and why shouldn't they?" Black anger glared at her and Deacon. "They're still jawing on you two from the last time he was here."

"I—"

"Don't." Colin stopped Deacon cold. "You ruined my sister, and if she hadn't convinced everyone that the two of you up 'n married in Houston, I'd have chased you to Hell and back to make sure you did right by her. She might have done wrong by you with this sham of a marriage, but you ain't exactly innocent, either."

Deacon stiffened. "While I admire your devotion to your sister, rest assured I did not ruin her."

"No?" Colin grunted out a snort. "Well, you sure as hell didn't do much to protect her, did you?"

"What are you talking about?" Rhea stepped between the two men. "I don't need him to protect me."

"Well you need someone to do it! Everyone in town saw the way you let him touch you, for God's sake." Colin's face twisted into a look of complete disgust. "And if that's how you let him behave in public, it doesn't take much to guess what went on when the two of you were out here alone."

"It wasn't like that." Rhea reached to touch him, but he pulled away.

"Doesn't matter now, does it?" He grimaced. "With him back, it'll give you a chance to silence some of that infernal tongue-waggin'."

He stormed out of the house, slamming the door hard enough to make the window rattle. In the quiet that followed, Deacon dropped back in his chair, scraped up every last bit of egg and then finished off Colin's ham as well.

"The man's right, you know."

"Don't—"

"You've put him in a bit of a predicament, what with him being the law and all." Deacon slouched back against the chair and started to cross his arms over his chest, but after a sharp wince, decided against it. "Seems only right that you do whatever he says until we can clear up this mess."

She snapped up the plates and forks and tossed them none-too-gently into the washtub. Everything had been fine yesterday morning, right up until the smug little devil walked through her front gate.

"Why aren't you angry about this?" she asked. "Any other man would be furious about what I did."

"Colin's right," he said, offering her a look of pathetic false innocence. "I did wrong by you the last time I was here, and I regret the trouble it caused."

"You have a regret?" She snorted, then turned her back to him. The blasted dishes wouldn't wash themselves. "Since when?"

He didn't answer for a moment, but when he did, his voice was softer than she'd ever heard it—almost to the point of being emotional. Almost.

"Rhea. You know who I am and what my limitations are. But good or bad, surely you must know how much I enjoy you."

"Enjoy me?" A sound, half laugh, half choke, ripped from Rhea's throat before she could stop it. "How flattering that you consider me part of your life's entertainment."

"Oh come on now." He covered the distance separating them in less than two strides and stood close behind her. Too close. "You had some fun with me, too."

His scent tickled her nose, his voice a whisper against her neck, and though he didn't actually touch her, his warmth surrounded her, blanketing her in that all-too familiar sensation that she was melting right where she stood.

"Yes," she admitted when she found her voice. "We had some fun. But that was a long time ago."

"Not long enough that either one of us forgets what it felt like." His words caressed her skin, leaving shivers in their wake.

Rhea gripped the edge of the washbowl, trying to steady herself. "I remember it well," she murmured.

He trailed his finger along the side of her neck, lifting a strand of hair, and breathed a kiss just below her ear.

"I also remember what it felt like when you took up with Salma, then left without so much as an apology or a good-bye." She shrugged him away and then stumbled out of his reach. "I can't go through that again."

"Rhea . . ." He stepped toward her, that damn crooked smile of his doing its best to win her over again. "That night with Salma—"

"Don't." Taking a breath, she found her balance and looked him straight in the eye. "I don't want to talk about her. I just need to know if you will do as you said and stay long enough for us to figure a way out of this mess I've created."

"Do you want me to stay?"

She took in a long slow breath and exhaled it even slower. "I would be . . ." The words stuck on her tongue.

"You'd be what?" His grin widened, his blue eyes taunting her.

Fine, she'd say it. Let him have his fun. It was only a matter of time before he'd leave again, anyway, and then she wouldn't have to put up with his teasing and prodding.

"Grateful," she ground out. "I'd be grateful."

"There," he said. "That wasn't so hard, was it?"

"You have no idea." She shoved past him and went back to work on the dishes, but his quiet laughter followed her.

"Be that as it may, if we're going to be married, you're going to have to at least pretend to trust me again."

It took her a second to swallow the lump that began to build in her throat. "I don't know if I can."

He seemed to ponder that for a moment, his smile fading, his head cocked slightly to the side. "I'm sorry to hear that."

"And I'm sorry I've put you in the middle of this predicament," she said, offering a silent prayer of thanks her voice hadn't cracked. "But like I said, I never in a million years expected to see you again."

"I know," he said softly.

Rhea lifted her shoulder in a small shrug. Not only had he left that night without so much as a good-bye, but before he left, he'd made a spectacle of himself as he climbed the stairs to Salma's room at the saloon.

Every man there had seen it, including Colin.

"That wasn't—" An odd look came over Deacon's face then; on a human, she'd have known it to be honest-to-goodness remorse, but on him, she couldn't be sure. "I can explain about that night."

"There's nothing to explain. You are who you are, and I should have expected as much." She cleared her throat past the lump that wouldn't go away and forced the starch back into her voice. "What I didn't expect was to be made a laughingstock. So while I'm sorry this sham marriage can no longer be kept a secret, I'm sorrier that I find myself needing your help."

She turned to face him, hands on her hips, her voice as even as she could manage. "So can I depend on you? Will you pretend to love me until we sort through this?"

"I'll do my best." His grin returned as he snapped the dish towel out of her hands. "I suppose the next best thing to having you for real is pretending for a while. What more could a man want?"

A chill twisted up Rhea's spine. Knowing Deacon, he'd want more—a helluva lot more.

CHAPTER FOUR

Deacon slipped the key into the lock and pushed the door open. It banged against the steep slant of the ceiling, making it impossible to open the door completely. He waved Rhea in ahead of him, then ducked to avoid cracking his head on the door frame.

Her description of the room above the store had been a slight exaggeration. It wasn't small. It was downright tiny.

To the immediate left, a wide cot ran the entire length of the room. The bed was unmade, but there were two matching gray blankets tossed in a heap at the foot and two thick white pillows at the head.

Deacon tried to suppress his grin. Two of them and only one bed. *Interesting.*

A small mirror hung on the opposite wall, and below it stood a circular table about the size of a large serving plate, upon which sat a blue washbasin and matching pitcher. A hardback rocking chair was near the large window, and two large brass hooks hung on the wall adjacent to the door.

Deacon took one step inside the room and stopped. "Home sweet home."

"Don't get too comfortable," Rhea muttered, setting

her small carpetbag on the bed. "Hopefully we won't be here long."

Two steps took her to the rocking chair, which she shifted slightly so she could see out the window while she rocked. Or maybe it was to avoid having to look at him; Deacon couldn't be sure.

She leaned her head back against the solid wood and eased the chair into a smooth gentle rhythm. A warm afternoon breeze fluttered through the thin white curtains, bringing with it the rank odors of horses and leather mixed with dust and wood shavings.

Rhea closed her eyes and breathed deeply. For the first time since he'd arrived, she almost looked relaxed.

"Don't you love the smell of spring?" she asked, her voice barely above a whisper.

Deacon frowned and moved next to her so he could see out to the street below. "If by 'spring' you mean dust and horse sweat, then no."

The town was alive with the hustle of people running their daily errands. A young couple, hurrying up the street, shot furtive glances over their shoulders before disappearing around the corner of the livery. A little girl in a bright blue dress and matching bonnet skipped down the boardwalk with her mother, both of their faces animated with excitement.

What could possibly give two people so much joy?

Deacon shook his head slightly. Humans were an odd bunch. And speaking of odd . . .

"Tell me," he said, turning to face Rhea, "if this room's been here all along, why haven't you or Colin moved in? It'd be much more convenient than going out to the house all the time."

"Colin won't come up here."

"Why not?"

Rhea shrugged. "Most of the time, I can't even get him to come into the store."

Interesting.

"Then why don't you live here?"

"And leave Colin by himself?" she retorted, her voice distant. "You've seen him. He needs someone to look after him."

Deacon fought back a snort. The only thing Colin needed was a sharp kick in the backside and a long hot bath. At least this morning he'd taken the bath, so that only left the sharp kick. Maybe Deacon could help him out with that.

"Seems to me—" he began, but Rhea cut him off.

"I have work to do." In one fluid motion, she was off the chair and heading for the door, her sunshine-yellow skirt swishing around her legs.

"Good. I'll help." He almost collided with her when she stopped in front of him. Her soft, clean smell distracted him for a moment, tempting him to lean closer and inhale the scent straight off her skin, maybe from that spot right below her ear.

Giving himself a hard mental shake, he righted himself and grinned down at her. "Nice to see you wearing something other than black, by the way. It's not your color."

"I don't need your help." If the distrust in her eyes wasn't enough, it practically seeped from her voice.

"Of course you do. So long as we're married, what's yours is mine and what's mine is yours." He tipped his head a little and grinned wider. "Of course, I don't actually own anything, so I suppose it's more accurate to say what's yours is ours."

Using the tip of her index finger against his chest, she shoved him none-too-gently back into the center of the room. "You listen to me, Deacon." Anger snapped in her eyes as her finger jabbed him over and over again. "We are *not* married, and once I can figure a way out, we can end this charade."

"Just remember," he countered, loving her fiery glare, "you're the one who started *this charade*." She would have made a great devil.

"I remember just fine, thank you very much." Her glare hardened and her spine stiffened. "But if you'd stayed away like you should have, I wouldn't need your help at all."

"Come now, Rhea." He wrapped his hand around her finger and pulled it to his chest. "Of all the methods you could have used to save your family name, for some reason, you chose to 'marry' me. Don't you think that's peculiar?"

"I was desperate!" She tried to jerk her hand free, but he tightened his grip. It was rather nice to touch her again. "And you know I had to use you—you're the reason I was in the fix to begin with!"

Rhea could blame him all she liked; they both knew the truth. Nothing had happened between them that she hadn't wanted.

"Calm down," he said softly, "and just listen."

"Let me go." The vein in her neck pulsed harder, faster. Had it really been eight months since he'd kissed that spot? Sometimes, when he thought about the time he'd spent with her, it seemed like only yesterday. Other times, like now, when he itched to kiss that spot again, it seemed like a lifetime ago.

With a sigh, he set her free, but she didn't move away as he'd expected. Instead, she stood there, toe to toe with him and looking up at him with eyes that simultaneously blazed blistering fury and ice-cold fear.

It was nearly impossible to think straight when she

was within his reach, and if she knew what was good for her, she'd hightail it out of that room and not look back.

Deacon fisted his hands together behind his back. "Like it or not, you made me your husband, and here I am—at least for the time being."

"You could leave again."

If he were capable of human emotions, those four little words could have wounded him deeply. Luckily, it was more of a sharp, painful nick than an all-out wound.

"I'm not going anywhere."

"Why?" she cried, slumping down on the edge of the bed. With a quick glance at the open window, she lowered her voice. "Why can't you just leave? It's not as though you've never done it before."

"Two reasons," he said. "The first seems obvious."

By the way she arched her eyebrows, it must not have been obvious to her.

"What would it do to the remnants of your reputation if I were to leave you now? Or worse, *divorce* you?"

"We can't get divorced," she answered weakly. "We're not really married."

"They don't know that." He jabbed his thumb toward the window. "As it stands now, the only things affording you any respect in this town are your parents' store and your apparent marriage to me."

"It's *my* store," she snapped. "I'm the one who keeps it running."

"Of course," he said. "But no *good Christian* in this town would ever do business with a divorced woman, would they?"

Hesitantly, Rhea finally shook her head.

"And before you even suggest the idea that I 'die' again," he said, "think about how it would look if your darling husband died twice—both times quite unexpectedly. Surely someone would suspect the merry widow of misdoings, and we certainly don't want them investigating you or the details of our marriage, do we?"

"No." She sighed, toed the floor and shrugged. "What's the second reason?"

"Beg your pardon?"

"You said there were two reasons you couldn't leave."

"Right." He crossed his arms over his chest and widened his stance. "I don't want to."

Who knew telling the truth could be so easy?

Rhea shot off the bed, her voice a barely controlled yell. "You don't want to?"

"Correct."

"I don't give a flying fig what you want," she fumed, pushing him in the chest again. This time he didn't move. "I certainly didn't want the *devil's son* to come into my life, but you did. I didn't want you to"—she ground her teeth together—"touch me or seduce me, but you did. And I didn't want you to humiliate me and then leave without so much as an apology or . . . or a goodbye, but *you did*!"

By the time she'd finished, the fury in her voice had cracked, changed. It was a feeling he knew all too well.

Sorrow.

"Yes," he admitted. "I did come into your life uninvited. And I did take advantage of you to a certain degree, but you can't stand there and tell me you didn't want it as much as I did."

"I . . . but . . ." Even in her anger, she was the most adorable creature he'd ever seen. "You still humiliated me."

"Yes, I did. And it's something I'll regret for the rest of eternity." He couldn't help smiling at the irony of it all. There he was, telling her the truth, and she didn't believe a word of it.

She dropped her hand and moved away from him, but he pulled her back. Turning her face to his, he fingered loose hair back from her face and smiled.

"You're trying to hate me," he said, "and rightly so. But I can explain about Salma—"

"Don't." Her eyes closed for a long moment, but when she finally opened them again, there were no tears as Deacon had expected—just a haunted, bone-weary emptiness.

He'd have preferred the tears.

"Fine," he said quietly. "Then give me this chance to make it up to you. Let me act as your devoted husband. Once we get things sorted out, I'll be on my way and you'll never have to set eyes on my ugly face again."

"You're not ugly." Her teeth worried her bottom lip until the urge to kiss her almost overwhelmed him. "And I don't hate you, though God knows I've tried."

"Good." Deacon couldn't stop touching her hair. "So all that's left is to hope we're able to come up with a solution that doesn't involve the use of another firearm or"—he shuddered—"destroying any more of my clothes."

Was that amusement flickering in her eyes? A bit of shame, maybe? He brushed the pads of his thumbs over the smoothness of her cheeks. Even his favorite silk shirt didn't feel that soft.

"I'll be the perfect gentleman," he said. "You won't even recognize me." He raised his hand, palm out, as though taking an oath. "You have my word."

"Your word." She snorted, stepping away from him. "No offense, Deacon, but given who you are and our history together, I'd be as dumb as a post to take your word on anything."

Ouch.

He forced another smile and tapped her on the tip of her nose.

Smart girl.

Rhea smoothed her apron over her skirt and stepped out of the backroom, into the store. Ernest was showing Mr. Rowe the newest harness they'd just ordered in, and Mrs. Hale was fingering a bolt of pink sateen.

"Good afternoon, Mrs. Hale." Rhea walked straight toward her. "Is there something I can help you with?"

Ernest glanced in their direction, started to smile, blushed, and then turned back to his customer.

"My Polly needs a new dress." Mrs. Hale's smile pinched the corners of her mouth for barely a moment before it faded clear away.

Rhea suppressed a sigh. Girls in Penance, Texas, didn't need dresses made of expensive sateen, especially when the girl in question was Polly Hale. That girl would look beautiful in a plain old burlap sack, which was about the only thing her family could afford.

But Mrs. Hale had never been one to live within her means when it came to her daughter.

The woman nodded abruptly toward the sateen. "I have a pattern similar to one I saw the youngest Dietrich girl wearing last month, so I think twelve yards should do nicely."

Mrs. Hale's own dress, one Rhea sold her years ago, had long faded from navy blue to muted gray, but it was no doubt Mrs. Hale's best.

Clearing her throat, Rhea lifted a bolt of pink-and-blue gingham from the shelf and set it on the table in front of Mrs. Hale.

"This is a lovely fabric," she said, unrolling it a bit for the woman to see. "The blue will bring out Polly's eyes beautifully."

Mrs. Hale barely cast it a glance before patting the bolt of sateen she'd been admiring. "I'll take this."

"It is lovely," Rhea agreed, lowering her voice to a whisper. "But you could buy three yards of this gingham for the same price as a single yard of that sateen."

Mrs. Hale's pale lips pinched white. "That may be, but a plain gingham dress isn't going to attract the type of husband my Polly needs, is it?"

"Husband?"

"Yes." The woman's voice faltered for a second. "We've decided to send Polly to Houston to live with my aunt. She has no hope of finding a man of wealth in Penance, does she? In Houston she will have opportunities we can't possibly give her here."

"But what about . . ." Rhea glanced quickly at Ernest, whose complexion had turned a horrible shade of gray.

"It's decided." Mrs. Hale nodded once for emphasis. "She's leaving at the end of the month."

"I see," Rhea said quietly. "I'll certainly be sorry to see her go."

Ernest's mouth opened, but he didn't speak. Rhea offered him an apologetic shrug before unrolling the sateen across the table. Using her tape, she measured out twelve yards and cut carefully.

When she'd folded it neatly and replaced the bolt, she turned back to Mrs. Hale. "Is there anything else?"

"No. That will be all. On our account if you will." A tiny tear slipped from the corner of Mrs. Hale's right eye. "I'm sorry if I was short with you. It's just . . ." She dabbed her eyes with a threadbare handkerchief. "I'm going to miss my girl."

"Yes." Rhea turned the woman away from where Ernest stood. "I'm sure."

As she wrapped the fabric in brown paper, Mrs. Hale stared unseeing at Rhea's fingers. But the second Rhea brought out the accounts book, the woman snapped up her package and beat a hasty retreat to the door.

Rhea watched her go, then nodded in Ernest's direction. The boy had been so distracted he'd completely forgotten his customer.

"You'll never get paid for that." Deacon's voice, so close behind, made her jump.

When she'd caught her breath, she shrugged. "You don't know that."

"Yes, I do," he scoffed. "And so do you."

"Mr. Hale pays what he can every month," she whispered. "He can't help it if his wife has such expensive taste."

Mr. Rowe finished examining the harness, shook his head at Ernest and took his leave. The door hadn't even closed behind him when a new customer blew in.

All the years her parents owned the store, Rhea had seen a great many different people, but never one like this. Ernest openly gaped as the woman made her way toward Rhea and Deacon.

The woman's face, stunning and perfectly molded, was surrounded by a mane of wild red hair she hadn't even attempted to tame. Her eyes, the color of deep jade, glanced around at the items on display, never paying much attention to any one thing. But it wasn't the woman's hair, face or eyes that made Rhea and Ernest gawk.

The woman was dressed top to bottom in men's clothes! Her blue chambray shirt was tucked into a pair of denim trousers, complete with suspenders, and a red kerchief was tied around her neck as though she'd just come in from a cattle drive.

Behind Rhea, Deacon sucked in a sharp breath and then proceeded to choke on it, forcing him to duck into the backroom.

Rhea took a moment to gather her thoughts before greeting her new customer.

"Good afternoon." She smiled. "Is there something I can help you with today?"

The woman stopped, eyed Rhea from head to toe and grinned. "You must be Rhea."

"Yes . . ." An odd feeling coursed through Rhea's body, but she shook it off. Of course she felt odd— besides the fact the woman used Rhea's given name as though they'd been friends for years, she was wearing trousers, for goodness sake!

"I'm Kit." The woman spoke as if those two words explained everything. "I've heard a lot about you."

"Oh." From the corner of her eye, Rhea could see Ernest still gaping. She shot him a sharp look, which was enough to send him scurrying back to the harness he'd left out. "It's a pleasure to meet you, Kit."

In the backroom, Deacon continued to choke.

"What do you have by way of suits?" Kit's voice was feminine, yet slightly raspy, almost as if she had a sore throat.

"Suits?"

"A man's suit. Black or gray silk if you have it." She nodded distractedly. "I'll need some boots . . . and one of those funny little hats—"

Rhea could barely hear her over Deacon's carrying on.

"I'm sorry," she said. "If you'll excuse me, I'll have Ernest help you while I go make sure my . . . husband . . . hasn't coughed up a lung."

Kit's laughter made Rhea laugh, too, as she waved Ernest over. "Miss Kit is in need of a gentleman's suit. Please show her what we have in stock as well as what's available to order."

With a slap on the back to get Ernest moving, Rhea hurried to check on Deacon.

"For goodness sake, take a breath." From the small pitcher on the table in the corner, she poured him a glass of water and held it out until he took it.

"I would if I could," he choked, "but I wasn't expecting to see . . . that . . . come through the door."

"She's beautiful."

"She's wearing men's clothes," he whispered hoarsely, shaking his head in disgust. "In public."

Rhea leaned back against the wall and sighed. "Isn't it brilliant? If it wouldn't scare off all my customers, I'd trade in these cumbersome skirts and petticoats for some of those trousers myself."

Deacon swallowed his water, set the glass down and moved directly in front of Rhea, trapping her against the wall. His eyes sparked with mischief, and his lip curled in a challenging half smile.

"No wife of mine is going to wear men's trousers and horrid flannel shirts."

"And no 'husband' of mine is going to tell me what I can and cannot do," Rhea bristled. "Rest assured, I'll do what I want whenever I want."

Why did he have to stand so close? He used up all the oxygen, making it impossible for her to breathe normally.

"Of course you will." His blue eyes pierced through her as he fingered the end of her braid. "So tell me, wife, what *do* you want?"

To start with, she wanted him to stop looking at her like that, as though he'd die if he didn't kiss her right then and there. More than that, she wanted to stop feeling the same way. And she really wanted him to brush his hair because the way it was now, all tousled and standing up, it was far too tempting to reach up and smooth it back into place.

The tip of his nose brushed over hers, then across her

cheek. No other part of his body touched her, yet she felt him everywhere, from each strand of hair right down to her toes. Her blood pumped harder, her heart tipped and her brain swirled.

This wasn't right. She didn't want this, didn't want him to touch her like . . . oooh. His lips whispered over her jaw, grazed her earlobe, then danced down her neck to where her pulse throbbed. Tipping her head to the right, she offered him more, silently begging him to take it, to kiss her like that again.

Oh no, this wasn't right at all. This was exactly what she'd been trying so hard to forget. The way each touch scorched her skin, each breath sapped more of her strength.

"I—" She pressed her palms against the wall on either side of her for balance.

"Hmm?" He nibbled soft kisses against her earlobe, rested his cheek against hers and whispered against her neck.

Her senses swirled and tumbled, taking in everything that was Deacon. His clean masculine scent overwhelmed her, and his touch left shivers in its wake. All she could hear was his breath, quick and labored, and all she could see was his face; those deep blue eyes asking her to give him what they both wanted, while those seductive lips tempted her beyond reason.

All that was left was to taste him.

Rhea turned her face to his, seeking out what she was suddenly so desperate for. He smiled against her mouth, teasing her with featherlight brushes, until she wrapped one of her hands around his neck and dragged him closer.

He took the kiss deeper, longer, moving his mouth over hers again, harder and more determined, until she gave back with everything she had.

Her pulse pounded, and her heart ached inside her chest. If only he'd touch her . . .

She arched toward him, but his hands remained where they were, pressed against the wall on either side of her head. He was trying to drive her mad, and it was working—but she wasn't about to let him win that easily.

With deft fingers, she released two buttons on his shirt and slid her hand inside. His breath hitched, his muscles flexed, and an instant later, he pressed into her touch. Someone moaned, but she couldn't be sure who.

The sound must have startled him, because he slowed the kiss, pulling her gently back to reality.

"Interesting," he murmured. "It would seem we both want the same thing."

If she could breathe, she'd set him straight on exactly what she wanted . . . though it seemed to have changed drastically in the last few minutes.

If only she could breathe!

Deacon gazed down at her. Dark storm clouds brewed in his eyes, a tempest that both surprised and frightened her.

"Deacon." It was all her parched throat could manage before her tongue froze again.

"Sweet little Rhea." He smoothed his thumb across her cheek and looked down at her with such tenderness, it made her heart ache. "You best get back to your customer."

He staggered back a step, righted himself and retreated up the stairs to their room.

Curse him.

Or, more to the point, curse herself! She wasn't the type of woman to swoon over any man—especially the likes of Deacon. He was a rat—a charming rat, and one who could obviously kiss the sense right out of her, but a rat nonetheless. He'd humiliated her once. She couldn't afford to let it happen a second time.

She needed to be stronger this time. How many times had she told herself that in the last twenty-four hours?

But damn, that man could kiss!

Rhea was still standing where Deacon had left her when Ernest came in a few minutes later.

"Miss Rhea?"

She closed her eyes, inhaled deeply, then stepped away from the wall, the only thing that had supported her all this time.

"Ernest," she said, pushing through the haze she'd been in. "Were you able to help Miss Kit?"

"Yes, ma'am. She took the entire black suit, plus a new shirt, a vest and a pair of boots. She even took one of them new bowler hats your husband seems to be so fond of."

Something niggled at the back of Rhea's mind, but she pushed it aside. It didn't matter what the woman purchased; all that mattered was if she paid for it.

"How did she pay?"

"Cash."

"Really?" Rhea stared down the aisles of the empty store toward the closed door. "That's good, then."

It was another minute or so before Ernest cleared his throat loud enough to get her attention.

"If there's nothing you need," he said, "I best be getting home. Ma likes her supper early these days."

"Of course. Thank you, Ernest." Then, before he could leave, she lifted the small jug of milk she'd taken from Colin's this morning and held it out to him. "Please take this to your mother. And tell her I said hello."

"Thank you, ma'am, but it ain't right for you to keep givin' us things like that."

"Of course it is," she said, smiling. "It'll just go bad sitting here." The anticipation on his face was almost enough for Rhea to give him Colin's cow entirely. "Please, Ernest. I'd hate to see it wasted, and you worked hard today—you deserve a little treat."

After a moment's hesitation, he bobbed his head slowly. "Thank you, ma'am. I'm sure it'll make Ma happy."

"I'll see you tomorrow then."

"Yes, ma'am."

"And Ernest." She reached out to touch his arm. "I'm sorry about Polly."

A deep red flush shot up the boy's neck and cheeks. "Weren't like we was engaged or anything."

"Maybe not," she said. "But I'm still sorry."

Another quick head bob and he was gone. Rhea locked the door behind him and then set to tidying up.

She swept the floor twice, washed the countertop and the candy bins, then spent a great deal of time sorting through the mess on the sewing table. Bolts of fabric, ribbons, lace, patterns and strings of beads covered the table in a giant haphazard mess. Right in the middle of that mess sat a huge glass bowl filled with buttons, every size, shape and color a person could possibly need. And if they weren't enough, there was another box of buttons underneath the table.

It must be horribly frustrating for her customers to stand there and sort through the whole bowl until they found the color or size they needed. She had time now, and tedious though it might be, she'd get them sorted.

Anything to make her customers happy. And anything to avoid going upstairs.

She dragged a stool over to the table, gently poured out the bowl and set to dividing its contents into different piles. It was amazing anyone had ever been able to find what they were looking for in that jumble. An hour later, she stood and tried to stretch the pain out of her neck and shoulders. Her eyes, dry and aching, begged to be closed, but she couldn't do it. Not yet.

If she closed her eyes now, she knew there was only one face she'd see, and she wasn't nearly ready to deal with that.

In fact, she should probably sort the box under the table, too . . .

"Rhea." Deacon's smooth voice floated across the room. "You can't hide down here all night."

"I'm not doing anything of the sort." Drat—she'd just thrown three yellow buttons in with the red. "I'm working."

"Working?" He moved so furtively, she didn't realize he'd moved at all until his arm brushed hers. "After all the years your family's owned this store, you suddenly find it pressing to sort that bowl of buttons?"

She sniffed and instantly regretted it. His scent was almost as seductive as his touch. "It should have been done a long time ago."

"Yes," he answered quietly. "I imagine there are plenty of things that should have been done a long time ago. And while I applaud your sudden desire to organize the chaos around here, I doubt very much that sales have suffered because women can't find the exact button they need."

He picked up a bright blue button with scalloped edges, fingered it gently and tossed it in with the rest of the blue ones.

Why did he have to stand right at her shoulder? Didn't he know how distracting he was? Rhea frowned. Of course he knew.

"You could help." She reached under the table and pulled out the other box of buttons. "There's plenty that need sorting."

His mouth turned up in a grin, but instead of being his usual cocky smile, it looked as though he'd simply cut it off someone else's face and fastened it to his own.

"Thank you, no," he finally answered. "I'd hate to hurry you along when you're obviously so determined to hide down here instead of coming upstairs to sleep."

"Don't be ridiculous." As she turned away, he snorted softly. "I'm not hiding, and I'm not tired."

"Says the woman who can barely stand up straight."

"I'm fine."

"Liar." His one word, whispered so quietly into her ear, reverberated through her brain.

She tried to shrug him off, but he lingered near her ear, not touching her or even speaking; just hovering.

Rhea lifted a handful of buttons out of the box and set them in a pile on the table. One by one, she sorted them into their respective piles, then reached for another handful. Maybe if she ignored him, he'd go back upstairs and leave her alone.

But, of course, that would go against everything Deacon was made of.

Without a word, his hands folded over her shoulders and began to knead them; slowly at first, then stronger, deeper. For the first few minutes, she continued to sort buttons with slow precision. But it wasn't long before she slumped down on the stool, crossed her arms on the table and rested her forehead on top of them.

Shifting slightly behind her, he repositioned his hands without ever losing contact with her back.

He rubbed harder, pushing, smoothing and pressing until each knot loosened. It was, undoubtedly, one of the stupidest things she could have let him do right then, when the taste of his kiss was still so fresh and she was so completely exhausted, but Rhea didn't care. His hands were magic to her muscles, a balm to every knot and kink she'd twisted them into over the last few days.

With her head down and eyes closed, she was boneless, pliable and eager for more of Deacon's attention. The devil had offered her a few moments of heaven right there in her store, and she'd willingly accepted. What harm could it do? As long as she didn't look at him, as long as he didn't move suddenly and send his intoxicating scent swimming through the air, she'd be fine.

Oh yes, she'd be perfectly fine. A soft moan escaped with her next breath. When had she ever been this relaxed, this—

As suddenly as he'd started, Deacon stopped and dropped his hands to his sides.

In her state of repose, it took a moment to gather the energy and strength to sit up and look at him; but that was all it took to bring every knot, every kink he'd just worked out of her muscles, screaming back.

Confusion and frustration mixed with forced calm and covered with a pained smile stared back at her—all feelings she understood and recognized because each one was thrashing inside her as well.

Deacon cleared his throat softly. "I'd best leave you to your buttons, before I make you do something you'll regret."

She chuckled, a harsh sound that pained her throat. "And you'd best get it out of your head that you have any control over me or what I do."

This time his smile reached all the way into his eyes as he tucked her hair behind her ear. "Even if I could, I wouldn't want to control you. But it's perfectly clear you enjoy me as much as I enjoy you. Why not just admit it?"

"Oh, I enjoy you well enough," she snapped. "I'm just not going to let myself enjoy you too much this time. I've been down that road before, and I'd rather not travel it again."

"You say that, yet you steered us both back down that road when you chose me as your husband." He crossed his arms over his chest and leaned back against the table behind him. "Perhaps you wish we were married for real."

"Perhaps not!" She pushed her button piles farther apart, then poured another mound to be sorted. What had she been thinking when she started sorting this mess? She squeezed her hands into fists to stop their trembling.

Too late.

Deacon covered her hands with his and leaned closer. " 'The lady doth protest too much, methinks.' "

She jerked her hands away and glared up at him. "Don't touch me."

"You wanted me to earlier."

"I never—" She pushed hard at his chest, but he didn't budge.

"No matter how long you try to hide from me, Rhea, we both want the same thing."

"I'm not hiding from you!"

He lifted a handful of buttons and let them slide between his fingers. "Liar."

Before she could fire a retort, he turned on his heel and disappeared through the backroom.

When she heard the door close upstairs, Rhea expelled her breath in a huge rush. God help her, that man was going to drive her mad. The fact he knew just where to touch her was aggravating enough, but to have her traitorous body react so wantonly—and so quickly—was downright infuriating.

She ran her tongue over her suddenly parched lips—lips still flavored with Deacon's kiss—and shuddered.

Oh, how she'd missed his touch this past year, and God help her, she'd missed his kisses. She didn't want to, but there it was.

She wanted to hate him for it.

All these months later, she could still feel every detail about their last day together. The air, still warm after a brief storm, held the lingering scent of a quick rain over the too-dry ground.

They'd barely spoken as they walked home from the restaurant, but she hadn't needed words. All she needed was the feel of his thick calloused fingers twined through hers. All she needed was to know how he felt, and he told her every time he looked at her.

Rhea squeezed her eyes shut, but the memory remained, singed into her brain. The overwhelming desire she'd felt for Deacon shone straight back at her through his blue eyes. It was a hunger she couldn't explain. All she knew was that it went far deeper than anything physical.

Unlike most of the men in town, her brother included, Deacon let her be who she wanted to be. He didn't try to control her, he didn't try to silence her when she had something to say and he didn't condescend to her.

He treated her with a surprising amount of respect given who he was, and that was perhaps what made her love him even more.

Yes, she loved him, devil and all, and she'd been so sure he loved her too, especially that last night. That last night . . .

Rhea slumped over the table, burying her face in the crook of her elbow. She'd been ready to give herself to Deacon, to give him everything he wanted and to take everything she wanted, but he'd walked away, leaving her alone, confused and humiliated. If that wasn't enough, he'd taken himself straight to the cursed saloon and into Salma's willing arms.

Rhea sucked in a sharp breath. How could it still hurt so much after all this time? After all that time spent trying to hate him . . . and she'd come so close to succeeding, too. If only he hadn't shown up on her front porch, smiling that crooked smile and whispering kisses over her skin like butterfly wings.

It didn't matter. Kisses aside, there was only one thing that mattered.

Survival.

If she wasn't careful—very, very careful—she would never survive the heartbreak he was sure as sin going to leave behind him again.

CHAPTER FIVE

Minutes ticked by. Deacon thought it was probably good that Rhea hadn't come upstairs straight away because he would have been hard pressed to keep his hands to himself.

But the longer she stayed away, the more difficult it became to think of anything—or anyone—else. Sweet little Rhea.

What the hell was he going to do about her?

Maybe he'd been wrong to come back; maybe he should have just left well enough alone. He'd never done something like this before, something to ease another soul's pain. And if he'd known it was going to be this difficult, he might have saved himself the trouble.

The plan had started out so simple: He'd come back, tell Rhea the truth about Salma, she'd see the reasoning behind his lie and stop hurting, and then he'd leave again. What could be easier?

He stood in front of the mirror, his hands gripping the small round table as he leaned closer.

"You're not supposed to still be here," he muttered to himself. "In and out—that was the plan."

He blinked back at his reflection and sighed. Stubborn cuss of a woman hadn't let him explain anything!

Instead, his mouth had been otherwise occupied with kissing her. And more than that, she'd kissed him back.

Deacon's throat burned raw. He wanted to stand next to her, to watch the passion build in those amazing eyes of hers and to be the one who took her so far past that passion she'd never see straight again.

He wanted to hear her breath hitch when he touched her, to make her sigh when he kissed below her ear and to somehow, despite everything, make her laugh again.

It might be selfish, but that was who he was, and there was no denying it. He wanted Rhea more than he'd ever wanted anything in his long miserable life. And no matter how much his father tried to lash it out of him, he'd always want her.

Deacon's throat burned hotter, his scars prickled tighter than ever. If there was any chance he could give her what she wanted . . .

He pressed the heels of his hands against his eyes and spun away from his reflection. Of course he could give her what she wanted. It was simply a matter of repairing her heart so she could go off and fall in love with someone else. A human husband, one who could give her a home and lots of little human children. Somehow, he'd have to help her find that—even if it meant an eternity of misery for himself.

Deacon stretched out on the cot, staring up at the ceiling. It was a wonder humans did any good deeds at all, if this was how it left people feeling. Trying to make her happy was leaving him miserable!

He'd known all along he could never have Rhea, but he was the devil's son: he wanted what he wanted, and nothing else mattered.

But Satan's teeth, something else did matter this time: Rhea.

Half an hour later, her boots sounded on the stairs,

but it was almost another minute of quiet before she finally opened the door and walked in.

Deacon fought to keep his breathing steady and remained where he was, stretched out, ankles crossed, and his uninjured arm curled behind his head.

"Finished already?" he teased. "I half expected you to throw a bedroll down behind the desk."

"I considered it."

Honesty—a surprising tactic. "So why didn't you?"

Rhea closed the door behind her and turned up the wick on the lamp. Even with her face half-hidden in shadows, there was no mistaking the strain in her clenched jaw.

"And have you think you'd scared me off?"

Deacon couldn't hide his smile as he sat up and swung his feet to the floor. "I've known you to be a lot of things, Rhea, but scared of me has never been one of them."

She simply arched her brow in response.

"It's late," he said. "I'll give you a minute to ready yourself for bed." As he pulled open the door, he stopped, turned and waggled his brow. "One minute."

He walked the length of the store slowly, paused to admire her button work and then stepped outside onto the deserted boardwalk.

The air was still, the town all but asleep except for the lights and muted sounds drifting from the saloon at the entrance to town.

He inhaled a long breath and stared up at the star-filled sky. The last time he'd seen so many stars had been that last night with Rhea, the night he'd seen straight into her soul and she'd seen into his.

An ache he couldn't explain began to spread throughout Deacon's chest. In that brief glimpse, he'd seen everything so clearly. Everything Rhea felt for him, every bit of light that burned in her soul for him, burned in his soul for her.

He blew out a long slow breath, fighting the smile that twitched against his lips. The punishment for that indiscretion had almost killed him, so why was he smiling? And why did warmth spill through his veins?

Everything had been so simple before Rhea came into his life. So simple, so predictable, so tidy.

"Stop it," he muttered into the darkness. "Focus."

He straightened his jacket, tugged his cuffs a little and frowned. Tomorrow he'd pick out a new suit and throw this embarrassing set of rags in the nearest fire. He'd never owned a suit for so long, and he'd be more than happy to see the last of it.

He backtracked through the store and up the stairs, knowing what he'd find even before he opened the door. Rhea had turned the lamp off completely, leaving the room awash in broken moonlight and darkened shadows. She lay huddled on the far side of the bed, wrapped head to toe in one of the blankets.

"Comfortable?" he asked.

"Very," came the muffled reply.

It would take him less than a heartbeat to rip that blanket off her. He was nothing more than the devil's son, after all, and she *was* his wife. Instead, he hung his hat on one of the hooks by the door and toed his boots off one at a time.

"Did you happen to bring the rest of that laudanum?" he asked, easing his jacket down his injured arm.

Her face peeked out from beneath her blanket. "No, I thought you did."

With a bit of a grimace, he slid his other arm out and hung the jacket on the back of the rocking chair.

"Does it hurt a lot?" The remorse in her voice almost made him feel guilty for playing up the pain.

"Not as much as yesterday, but enough that I wish you'd brought the laudanum."

"I'm sorry." She spoke so quietly, Deacon almost missed it. "I never meant to hit you."

In the silence that followed, he undressed down to his shirt and drawers and slid into bed beside Rhea. Before he'd settled, she moved farther away, so her back was pressed up against the wall. Deacon pulled the other blanket up to his waist and sighed.

Not exactly how he'd imagined spending the night with Rhea, but it was a damn sight better than that porcupine quill bed she used at Colin's.

"Deacon?"

"Hmm?"

"Why did you come back?" She shifted her blanket a little until she was able to pull her arm out and lean up on her elbow. "Does it have something to do with your scars?"

The mere mention made the old wounds prickle again.

"Indirectly."

"You don't have to hide them from me," she said. Though her voice was low and gentle, thankfully he couldn't detect any pity. Even so, he wasn't about to take off his shirt. She'd seen them once; that was enough for now.

"What did you do to make him hurt you that way?"

Waves of exhaustion began to lick at his senses. "My mere existence is usually enough reason for him."

"Oh."

It had been a long time since he'd been so tired, and even longer since he'd felt safe enough to fall asleep. Too bad Rhea was keeping herself tucked up on the other side of the bed. Having her curled up next to him would make everything worthwhile.

If he didn't go to sleep—and soon—he'd roll over and make Rhea his wife in the only way that mattered to a man, human or not.

He inhaled long, slow breaths, each one pulling the blanket of sleep deeper through his body until his mind eased into the drowsy pre-slumber state of calm he'd longed for since he'd last spent time with Rhea.

As he drifted off, his last conscious thoughts were of her: the way she responded to his kiss, the ache in her voice when she spoke of his scars and the all-encompassing need he had to wrap his arms around her right then and there.

Instead, he pulled the blanket higher and let sleep take him. It was better for both of them that way.

"I bought you a present." Kit handed him a large package wrapped in brown paper, then reached down and lifted two more.

Deacon eyed the package warily before allowing her into the room. "Why?"

"Because you're obviously in dire need."

"Dire need?" He opened the wrapping to reveal a handsome black silk suit and a crisp white shirt, complete with a tidy row of small mother-of-pearl buttons. Boots polished to perfection were in the second parcel, and the third held a fashionable new black bowler hat.

"Excellent choice," he grinned. "And yet so completely unlike you to do something this . . . congenial . . . for no apparent reason."

Kit shrugged indifferently. "It just seems wrong to see you wear the same dirty clothes as long as you have. And besides"—she sniffed the air around him, then crinkled her nose—"you stink."

"I do not stink!" But his sister was right; he hadn't been paying much mind to his appearance since Rhea shot him. That would have to change. He couldn't have anyone else see him in his present rags. After all, humans were impressed by appearances—and up until recently, his appearance had been more than just a little impressive, if he did say so himself.

"I'd rather hoped you would have used some of that money on a new wardrobe," Kit said, cocking her brow toward the unmade bed. "Guess you got . . . distracted."

He had been distracted—just not in the way she thought.

"It's bad enough you came here to do something good." She shuddered. "But you can't even focus on that—all you've done since you arrived is moon over this woman like you were a . . . a human!"

"I'm not mooning." There was that unexplained smile again. What was wrong with him?

"Call it whatever you like," she said. "But if you don't end this quickly, you're going to lose everything."

"I've already lost everything," he muttered, slipping his arms into his old suit jacket. No point in putting on the new one until he was fit to be seen in it.

Kit paced by the window, keeping her eye on the street below. "He can still take your life."

"You mean he hasn't already?"

She whirled to face him. "How can you be so flippant? You're risking everything just by coming here and instead of ending it clean and simple, you're dragging it out as if there wasn't anything at stake."

"She needs my help." He crossed his arms and stared down at her. "And I risk nothing by being here."

Kit's mouth opened, but no sound came out right away. "Do you think Father is going to let you linger here as long as you like?"

"What does he care where I 'linger'?" He shouldn't use such a tone when speaking about his father, but it was too late to take it back. "He's the one who kicked me out of Hell and stripped me of my powers."

"Don't pout." It was unlike Kit to sound so testy. "You know you'll get them back eventually."

Deacon shrugged indifferently. "Regardless, I won't rush through this, Kit. I'm staying as long as Rhea needs me, and if you think you're being here is going to hurry me along, you're wasting your time. And mine."

Her eyes narrowed, looking for the smallest crack in his confidence. Good thing he knew how to hide them, otherwise she'd find more than just a few small cracks; she'd see huge gaping crevices.

He could say whatever he liked, but the truth was unavoidable. His father would use whatever means necessary to tempt Deacon back to Hell, and if past experience was anything to go by, it wouldn't take much.

In fact, Deacon had no doubt just fallen into the first trap—accepting the new clothes from Kit. She'd never done anything like this before.

After a long moment, Kit sighed and shook her head slowly.

"Do it any way you like," she said. "So long as you understand he's not about to let you dally with this woman. He's going to expect you to come back, and probably soon, so you'd best be ready."

"What if I don't want to go back?" There were few times Deacon wished he could take his words back, but this was one of them.

"Not go back?" His sister's expression went from confused to enlightened in less than a breath. "You're not Lucille," she said. "You can never have a life with this human woman."

It wasn't anything Deacon didn't already know, yet hearing her say it gnawed a giant hole in his stomach.

"You forget who you're talking to," he forced out.

"I am well aware of what can and cannot be in my life. I've suffered the consequences of his wrath more times than you can even imagine, and you can bet I'm not looking to put myself through it any more than I have to."

"A few days ago, I would have believed that, but you haven't been yourself since you came here." She didn't blink. "Just remember this—Lucille's human was at a huge disadvantage when he finally learned the truth about her. Your woman is not."

"What are you talking about?"

"By the time he discovered who Lucille was, he was already so in love with her that he was unable to hate her." Kit nodded decisively. "Your woman already knows the truth. She *chooses* to love you, which means she can choose to stop anytime she wants. She holds all the power."

Deacon didn't understand much about love, but he'd known all along that Rhea was the one with the power; she'd always had it when it came to him. Just because he knew it, didn't mean he needed Kit knowing it. Best to steer her off course a bit.

He cleared his throat and cocked his brow at Kit. "What difference does any of this make?"

"Oh, for the love of . . ." Kit clicked her tongue at him as though he were a witless child. "It makes all the difference. If you're so bent on stopping the pain in her heart, this is exactly what you need. Make her choose to 'not' love you."

Not love him? That wasn't what he wanted. He just wanted her to be happy again; granted, that would mean she'd have to find that happiness with another man, but it didn't mean she'd have to stop loving *him*, did it?

Ugh—humans! Why did everything have to be so complicated?

"Look." Kit sighed dramatically. "While I'm enjoying

myself at the poker tables in this town, it would be better for both of us if you would hurry things along a little. I'm on a bit of a schedule."

Of course. "How long did he give you to bring me back?"

"At the rate you're going?" she griped. "Obviously not long enough."

"Rest easy, Kit." He spoke slowly, carefully selecting each word. "I will end this with Rhea, but I will do it my way, at my own speed, and not because you're worried about your schedule."

Deacon needed to get her out of the room before Rhea walked in. "Thank you for the clothes, but as you so eloquently pointed out, I need a bath." He lifted the new clothes into his arms and held the door open for Kit to pass through ahead of him.

"Pay the extra and get a shave, too," she said, patting his cheek. "Women don't like whiskers."

Before her toe crossed the threshold, she'd vanished.

Deacon waved her off and made his way to the bathhouse behind the hotel. In a matter of minutes, he was up to his armpits in a tub of scalding hot water, a brandy-dipped cigar clenched between his teeth and a new bar of sandalwood soap on the shelf beside him.

For an extra four bits, the attendant, Kwan, shaved the offending whiskers from his face, all the while chattering on in Chinese as though Deacon should understand every word.

Deacon leaned back against the curve of the tub and puffed out large rings of cigar smoke. As much as he hated to admit Kit was right, she was. Dragging this out wasn't going to make it any easier. He'd stay until they sorted out the marriage mess, but the moment that was cleared up, Deacon would need to be ready to leave Rhea once and for all.

It was only fair.

Kwan indicated for Deacon to sit up, then pointed at the bandage and rattled off another few comments Deacon couldn't understand.

"Do you speak English?"

The other man's only response was to blink.

"Probably just as well," Deacon muttered.

With swift and skillful hands, Kwan unwrapped Deacon's shoulder, then leaned closer to study it. He pointed a long crooked finger at it, grinned an almost toothless grin and nodded.

"Guess you heard, huh?"

Kwan's grin widened over his reply. "Miss Way-ah."

Deacon's own grin surprised him. "That's right. Miss Rhea."

More mysterious sounds fired from Kwan's throat, none of which made any sense to Deacon.

"Bet your wife doesn't shoot at you, does she?" Deacon clamped his teeth tighter on his cigar and inhaled a long drag. "But I bet you've never given her reason to, either."

Kwan bent over Deacon's shoulder, pressing a scalding cloth around the edges of the wound.

"Gah!" Deacon gripped the sides of the tub until his knuckles ached. "If I were a paranoid man, Kwan, I might think you'd been trained by my father."

Kwan sniffed the wound, muttered, pointed and shook his head.

"I don't know." Deacon shrugged his good shoulder. "I came back to help her and she shot me."

"Howp?" Kwan worked the word around his tongue before letting it slide off.

"Yes." Deacon nodded. "Help." He yanked the cigar from his mouth and squeezed it between his fingers until the end almost completely flattened. "Of course,

I've never actually helped anyone before—but surely it's not always this complicated."

Kwan grunted, pulled the cloth from Deacon's shoulder and hurried from the room. A moment later, he returned with a tiny lidded pot and set it on the floor next to the tub. "Howp?"

"Yes," Deacon repeated. "It's a long story, but I thought I needed to make her hate me. That didn't quite work the way I expected, so now I need to make her not hate me. Understand?"

Kwan's round face wrinkled in a deep frown. Of course he didn't understand. The man only knew three words of English.

"Howp." With an impatient jerk, he pulled the cigar from Deacon's fingers, tossed it in a nearby spittoon, then pushed the tiny pot into his hand and nodded. "Howp."

"What is—?" He lifted the lid and would have dropped the entire pot of ointment in the bathwater if Kwan hadn't reacted so quickly. The rank stench of rot combined with some kind of exotic spice assaulted Deacon's senses long after the other man slapped the lid back on and forced Deacon to take it again. "What the hell is that?"

Kwan's laughter filled the room, but he didn't answer—not even in Chinese. Instead, he pointed at Deacon, pinched his own nose, then pointed back at the pot.

"Nice of you to warn me," Deacon muttered as he pinched his nose shut. He might not be able to smell it, but breathing through his mouth wasn't any better. It was almost as if he could taste the smell, and it was all he could do not to gag.

Using a tiny flat stick he'd pulled from his tunic pocket, Kwan dipped it into the pot, then gently dabbed the offensive ointment on Deacon's wound. It burned and soothed all at the same time.

Oddest damned thing.

"You howp Miss Way-ah." Kwan kept his attention on Deacon's shoulder, carefully dabbing tiny bits of ointment all the way around the wound, then rubbing it in with his pinky finger.

"Y-yes." Deacon sucked in a breath as the next dab of ointment singed his skin. "I'm trying."

He closed his eyes and forced long even breaths in and out of his lungs. "It'd be infinitely easier if she weren't as stubborn as an old mule."

Kwan muttered in Chinese, but never lifted his head.

"If she'd just let me explain about Salma—"

Kwan's fingers stilled. He frowned up at Deacon, tsked, then went back to work.

Deacon sighed. "Nothing happened! I thought it was best for Rhea if I ended it that way. Obviously I was wrong, and now she won't even listen to the truth."

Head bowed over his work, Kwan continued to mutter under his breath, and it didn't matter that Deacon couldn't understand him—the tone made it pretty clear what he meant.

"I want to make it right," he said, then frowned. Why was he explaining himself to a bath attendant who didn't even speak the same language? "Her heart is pained because of me. If I can ease that pain, then her heart won't hurt anymore, and I can leave her in peace once and for all."

A sharp knot tightened around his heart, making Kwan's ointment seem like nothing. It actually took Deacon several moments before he realized Kwan had stopped his ministrations. The man's frown was as fierce as Deacon had ever seen, and his thin little body had snapped upright so he looked more like a long narrow rod.

"What?" Deacon frowned back at him. Who was Kwan to judge him? "It's the right thing to do! Since I'm the one who hardened her heart, I'm the one who must soften it so she is free to love again. Why can't anyone else understand that?"

Before Deacon finished speaking, Kwan flew into a tirade of Chinese, his tongue racing so fast that it all came out sounding like one long angry word.

As he ranted, he wrapped a clean bandage around Deacon's shoulder and upper arm, being none-too-gentle about it either, and tucked the end beneath the folds.

"You no howp." Grabbing up the tiny pot, Kwan marched out of the room and slammed the door behind him, leaving Deacon alone in his rapidly cooling bathwater.

What did Kwan know anyway?

Deacon washed his hair and scrubbed the rest of his body twice, careful to keep the new bandages dry.

Feeling like a new man, he climbed out of the cooling water and stepped into his new suit. Ah, there really was nothing better than the feel of new silk. Well, perhaps there was one thing, but since he couldn't walk around with Rhea draped over his chest, the silk would have to do.

He set his new hat on his head, left his old clothes bundled in the corner and stepped out into the street.

Now that he no longer looked like a vagabond, he could hold his head up in public. First stop—the sheriff's office.

The building was little more than a brick box, complete with a cell made of rusty bars and a scratched and scarred old desk in the corner. Handbills hung in haphazard design over the walls, and a long, heavy looking rifle stood propped in the corner.

Colin slouched in his chair, his booted feet crossed over the corner of the desk, a cup of coffee in one hand, and a piece of paper in the other.

"Colin." Deacon stepped inside the building, but didn't dare touch anything; the resulting dust storm would no doubt settle on his new suit and ruin the effects of his bath.

"Well, look at you," Colin snorted. "Helping yourself to the goods at the store already, are ya?"

Deacon curled his fingers around the lapels of his jacket and grinned. "It was a gift, actually."

"A gift?" He ran his hand over his mouth and scratched his whiskers. "Guess you've got Rhea feeling pretty guilty about shootin' you if she's willing to splurge on a suit like that."

If Colin wanted to think it had been a gift from Rhea, so be it. It saved Deacon from having to explain about Kit.

"I was wondering," Deacon said, "if you've had any ideas on how to rectify our . . . situation?"

Colin's boots hit the floor with a loud thud. "Nothin' yet."

A wave of relief washed over Deacon, but he kept his expression neutral. "Very well." He turned to leave, but Colin stopped him.

"How's Rhea?"

"She's fine." Irritation gnawed at Deacon. Colin might be in his rights to ask, and he might even be in his rights to ask in that tone of voice, but it didn't mean Deacon had to like it.

"Listen." Colin rose from his chair and made his way across the small room. "What Rhea did with this whole marriage thing was wrong, and she's gonna have to deal with whatever happens. But that don't mean you got any right to mistreat her."

It took the better part of a minute for Deacon to see past the fire burning in his sockets. "I am *not* mistreating her."

"Maybe not physically."

"Not in any way," he ground out. "Your sister and I have an understanding."

"The only understanding I'm interested in is the one between you and me," Colin said, jabbing his finger against Deacon's shoulder. "You've battered her reputation enough. When you 'die' this time, you'd do well to stay dead."

Deacon gritted his teeth to stop from grimacing every time Colin's finger jabbed his wound.

"Calm down, Colin," he said. "This will be my last visit to your town—and your sister."

"Good."

"Good."

Deacon turned sharply and made his exit. From there, he headed directly for the store. He had a sudden overwhelming need to see Rhea; not to talk to her or even touch her, though that would be good, too. He just needed to see her.

Weak, that's what he was. And every minute with her was making him weaker.

People crowded down each aisle of the store, yet few seemed interested in any of the merchandise. Ernest and Rhea were both busy with customers; he, at the counter facing Deacon, and she in the far aisle, paging through a catalog with a woman in a fancy green dress.

The rest of the crowd seemed to be hovering, chattering aimlessly and waiting for something—or, more likely, someone.

Him. Their modern-day Lazarus.

At the sound of the door opening, every head turned in his direction. The ensuing silence lasted less than two seconds before the entire room burst into a flurry of buzzing, whispers and pointing fingers.

Humans.

Fighting back a curse, he pulled his hat off and started up the aisle nearest the button table. Halfway past it, he paused. All the buttons Rhea had spent so long sorting were now back in the bowl, a jumbled mess of colors and shapes. What the—

Ernest came around the counter and marched straight toward him, brushing by customers as if they weren't even there. His complexion was a disturbing reddish purple color, and it seemed his eyes were about to bulge right out of their sockets.

"Something wrong?" Deacon asked.

"You've got nerve." Ernest came to an abrupt halt right in front of Deacon. He kept his voice low, but there was no mistaking the blatant animosity. "Do you think I'm gonna let you—"

"Pfft." Deacon brushed him off without a second glance. Whatever was bothering the boy would have to wait until the crowd dispersed.

"Mr. Deacon!" The voice came from a slightly hunched older woman with snow-white hair and a curious twinkle in her eye. People throughout the store turned in their direction, including Rhea, who glanced over, started to smile, then stopped, her mouth frozen in a twisted half curve. As Deacon watched, Rhea's eyes flickered to Ernest, then to Deacon, before she blinked rapidly and returned her attention to her customer.

The old woman smiled brightly and held up hand for Deacon to take. "I'm Mrs. Foster, an old friend of Rhea's parents. It's a pleasure to finally meet you."

Hiding his grimace, he shook her hand quickly, all the while trying to catch Rhea's eye again.

"Of course, your face and name are familiar to me," the woman was saying, "since you've visited our town before, but we've never been formally introduced."

"No," he answered, forcing civility into his voice. "We haven't."

"We're all so happy you've come back," she said, "though I imagine it was quite a shock for her to have you suddenly appear after all this time."

"I'm sorry?" He looked around for Ernest, who had taken his angry glare to the far corner of the store to help another customer.

"Rhea," the woman said with an exasperated sigh and a brief nod in Rhea's direction. "I'm sure that's why she . . . I mean, the shooting and all. Must have been the shock that made her do it."

Deacon blinked through the fog in his head.

"Yes," he finally answered with a grin. "Shocked. That's exactly it. I don't think I'll ever forget the look on her face."

"I guess we're just lucky she didn't have better aim."

"Yes," he laughed. "Very lucky indeed."

"Forgive me for asking," she went on, "but I'm most curious to know where you've been all this time, and why Rhea would believe you were dead."

"Did you ask her?"

Mrs. Foster shook her white head slowly. "I didn't want to pry, you know."

Of course she did, the nosy old bat.

Several other customers moved closer. Some had the decency to feign interest in nearby merchandise, but most simply stared and leaned in, straining to hear.

The urge to tell them the truth was almost too much. But the last thing Rhea needed was for the old biddy to have a stroke in the middle of her store, so he did what came naturally.

He lied.

"I was in Houston, recovering from a nasty injury that did, in fact, almost kill me."

He offered her a short, condescending smile. "Sadly, my attacker thought to inflict more harm by prematurely declaring me dead to the world. Thus, word was passed to my poor unsuspecting wife."

"Oh dear." Mrs. Foster's watery eyes widened. "How perfectly awful."

"You have no idea."

She shifted her reticule to the one hand and used the other to steady herself against the button table. "But once you'd recovered," she said with a frown, "why didn't you wire her with the good news?"

Deacon suppressed a sigh and forged on with the growing lie. "I'm afraid," he said, lowering his voice, "my injury was brought on after an unfortunate incident with a group of gun-toting card players."

"Oh my goodness," Mrs. Foster gasped softly. "Did you . . . surely you hadn't . . ."

"Did I cheat?" He cast a furtive glance around at the growing group around them, then leaned closer. This was more fun than he'd imagined. "To my eternal shame, I did, so you can understand why these particular gentlemen were intent on causing me significant bodily injury."

The old lady clutched her reticule to her chest.

"Fortunately," he whispered, "I was discovered by some Apaches."

He gave the old woman a moment to catch her breath at the mere mention of natives.

"Perhaps they thought to ransom me, or perhaps they had some other purpose for keeping me alive, I don't know. What I do know is every day I lived in fear for my life, even as they tended my injuries and nursed me back to health."

Mrs. Foster's mouth hung open. "But Apaches don't do that . . . they're savages!"

"Exactly." He nodded. "So you understand my fear. I could never be sure if it was medicine or poison they were feeding me. Never sure if their knives were going to be used on my beard or my throat."

The old woman grabbed her own throat as if Deacon were slicing it open right there in the store.

"For some reason," he continued, "the chief took a liking to me. But because we didn't speak the same language, it took a long time to make him understand I had a wife waiting for me."

Deacon raised his brow and forced a look of admiration to his face. "They might be savages, Mrs. Foster, but even Apaches appreciate the quality of a good woman."

Her only response was to swallow hard beneath her hand.

"The chief eventually agreed to let me go, but because of my previous transgressions, I had lost all my money and had no one to borrow from."

"And the Apaches? They couldn't offer you any assistance?"

Deacon spoke with just a touch of condescension. "Mrs. Foster, you must understand, these people barely survive as it is, and even if they could have helped me . . ." Deacon tsked and shook his head. "I'd imposed on them for too long as it was, eating their food, sleeping in their tents, and I knew full well that I was lucky to still be alive. I couldn't possibly ask for anything else."

"So what did you do?" Try though she might to hide it, the woman's excitement over this titillating piece of gossip outweighed her concern for Deacon's welfare.

"The only thing I could do," he answered, standing up straight. "I walked back home to my wife."

The rest of the group gaped openly.

"You didn't!"

"I did." He nodded for emphasis, fighting back the laughter that tickled his throat.

"All the way from Houston?"

"I had to get back to my Rhea," he answered with a wink and a grin.

"You dear sweet man, of course you did." The smile that lit the old woman's face nearly blinded him. "And all this time, she's been thinking you were gone forever. The poor thing's been in terrible mourning, you know."

"Yes," he said, forcing a look of great concern. "I'm sure she was devastated."

Mrs. Foster patted his sleeve and nodded slowly. "We're all very glad you're here now. It's not right for a woman like Rhea to be widowed so young."

"No," he agreed. "It's not."

The old woman kept looking at him for a long moment, her face flushed with the excitement of his story. "Well," she said at last, "I best go, but perhaps we'll see each other again."

"Perhaps." He dipped a nod and hastened his retreat through the crowd to the backroom, trying to sort out the lie he'd just fabricated and the hostile glares Ernest and Rhea had been shooting him since he'd walked in.

The backroom, while not huge, was large enough to hold a small table and chair, as well as boxes and shelves of merchandise Rhea either hadn't inventoried yet or simply didn't have time or space to put in the store.

Looking around, it was a wonder she could find anything when she needed it. Organization was obviously not one of Rhea's priorities.

Perhaps a little help from him would soften her heart. He slipped off his jacket and replaced it with one of the long cream-colored aprons on the hook. Reduced to a store clerk; his father would no doubt find a great deal of humor in that.

Shelf after shelf, he emptied, washed down and replaced the items in proper order. Bolts of fabric were stored among bags of rice and cans of beans. How could that possibly make sense to anyone? No wonder her button bowl was such a disaster.

"Who is she?" Rhea's tight voice snapped his attention away from the case of cutlery he'd been wiping and sorting.

Instead of answering, he pointed toward the cutlery. "Forks and knives in the same box?" He shook his head, pushed the box aside and rose to his feet. "Honestly, Rhea, that's no way to run a store."

"Who is she?" With her hands fisted on her hips and her chin tipped up that way, she was like a compact ball of fury waiting to explode.

"Who?"

"*That woman.*"

Deacon frowned. "The old woman in the store earlier? She said she was an old friend of your parents. Mrs. Forster? Mrs. F-Something-Or-Other."

"Mrs. Foster," Rhea snapped. "And that's not who I mean."

Her eyes blazed fire. If she stiffened her spine any more, it would probably snap in half.

"Then who—"

"The woman who gave you those clothes," she seethed. "The pretty one in the denim trousers."

"Wha—" Deacon snapped his mouth closed. Damn Kit. "Oh, her."

"Yes, *her*."

He took a step toward her, but a blast from those eyes stopped him cold. "It's not what you think."

"No? Then what is it?"

"I think you need to sit down."

"Don't tell me what to do, and don't talk to me like I'm a child."

Deacon took his time untying his apron. With his back to her, he could release the grin that sprang to his face. Rhea was jealous. That shouldn't make him happy, but it did.

It made him *very* happy.

"I'm waiting." Her toe tapped out her impatience against the floor. "You knew who she was when she came in yesterday, didn't you? That's why you hid back here."

"I did not hide," he lied, forcing the smile from his face before he turned back to her. "But yes, I knew who she was."

"Is she—" Rhea's voice cracked slightly, but she swallowed quickly and tightened it again. "Are you and she . . . ?"

"Rhea." He held out his hands, but she ignored them. "I would never do that to you."

Even as the words fell from his tongue, a flash of something worse than anger flickered across her eyes. It was a flash of physical pain, and the only reason he recognized it was because he'd felt his first physical human-type pain the other day when she'd shot him. The rip of pain he'd just watched shoot across her face and deeper into her eyes was the exact same rip he'd felt when the bullet hit him.

But how could words cause that kind of pain?

"Yes, you would." Rhea blew out a short breath. "She's

obviously someone important to you, or you wouldn't have accepted such an expensive gift from her."

"I don't know that I'd use the word 'important,'" he said, "but she does play a significant role in my life."

"You rat!" Rhea's fists came down on both his shoulders, making him suck in a breath and dodge out of her reach. "It wasn't enough that you humiliated me with Salma, but you've been in town less than two days and you do it again with that . . . that *Kit woman*."

"Whoa." He ducked away from her next swing, then grasped both of her wrists in his hands. "Listen to me, Rhea. Just listen."

She continued to struggle until he wrangled her arms behind her back and held her up against his chest. What a hellion she was!

It was wrong to let her think this way about Kit, but her jealousy soothed his ego and also reinforced what he'd been thinking all along. If Rhea was envious, it could only mean one thing: she really did have feelings left for him. A sigh of relief threatened to escape, but he swallowed it back and smiled down at her.

"Kit is nothing like Salma, but I'm sure she'd find some humor in your thinking so."

"Don't lie to me, Deacon," she spat. "Ernest sold her the very suit you're wearing, so don't try to deny anything."

Tears clung to her lashes, but did not fall. Even her tears were stubborn.

"I don't deny it." He moved her wrists into the grip of his left hand and wiped one of her eyes with his right. She tried to jerk her head away, so he waited until she'd settled again, then wiped her other eye. "Kit gave me this suit—and she chose very well, don't you think?"

"Women don't just give expensive gifts to men without expecting something in return, Deacon." She continued to struggle, but he held her fast. "And I can just imagine what you gave her as payment."

Deacon threw his head back and laughed. "What a dirty little mind you have."

"This isn't funny," she snarled. "You said you'd act like my husband until Colin figured out a way—"

"And I'm doing that."

"You might have let me in on the fact you weren't going to give up your women friends while you played the part."

He laughed again. "Kit is not my 'woman friend.'"

"No?" Disbelief oozed from her voice. "Then who is she?"

Deacon slid his thumb across her cheek again, for no other reason than he wanted to touch her skin, to feel the heat, the anger and the softness.

Could he risk telling her the truth? Satan's children didn't just show up for no reason, and with two of them in the same town, Rhea would have every reason to suspect the worst.

On the other hand, if he lied about Kit now, how could he ever expect Rhea to believe the truth about Salma? It was a gamble either way, and Deacon was not the gambler in the family. That had always been Kit's area of expertise.

"Deacon—" Rhea tried to wrench free, but he didn't release her. Not yet. One more touch—that was all he wanted. That was all he'd ever want. One more, and then one more again.

With a great deal of reluctance, he released her arms and waited for her to slam him in the shoulder again. It didn't happen.

"She's my sister."

"No." Rhea took a step backward. "You're so . . . and she's so . . ."

All he could do was shrug. "I know."

Her cheeks paled and her voice quivered as she reached for the back of the chair. "W-why is she here?"

"Rhea—"

"Tell me." She took in a large gulp of air. "Is she here for m-me?"

"No!" He rushed forward, but she held him off with a raised hand.

"Then wh-who?"

"Me."

"You." She looked as though the air had been sucked out of her lungs. "You're leaving."

"Eventually, yes." He spoke quietly, hoping it would make the truth easier to hear. "I told you before I was only staying for a short while."

The sound that ripped from her throat came out as part chuckle, part sob. Deacon took her hand between his own and held on tight.

"I'm sorry, Rhea."

"You're sorry." The words were like acid on her tongue. "Not nearly as sorry as I am."

CHAPTER SIX

Breakfast the next morning was a horrid affair. Rhea forced herself to swallow the last dregs of her coffee while Deacon sat across from her, smiling to the other diners as though all was right with the world.

What did any of them know, anyway?

She wiped her mouth with her napkin, then set it on her plate. "I have to open the store."

"Can't Ernest do it?" Deacon's plate remained half-full.

"He comes in late on Saturdays."

For the benefit of the other diners, Rhea politely excused herself, then made for the restaurant door. Half a dozen steps down the walk, Deacon's hand wrapped around her arm.

"Now what kind of husband lingers over breakfast while his poor wife is working herself into an early grave?" In one firm but smooth movement, he had her hand curled around his bent elbow. "It looks like I'll be helping you this morning."

Rhea kept her voice low and out of anyone else's earshot. "But you might get your fancy new clothes dirty."

They passed Mrs. Hale and her two young boys, both

covered in dust and chasing a skinny old wooden wheel down the sidewalk.

Deacon settled his hand over Rhea's and squeezed gently. His skin was warm against hers, his fingers longer, thicker and much stronger. It was an odd sensation to have her hand pressed between the warmth of his hand and the cool silk of his sleeve.

"Don't you worry about the clothes," he replied, bobbing a nod at Mr. Worth as he swept the walk in front of the newspaper office. "Kit has plenty of money. She can always buy me more."

"Why, you—" The toe of her boot caught on an uneven plank, but Deacon steadied her without missing a step.

Rhea curled her fingers into his arm until her nails threatened to damage his precious suit. They both nodded a greeting to a man who stepped out of the bank, and carried on their pretense of civility until they were inside the store. Deacon closed and locked the door behind them.

"What are you doing? We need to open."

"Not yet." He took her arm again, this time not so gently, and dragged her toward the backroom.

He pulled the curtain that divided the store from the back, thus preventing any prying eyes from watching through the windows.

When he turned, he stared at her with icy fury. His expression should have frightened her, but all it did was fuel her own anger. *He* was mad at *her*? Half of this mess was his fault!

"Sit down." He jabbed his thumb toward the only chair in the room, an old wooden ladder-back with one leg shorter than the others.

"Don't tell me what to do," she shot back. "I'll sit

when I'm good and ready to sit, and not a moment sooner."

The anger simmered unwaveringly until she finally slumped down on the chair and folded her arms.

"Thank you." His voice was tight and frustrated. "Let's get something straight now."

Rhea crossed her arms over her chest and pursed her lips. If he thought for one second she was going to believe anything he said . . . oooh, he had a lot of nerve!

Deacon cupped his hands behind his back and began to pace in front of her. "I was wrong to leave the way I did last time, I admit that. And while you may have felt justified in shooting me, it would have been nice if you'd given me a chance to explain myself first."

Guilt niggled the back of her brain. One day she'd have to learn to control herself when it came to Deacon. It probably wouldn't happen today or tomorrow—but one day.

"No one would have blamed you if you'd left me to the vultures," he said, "but you didn't."

She opened her mouth to speak, then clamped it shut. If this was his way of apologizing or thanking her, who was she to interrupt?

A few seconds later, Deacon stopped pacing and looked straight at her. "I'm sorry for leaving you the way I did last summer, and though I know you might not believe it, nothing happened between Salma and me."

Rhea was halfway out of her chair when he caught her by the arm again. "I don't have time for this, Deacon. I need to open—"

"Please." Maybe it was the way his fingers held her so gently, or maybe it was the soft pleading in his voice. Whatever it was, it stopped her from wrenching free of his hold.

Hesitantly, she sat down again, her mouth pinched tight to keep it shut.

"An apology can't make anything right, Rhea. No words can."

"You're right about that."

He seemed to resign himself to that. "So let me prove myself to you. Let me help you."

"Help me?" She eyed him cautiously. That darned handsome face of his looked sincere, and he sounded sincere, but still . . .

"Let me help at the store."

"No thank you."

"Why not?"

She barked out a dry laugh. "Mainly because you can't bear to be around people."

"Not all of them," he shot back indignantly. A moment later, he sighed and nodded grudgingly. "Okay, most of them."

"How would you serve the customers? Besides, if we let you loose out there, the store will be overrun with people just wanting to get a look at you. We'll never get any work done."

The muscle in his jaw tightened, his jaw set like stone. "If you don't want me near the customers," he ground out, "then I'll work back here."

"I don't need your help."

Deacon closed his eyes and inhaled a long breath. His chest expanded so much, she thought he'd burst the buttons on his shirt.

When he opened his eyes again, most of the anger was gone—or hidden, at least. With a cocked brow, he nodded toward the box of cutlery he'd been working on yesterday, and sighed dramatically.

"Forks and knives in the same box? Things like this are screaming for my help, Rhea."

The way his lips quivered against the smile he held back, the way the corners of his eyes crinkled . . .

"And by the looks of it, someone had the audacity to undo all your hard work with the buttons. Surely that must be remedied straightaway."

No. She would not find him charming; she would not smile back at him. But if he wanted to work, she'd darn well work his hide off.

"Fine." She nodded, maintaining her straight face. "You can organize the stock back here, but you will not, under any circumstances, come out front."

"Believe me, I'd rather sit down to dinner with Gabriel and his cronies than set foot on the other side of that curtain."

Rhea frowned. "Gabriel?"

That crooked little smile got bigger. "You know— big wings, shiny halo, that whole 'guess what, Mary?' thing."

Rhea sputtered and gaped, and when she couldn't contain it anymore, she laughed right out loud at the absurdity of it all. Angel Gabriel indeed.

"Can I open up now?" She pushed out of her chair again, but he still wouldn't let her pass.

"Not yet." His eyes, still sparkling, held her gaze steady. "Let me be nice to you."

Rhea choked on her next breath. He had to be joking.

"I'm not asking you to afford me the same courtesy." He cupped her chin in his hand and brought his face closer until the tips of their noses touched. "Just that you accept the kindness I offer you."

"Kindness?" She yanked back, narrowing her eyes at him. "I didn't think that was something your kind practiced."

The look he gave her sent pangs of guilt racing through her body.

"I'm sorry," she relented. "That was uncalled for. But put yourself in my place. You made a fool out of me in front of the entire town, yet you stand there expecting me to accept your 'kindness' without being the least bit suspicious. You must see how difficult that's going to be."

"No," he said. "I don't."

Oh, honestly. Could he really be that thick?

"I trusted you once," she said. "And look where it got me. I can't afford to have the town dragging my name through the mud any more than they already have."

"I'm sorry about before," he said quietly. "But people are going to think what they want to think, no matter what you or I do."

Rhea pulled two aprons off the hook and threw one at him. "That may be," she said, "but it doesn't mean I should give them reason to continue to trample my family's name. Stay back here, where no one can see you."

"Out of sight, out of mind?" he asked, smiling weakly.

"One can only hope," she muttered as she stepped through the curtain. "But somehow, I doubt it'll be that easy."

The three Dietrich sisters stood at the door, peering through the glass impatiently. Tying her apron as she moved, Rhea hurried down the aisle to let them in.

"Good morning, ladies. Sorry to keep you waiting."

Annabelle swept in first, looking as though she stepped right out of the pages of *Harper's Bazaar*. Her moss-colored day dress, complete with pearl buttons, lace trim and a large bustle, swished gently over her boots as her matching parasol tapped the floor in time to her steps.

"If this was our store," she sniffed, "it would never open late."

"I'm sure," Rhea muttered.

Donnelda and Suzanne strolled in behind their sister, each one's eyes searching a different corner of the store.

"Is there something I can help you with?" Rhea asked.

Annabelle looked straight through her as if she wasn't even there. "We wanted to check if you had any new earbobs."

"Not since you asked yesterday." Rhea smiled as sweetly as she could.

Annabelle gave no indication she'd heard a word of what Rhea said, but fixed her gaze on the curtain to the backroom. Donnelda and Suzanne wandered through the store with no obvious destination, even through the tools and housewares, for goodness sake, despite the fact neither had ever been introduced to the working end of a broom.

After several minutes of this nonsense, Suzanne sauntered toward Annabelle and raised an indignant brow before asking Rhea, "Are you working alone today, Rhea?"

"No, Ernest will be in a little later."

"I see." Suzanne's dark hair had been fashionably styled in a soft knot at the back of her head and covered with a bonnet so small it could not possibly serve any practical purpose. But it matched her fawn-colored dress, and that was probably all the reason she needed to wear it.

"Why is the curtain closed?" Annabelle made her way to the counter and openly stared at the obstacle she couldn't see through. "You never close it."

Donnelda hurried toward the front to see, too, sending her golden ringlets bouncing with each step. Unfortunately, Deacon chose that exact moment to drop whatever he'd been holding. A loud crash made all the women jump.

"Well, now," Suzanne said coyly. "I thought you said you were alone."

"No," Rhea corrected her. "I said Ernest would be in later."

"So who's back there?"

As if they didn't know. Rhea fought the urge to roll her eyes at the lot of them. If they wanted to put on a show, Rhea would play along, too. In fact, she'd give them a show like they'd never imagined.

"My husband," Rhea said, biting back as much of the bitterness as she could. "Surely, by now you've heard he has returned."

"Yes, of course," Annabelle murmured. "I believe Father mentioned something about it the other day."

All three women kept their gazes fixed on the curtain, as if willing Deacon to come out for their inspection. If they weren't so free with their money in her store, Rhea would have shooed them all out right then and there. They were about as subtle as a train wreck.

"He tires so easily these days," Rhea whispered loudly.

"Why is that?"

"It's been a . . . difficult . . . time for him since we were married," she said, amazed she could maintain a straight face as she spoke. "As you know, we were all led to believe he was dead, but in fact, he was simply hovering on the verge of death for months."

"Yes, we heard." Suzanne's brown eyes grew wide. "But we were told he looked just fine now."

"Yes, well, looks can be deceiving, can't they?" Rhea stepped behind the counter and cast a cautious glance at the curtain for good measure. If it was a story they wanted, a story they would get—one that would turn every eye away from her and straight onto Deacon.

"What do you mean?" Annabelle was doing a fine job

of looking indifferent, despite the fact her eyes snapped with excitement.

"My husband left a few pertinent details out of the story he told Mrs. Foster." She forced a frown and shook her head sadly. "Poor man."

"Details?"

Rhea nodded. "You will keep this in the strictest of confidence, of course."

"Of course." The three women leaned closer, eager to hear Rhea's story.

"The night before I was to leave Houston to come home, we took supper at a lovely French restaurant—"

"Oooh," Suzanne squealed. "Did you have escargot?"

Rhea's tongue froze. Escargot? What on earth was that? And did everyone eat it at a French restaurant? She gave herself a mental kick; one sentence into her story, and already she was caught.

Annabelle clicked her tongue. "Land sakes, Suzanne, what difference does it make what she ate?"

Suzanne flushed slightly and shrugged. "I've never met anyone who's actually tried them."

The other two women rolled their eyes impatiently. "Please go on."

"Yes, well, as I was saying," Rhea stammered, "we'd finished our supper and started back to the hotel when we were set upon by two very large men."

Donnelda gasped behind her hand, but Suzanne looked as though she would jump out of her skin from the excitement of it all.

"I was terrified," Rhea continued, "but my dear husband, he wasn't about to let any harm come to me." She forced her smile to appear wistful, as opposed to the dry smirk that came naturally. "He single-handedly fought off both of our attackers."

"He didn't."

"He did. Thankfully, he wasn't hurt in the fray, and we were able to make it safely back to the hotel."

"Then what happened?" Donnelda's eyes bulged from their socket. "How did he become ill?"

Rhea pressed her fingers to her lips, as though calming herself for a moment before answering. For the briefest of moments, a twinge of guilt twisted in her stomach. Her mother was no doubt spinning in her grave right then, listening as Rhea spun this web of lies.

Oh well. In for a penny, in for a pound.

"The next morning," she said, "he saw me safely on the stage, and that was the last I saw of him."

She paused, glanced at the curtain again, then leaned her head closer to the theirs, her voice low. "As I'm sure you heard, the two men from the night before were men my husband owed money to, and they caught up with him on his way back from the station."

"I find that odd." Suzanne frowned. "Since I've heard your husband comes from an influential family—surely they could have assisted him."

"Influential?" Rhea couldn't stop the grin that tugged at her lips. "Well, I guess that's one word for it."

"How much did he owe them?" Donnelda whispered.

Rhea opened her eyes as wide as she could. "Quite a bit, I'm afraid. And since he'd cheated them at cards, you can understand why these men were so intent on seeking revenge."

"So that's why they beat him so badly," Donnelda breathed.

Shuffling sounded from the backroom. Rhea held up a hand to shush them, waited until the noises stopped, then continued.

"The beating was only the start of it," she said. "After they'd taken their pound of flesh, they tied him to the back of a horse and dragged him twenty miles or more out of town."

"Oh my goodness." Even Annabelle's cool demeanor gave way to a bit of shock. If any of them stopped to think for a minute, they'd realize how preposterous the whole idea was.

"It gets worse." This was too much fun. "They stripped him naked first."

Three jaws dropped. Six eyes rounded as big as dish plates.

"And then they left him there, with no water, no food and . . ." She sighed. "No clothes."

When she thought they'd had enough time to absorb that juicy lie, she went deeper. "Luckily the Apache tribe found him and nursed him back to health."

"Apaches," Donnelda gasped, her expression a mixture of both distress and delight. "They're so vicious—he could have been killed."

"He was already as good as dead when they found him," Rhea said. "And long after they got him back to their camp, he was delirious and half crazed with fever."

"No."

Rhea nodded. "None of the Indians spoke English, and my dear Deacon didn't speak their language, of course, so there was no way to communicate, no way to get word back to me."

"You poor dear." Annabelle reached to pat Rhea's hand. "How awful."

"The worst part," Rhea said, "was being told he'd been killed in an accident, when all this time he was alive and suffering." She covered her eyes with one hand and forced a slight sob. "If only I'd known, I could have sent Colin to bring him home to me."

"How is your brother?" Donnelda's sudden question made them all stop and stare for a moment.

"Well, he's fine, thank you." Rhea frowned a little, then added, "I'll be sure to tell him you were asking."

A flash of embarrassment crossed Donnelda's face, but she quickly recovered and returned her attention to the scandal at hand.

"What about your husband?" Suzanne pushed. "Did he really walk all the way back?"

"Every step." Perhaps she should consider writing a dime novel one day.

"Oh my." Donnelda looked as though she'd faint right there in the store. "That is so romantic."

"Yes." Suzanne nodded. "It is."

Annabelle didn't look so convinced. "So why on earth did you shoot him?"

Rhea pressed her hand over her heart and forced a look of affront. "What would you do if a man you believed to be dead suddenly turned up on your front porch?" she asked. "For all I knew, he was the devil himself."

That put the little busybody back in her place for a minute. They all stood in silence for a long moment, staring at the curtain. Finally Annabelle cleared her throat quietly. "Does he always stay back there?"

"Most of the time," Rhea said solemnly. "I'm afraid he hasn't completely recovered from the shock of everything's that happened to him." She opened her eyes a little wider and tapped the side of her temple.

"You mean—" Donnelda started.

"He's mad?" Annabelle finished.

Rhea nodded slowly. "Still as handsome a man as God ever put on this earth, but his mind isn't what it used to be. We're hopeful, now that he's home, we can help him make a full recovery and he'll soon be as right as rain."

After another few minutes of curtain-staring, Annabelle gathered her wits and blinked several times.

"That is certainly a distressing story, Rhea. I hope he recovers soon."

"Yes." Rhea smiled brightly. "Thank you."

"Perhaps I'll check back tomorrow for those earbobs."

"You can check," Rhea answered, "but I'm not expecting any new shipments for a while yet."

Her words went unacknowledged as all three women were already sashaying toward the door, whispering furiously among themselves. When they'd finally left and Rhea was once again left to the quiet of her store, she exhaled a long breath and grinned.

She'd made some rather fine adjustments to Deacon's story, if she did say so herself. If they were going to gossip about her, at least it wouldn't be the pathetic truth.

"So let me get this straight." Deacon's voice from behind the curtain made her start so suddenly, she knocked one of the candy jars sideways and had to scramble to right it. "After defending your virtue, I was beaten, stripped naked and left for dead out in the middle of the desert, causing me to lose most of my mind."

"You were listening!" She tugged the curtain open a little to find him sitting on the chair with his arms crossed and his crooked grin mocking her.

"A story like that," he answered, "was too good to miss."

"Your version was fine." She couldn't help grinning, too, as she moved away from the curtain and back to the counter. "It just lacked the extra little spark that made it more about you and less about me."

"I especially enjoyed the part about me being so handsome. 'As handsome a man as—' " He leaned forward and pulled the curtain open a bit more. "If only they knew God hadn't put me here."

"Yes," Rhea retorted, rolling her eyes. "Let's tell them that."

She stared at the door the girls had walked out and chuckled. "You should have seen their faces. They'll be talking about you for months."

"Lying well is a talent," Deacon said. "And while I'm impressed with what appears to be your natural ability, don't you think your good friend Mrs. Foster is going to be a little put out that she didn't get to hear the added details firsthand?"

She didn't even try to hold back her laughter this time. "She would have had apoplexy right there by the buttons if you'd even thought about saying some of the things I did."

Turning slightly, she was able to keep an eye on the door, while still keeping Deacon in her peripheral vision as she went over the accounts book.

"You're probably right." He stretched his legs out and crossed his booted feet at the ankles. "And while that may have been unfortunate, it would have given the town vultures someone else to stare at for a while."

"The last thing we need to do is make trouble for anyone else." Rhea chuckled. "Especially when it's all just a wild made-up story."

"About that wild made-up story." Deacon's eyes snapped with mischief. "There's something about your version that I find myself wondering about."

"What's that?"

He stretched to his feet, leaned against the door frame and grinned. "How much time do you spend imagining me naked?"

"What?" She jumped away from him and bumped into the counter. He remained hidden behind the curtain, which was just as well because Mrs. Foster and Mrs. Worth were standing outside on the boardwalk. If either caught sight of Deacon, there'd be no getting rid of them.

"You truly are mad," she growled.

"Me?" He laughed; the sound—deep and velvety— bounced off the walls. "You were the one detailing how handsome your husband is, even naked. Wasn't me."

"Ugh," she huffed.

"Huff all you like," he needled. "We both know what you're really thinking, don't we?"

"What I'm thinking is that you truly are a lunatic," she seethed. "And before you say another word, you should know Mrs. Worth is heading this way."

He darted back out of sight, tripped on something, cursed and scurried as far away from the curtain as he could.

Who did he think he was, suggesting she spent any of her time thinking about him naked? She'd only used the idea as fodder for her story. It wasn't as though she wasted her precious time thinking on such a thing. Not much, anyway.

CHAPTER SEVEN

Sunday morning couldn't come soon enough for Rhea. Finally a day where her cheek muscles wouldn't ache from holding a smile she didn't feel; finally a day where she could hide away from the entire town without having to answer questions.

Before she poked her head out from under the blanket, she knew she was alone. The room was too quiet, the air too still and the other side of the bed too empty.

For the better part of the past week, she and Deacon had spent almost every minute together, and while she'd felt overwhelmed and distracted by his constant presence, not having him beside her when she woke up was worse. Much worse.

She fumbled her way out of the blanket, took her hairbrush and made her way to the rocking chair. The morning sun teased the horizon, casting shadows over the street below as Rhea repeatedly pulled the brush through her hair. When was the last time she'd simply sat down and enjoyed the quiet of a Sunday morning? When was the last time she'd wanted to?

Any woman would be glad to have the chance to do just that, so why was she feeling so restless? She needed to be up and doing something, making better use of this time.

Just as she pushed out of the chair, the door creaked open and there stood Deacon, a basket in his arms, looking as neat and proper as he always did.

Not only neat, but dressed in yet another new suit. Ernest hadn't mentioned selling it, but Rhea recognized it as the last gray one she'd had in stock. She sure hoped someone paid for that one, too, because she certainly couldn't afford something so fine.

As she took a step toward him, it hit her; the reason Deacon stood there staring at her openmouthed was because she was only wearing her plain cotton nightgown; no wrapper, no shawl or anything. And while she'd lain in bed next to him all these nights, he'd always waited until she was tucked in before he came into the room.

Rhea grabbed for her blanket and wrapped it around her shoulders as Deacon muttered under his breath.

"I'm sorry," she said. "I was just sitting in the window—"

"Like *that*?" He stepped inside and kicked the door closed.

"What . . . ?"

"Nice of you to treat the whole town to yet another scandal," he said, his voice tight. "But next time you might think to cover yourself first."

"No one can see me when I'm in the chair," she argued.

"That's all very well," he said. "But when I came in, you were standing right in front of the window."

"So?"

"So," he almost growled, "anyone who cared to look up would have seen clear through your nightgown."

"Oh." For the amount of heat that raced over her

skin right then, she half expected to burst into flames. "I wasn't thinking."

Thankfully he didn't comment further. Instead, he set the basket on the end of the bed and hung his hat on one of the hooks.

"I brought breakfast," he grumped, tugging a cloth from the top of the basket. Inside were two plates of ham, eggs and bread, cutlery and a small blue-and-white checked tablecloth.

He spread the cloth on the floor, then set the plates on top.

"Breakfast picnic," she said quietly. "Interesting."

"It's a damn sight better than sitting in that restaurant again and having every busybody in town stare at me while I try to eat." He took a breath and waggled his brow at her. "Apparently they've never seen a madman up close."

Rhea took the fork he offered, then arranged herself on the corner of the cloth, careful to keep herself covered with the blanket. He waited until she was settled before starting his meal.

"Well," she said after a while, "I guess the gossips will find something else to talk about eventually, won't they?"

He shrugged.

"And a lady should never complain when a gentleman brings her food."

"If that's your way of thanking me, then you're welcome." The gruffness in his voice faded a little, but not completely.

As Rhea ate, she struggled to keep the blanket up. It wasn't the easiest thing in the world to wrangle her food up onto her fork without the use of her knife, but that would teach her not to lounge around in bed so long. Every other morning, she'd been up and dressed before Deacon opened his eyes.

His gaze seemed fixed on her throat, making her horribly self-conscious each time she swallowed.

"The store's closed today?"

"Yes."

"Good." He nodded briefly. "Then let's get out of this blasted town for a while."

"Where will we go?"

"Doesn't matter." He swallowed the last of his eggs and wiped his mouth. "Let's go for a ride somewhere. Anywhere."

She started to object, then stopped. Maybe a ride was just what she needed to sort out her thoughts. With all the customers—both buyers and snoopers—who had come through the store over the last few days, she hadn't had time to sort out the mess she was in.

Today could be the perfect time to do just that.

"Sounds lovely," she said. "I'll need a few minutes . . ."

Deacon was already stacking the dishes in the basket.

"I'll return these to the restaurant and rent us a buggy. Will that be enough time?"

"Yes." Her nerves twitched uncertainly. It wasn't as though she'd never been alone with Deacon before, so why did her stomach flutter this way?

And for goodness sake, why didn't her head remind the rest of her body that it wasn't supposed to feel anything for him? She pressed her hands against her stomach to quell the quivers.

If he was going to be nice to her, surely she could return the kindness without allowing herself to be charmed out of her boots this time. A tiny thread of doubt wove its way through her brain until she shook her head to clear it.

Stop it, she silently chastised herself. *Just stop it.*

All she needed to do was keep the whole fiasco with Salma at the forefront of her mind, and then she could fight off these ridiculous feelings she still had for Deacon.

In the meantime, she had another problem.

What should she wear?

The second the door closed behind Deacon, Rhea pulled her three dresses off the hooks and spread them out on the bed. Her yellow one was nice enough but looking its age, and she'd worn it the last two days in a row. The blue print had a large stain on the bodice, which hid nicely behind her apron when she was working—but she wasn't wearing an apron today, was she?

Her only other choice was the dark brown sateen, the dress she normally wore to Sunday service. With the reverend ministering to the outlying ranches, they hadn't had services in a couple weeks, but still . . . the dark brown was too close to black, and Rhea had worn black most of the year.

She hung the last two dresses back up and studied the yellow one again. It was a suitably fine garment and would do nicely for today.

Problem was, Rhea didn't feel like wearing anything she could best describe as "suitably fine." It had been a long time since she'd bought a new dress; surely it wouldn't be considered too extravagant if she bought one today.

She stopped, stared blankly at the wall and grinned. Who would question her purchase? Her parents were both gone, Colin wouldn't even notice and Deacon certainly wouldn't care.

She yanked the yellow dress over her head and fumbled with the buttons as she pushed her feet inside her boots.

Creeping through the store, she made her way directly to the ready-made ladies' clothes. Pretty, yet sensible. Surely there was something . . .

The plum-colored walking skirt and white shirtwaist would look smart together and would also be suitable for work.

It certainly wasn't anywhere near the fancy clothes the Dietrich girls wore about town, but dresses like those held little appeal to Rhea. What could a woman hope to accomplish during the day if she was constantly worrying about the size of her bustle or soiling her hem?

Back in the room, she ran her fingers through her hair, lifting it, twisting it and curling it around the crown of her head.

Why couldn't she have beautiful hair like Kit? Now there was a head of hair to be envied. Even tousled around her head in the messy way she wore it, it was amazing, and would no doubt be even more beautiful pinned up.

With a great sigh, Rhea let her own boring brown hair fall down her back. Boring old braid it would have to be.

"Leave it down," Deacon said quietly from the doorway.

"Oh!" She dropped the brush, and it skidded across the floor. "You scared me."

He crossed the room in two long, slow strides and slid his fingers through the beginnings of her braid, loosening it all over again. With slow, gentle hands, he fanned her hair out over her shoulders, rubbing the ends between his fingers.

"Definitely leave it down."

Rhea swallowed hard and forced her head to nod. Surely if Mrs. Foster saw her this way, she'd take it upon herself to remind Rhea of what was proper and what wasn't. But one last look at Deacon's face in the mirror, and all thoughts of Mrs. Foster vanished.

"Are we ready?" she asked, a little shaky.

Deacon didn't speak, just nodded and let her by. Outside, two sleek black horses were hitched to a shiny white oak phaeton. With Deacon's help, Rhea climbed inside and settled back against the soft leather seat.

How had he paid for the buggy? He'd told her that first day that he hadn't a penny to his name.

"Does Mr. Travis know we have his best buggy?" she asked.

"Of course. What did you think I'd done—stolen it?" He climbed up beside her and took the reins in his hands.

Rhea chose not to answer that question or further the conversation in any way. Best to leave well enough alone for now.

She shifted slightly in her seat, watching the horses' tails swish calmly and their ears twitch against a couple of pesky mosquitoes.

"Why are they acting that way?"

With a flick of the reins, Deacon set the horses off at a slow walk.

"What do you mean?" he asked. "They're being perfectly calm."

"I can see that," she agreed. "But if memory serves, animals don't usually appreciate your presence."

He grinned. "I told you, things have changed. Without my powers, I'm just like any other human to these animals."

"A human who's never driven horses before."

"They don't know that, do they?"

Rhea swallowed the retort that jumped to her tongue. They were going to have a nice day. Nothing else mattered.

The streets were almost empty, save for a few people lingering around the livery and two dirty yellow dogs sniffing the corner of the saloon.

"It's so beautiful this morning." She inhaled a long, slow breath and smiled. "I love the smell of spring."

"So you've said," he teased. "Still smells like dust and horse sweat to me."

The morning sun followed them west across miles of open land.

"Where are you taking me?"

"I have no idea." He shrugged over his grin. "The farther away from town, the better."

She pointed off into the distance. "There's a lake about five miles that way if you're interested. Trees for shade, a bit of grass for the horses."

"Any people?"

"Not usually this early."

"Perfect." He turned the horses southwest and settled back against the bench. As one minute stretched into ten, then twenty and more, the knot in Rhea's stomach grew in proportion.

"You're awfully quiet," he noted. "Is something wrong?"

"No," she hurried to answer. "Nothing. I think, perhaps, that's the problem."

Deacon laughed. "It's bad that we're having a peaceful morning together without arguing?"

"Yes. I mean no, it's not bad—just unexpected."

"Why? It's not as though we've never done it before."

"True," she conceded. "But as you've pointed out more than once, things have changed."

He pinched the reins tighter but didn't say anything. A minute later, the horses picked up their pace a little as the lake came into view. Deacon reined them in beneath a tall pecan tree and set the break.

"I'll help you down." He made his way around the buggy, lifted her down, then threw the reins around a low hanging branch.

"We need to unhitch them," Rhea said. "Unless we're leaving shortly."

"So long as no one else comes out here, we're not going anywhere for a while," he said, then grinned sheepishly. "But I've never had to unhitch an animal before."

It was times like these when Rhea could almost forget where he came from. He seemed almost . . . innocent.

She pushed her hair back over her shoulders and set to work on the harness. Deacon watched what she did and mimicked her actions on the other side. Soon enough, the horses were free and hobbled in the shade.

Taking her by the hand, Deacon frowned as he led her toward the water. "You have a bit of dirt just . . . there."

Rhea glanced down at her blouse to find a gray smudge across her chest. If she hadn't been distracted by Deacon holding her hand, she might have taken more time to worry over the stain. As it was, she brushed off as much as she could with her free hand and ignored the rest.

Her hand was still tucked in Deacon's as they found themselves a spot of thick green grass to sit on.

"I'm sorry about your blouse." It wasn't like Deacon to apologize for anything—especially when the offense was not his.

"It's just dirt. It'll wash out."

"I know that, but you . . ." He averted his eyes and shrugged. "It's new."

His thumb moved in slow circles over her knuckles, causing the blood in her veins to swirl in the same motion.

"Y-yes," she stammered. *Think of Salma. Think of Salma.*

"Thank you."

"What for? I've hardly done anything in the past few days that you should be thanking me for."

He finally looked at her, and what she saw made her want to dive into those eyes and never come back.

Salma Salma Salma Salma.

This was the same man who'd left her shattered last summer, the same man who was going to leave her shattered again if she didn't keep Salma's face in mind.

"You took the trouble to dress up for me," he said. "I didn't expect that."

"I-I—"

"And you're letting me be nice to you." He tried to smile, but failed.

Drat. How could she possibly keep up the illusion of aloofness if he was going to look at her like that?

"It's been a trial, too," she teased. "For goodness sake, breakfast brought to my room and a ride to the lake on the most beautiful day of the year." She squeezed his hand gently. "I don't know how much more of this I can take."

Deacon pulled her hand up to his chest. Finally, at long last, his cocky grin was back. "Are you mocking me?" he asked.

She batted her lashes and smiled. "Never."

"Let's walk." He pulled her to her feet, then stood staring at her hair. "Shouldn't you have a bonnet or something?"

"Probably," she replied, "but I've never been one who much liked hats."

"Surely you like mine, though."

Rhea stared at her boots for a minute before looking up at him and smiling self-consciously. "Hate it."

"But—" He pulled the horrid thing from his head, considered it a moment, then shrugged and tossed it to the ground.

That was better; now she could see his hair, she could imagine what it felt like to run her fingers through it . . .

Wait a minute. The Deacon she knew would never go anywhere without his hat, and he certainly wouldn't throw it on the ground because someone didn't like it!

"You could've told me you didn't like it," he said, tucking her hand under his elbow. "I'd tell you if you were wearing something I didn't like."

Perfectly good new clothes wasted. "You don't like this skirt?"

"I didn't say that, did I?" There wasn't even a hint of teasing in his voice now. "You get prettier every day."

"Aside from the giant smudge across my . . . blouse, the fact my hair is a complete disaster, and—"

Deacon stopped short, jolting her along with him. He cupped her face in his hands and looked straight into her eyes.

"Beautiful," he said. "Completely, thoroughly and altogether beautiful." Each word brought his face closer to hers until they were but a breath apart.

He was so close. He smelled like sunshine. And his hands . . . so warm, so gentle against her skin.

"Deacon," she whispered. "Why did you come back?"

"I missed you." His thumbs caressed her cheeks in slow tortuous circles. "I wanted to make things right."

Something prickled the back of her brain; she was supposed to remember something, but what? And did it really matter at this point?

"I missed you, too."

She pushed up on her toes, touching her lips to his, hesitantly at first, then slowly becoming bolder. Deacon didn't move, didn't try to control it, but instead let Rhea take her time. It was a heady feeling knowing she could do whatever she wanted, for as long as she wanted.

For that moment, Rhea didn't care one whit about what was proper, what wasn't or why any of it mattered. The cloudless sky, the crystal clear lake and the man she lo . . . enjoyed; it was a moment to cherish.

She leaned into him, her hands pressed flat against his chest as it thumped out its wildly erratic beat. Her breathing, labored and shallow, matched his gasp for gasp.

A low growl started in his throat, but still he didn't move.

"Deacon?" She'd barely murmured his name before he took control. His mouth slanted over hers, possessing her and loving her, while his hands still cupped her cheeks, his thumbs caressing her skin.

"I missed you," he whispered again, his voice aching and cracked. "I missed this."

Each breath she took was more painful than the last. God help her, but she wanted to believe him.

"Kiss me again."

"Rhea." Her name was a heartbreaking sigh from his lips.

His fingers moved through her hair, sliding over the length of it. He kissed her eyes, her cheeks and the sensitive spot just below her ear. Rhea couldn't have moved if she wanted to. Not a single ounce of strength remained in her muscles; not a single clear thought remained in her brain.

Seeking out his mouth, she opened to him, accepting his tongue as it teased her lips open and danced against her teeth. One of his hands splayed across her back, holding her tight against his chest; the other caressed the underside of her jaw, the side of her neck.

She needed to touch him, to feel the heat of his skin beneath her hands. She fumbled against the buttons on his shirt, but before she could release the first one, Deacon broke their kiss and stepped back.

Rhea staggered slightly, righted herself and looked up at him. What on earth?

Guilt splashed across his face even before he exhaled a long breath and indicated behind her with a raised brow.

Rhea turned slowly, still dizzy from his kisses and the way he'd ended it so abruptly. She didn't want to see whatever it was that caused Deacon to look at her with such regret and frustration.

Blinking through the haze in her brain, she found herself looking straight into Kit's exquisite face. Dressed in her denim trousers and chambray shirt, Kit looked completely at ease standing there in the midmorning sun. How had she snuck up on them so quietly?

Every beautiful thing about the day exploded around Rhea in a storm of regret. Kit was Deacon's sister. She had the power to appear and disappear whenever she liked.

"Sorry to interrupt." Kit's smile and raspy voice were a direct contradiction to her words.

Stumbling slightly, Rhea forced her legs to hold her upright as every ounce of happiness slowly drained to her toes.

If it wasn't embarrassing enough to be caught in a compromising position, it was beyond anything else to be caught in that position by Deacon's own sister.

Kit cocked her head to the side and grinned brightly. "Hello, Rhea."

"Kit." Bile churned in her stomach, sloshing back and forth with enough force to make her dizzy.

Kit's grin faded to a frown. "Oh no, he told you about me, didn't he?"

"Yes." Deacon's answer hung on the air as he moved in beside Rhea and slid his arm around her waist. Normally, it would have been a welcome support; but now, with Kit standing there smirking at them, Rhea couldn't shake him off fast enough.

"Deacon, Deacon, Deacon." Kit ran her fingers through her chaos of red hair, shaking it loose around her shoulders. "When are you going to learn? Humans don't need to know about us. It just complicates things."

"On the contrary," Rhea replied. "It makes things much easier knowing you're a . . ." She couldn't bring herself to say it out loud. "You're like him."

"Oh, please. I'm much better than he'll ever be."

"Better? Or worse?" Rhea shot back. "It seems you and I have different definitions of those words."

As if she wasn't confused enough about what she felt for Deacon, having Kit there only made it worse. She was a constant reminder that Deacon's time with Rhea was limited. But just how limited?

"Listen to me, Rhea." Deacon took a tentative step toward her. "You don't know what Kit's capable of, and without any powers, I can't protect you from her."

"Why would you need to protect me? I've given her no reason to do anything to me."

"That's true," Kit admitted, brushing grass from her trousers as she rose to her feet. "She hasn't. In fact, she was more than courteous when I was in the store the other day."

Deacon ignored her. "She doesn't need a reason to hurt you, Rhea. She'd do it simply because she can."

"Deacon!" The pained look on Kit's face didn't fool anyone. "What kind of a thing is that to say about your youngest sister?"

"Youngest?" Rhea repeated, her head twisting to stare from one to the other. "There's more of you?"

Kit's green eyes lit up like a mischievous child's. "You mean you haven't told her about Lucille? And here I thought you were being all truthful and good."

"Lucille?" Rhea pressed her hand over her chest.

"This just keeps getting better." Kit began to walk, taking slow deliberate steps around them.

"Be quiet, Kit." Deacon's voice was dangerously low.

"You have another sister?" Rhea could hardly look at him. "I can't believe you didn't tell me."

"I can't believe you shot him." Kit snorted. "That's my favorite part of this whole story."

"Yes, well, I apologized for that." Shame fired her skin until she was certain her cheeks must be completely scarlet. Thank goodness Kit didn't seem to take notice. Instead, she shot Rhea a quick wink and laughed.

"Why? We both know he deserved it."

The soft breeze caught Rhea's hair and blew strands across her face. She brushed them away and cursed herself sideways for leaving it down. What had she been thinking?

She hadn't—that was the problem. She'd let herself be tempted by that look in Deacon's eye and the promise of his bone-melting touch.

Foolish girl.

"What do you want, Kit?" Deacon turned in a slow circle, following Kit as she moved around them.

"Not a thing. Just wanted to say hello. I see you have another new suit." She didn't seem to mind the fact her hair was being blown around like a tiny tornado. And much to Rhea's chagrin, she had to admit the chaos only made Kit prettier.

"Which reminds me . . ." Rhea frowned at the scowl Deacon shot his sister. "While I appreciate your business, Kit, I hardly think he needed a second suit so soon."

"I didn't give him that one."

"But I thought—"

Kit shook her head. "Not me."

"Then who?" Rhea whirled on Deacon. "Oh my Lord, did you—?"

"No!"

"But you told me you didn't have any money, and if you didn't get the clothes from her and you didn't get them from me . . ." She backed away from him slowly, her heart plunging to her toes.

"I didn't steal it, Rhea." He started to follow her, but she shook her head. "Kit gave me some money."

"If that were true, she wouldn't have had to buy you that other suit; you could have bought it yourself."

"Excellent points, Rhea." Kit continued to walk in a wide circle around them. "I'd be very interested in hearing his explanations."

Deacon fired a look at his sister that was so fierce, so dark, it froze Rhea's breath in her lungs. Her fear must have shown on her face, because Kit laughed and rolled her eyes.

"Don't let his bluster and fearsome looks worry you," she said. "He couldn't hurt me if he tried. Unfortunately, I can't guarantee he won't hurt you."

"Rhea—" Deacon's hand wrapped around her arm, but she pulled away. The fact that he didn't try to hold on spoke volumes. "Don't listen to her. I told you why I came back. You have to believe that."

"I think it's time I went home," Rhea said quietly, backing away.

Deacon didn't try to stop her, didn't reach for her or say one word asking her to stay. And while the reasonable side of her brain found that to be a huge relief, the other side of her brain—the side ruled by her heart—screamed in misery.

How she wished she could shut off that side of herself, the weak side, the side she couldn't control when it came to Deacon.

Before she lost what was left of her nerve, Rhea lifted her skirt, turned toward town and started walking. It was probably a good thing Kit showed up when she did. Otherwise there'd be no telling what would have happened between Rhea and Deacon.

This way Rhea had time to think, to try and make sense of what her heart wanted and what her mind knew she couldn't have.

So far as she knew, Deacon had been truthful with her since he'd come back. He'd even admitted he'd be leaving soon. So what if he hadn't told her about Lucille? Could she blame him for that?

Being who he was, it only stood to reason he wouldn't be keen to tell her about his family.

He'd been nothing but kind to her since he came back, and Lord knew he didn't have to be, not after she dragged him into a pretend marriage. He could have just as easily turned tail and run, or worse, let everyone know the truth about their marriage.

But he hadn't. He'd taken up the role of her husband and had even put up with the stares and whispers that plagued him wherever he went.

Why?

Of course, he'd also said he came back to make things right. How could he do that if he was going to leave again?

Rhea straightened her shoulders and breathed deeply. She could walk from here to China and her heart still wouldn't have enough time to make sense of this.

Her heart might be confused, but her mind wasn't. Deacon wasn't staying—she knew that. She also knew she wouldn't get another chance to redeem her family name if it was ever brought to light that she and Deacon were not legally married. There would be no recovery from that. She'd be forced to give up the store, her last connection to her parents, and move far away.

As the idea took form in her head, her pace increased. The idea had actually been Deacon's, not hers. He wanted to make things right, and he'd already offered to do it, so all Rhea needed was a real marriage certificate and an understanding judge.

And she knew just the one.

CHAPTER EIGHT

Ernest poked his head through the curtain separating the store from the backroom and cleared his throat. "The sheriff wants to see you."

"Thank you, Ernest," she said. "Will you be all right for a little while?"

He nodded. "Been pretty quiet this morning."

"I shouldn't be long." With trembling fingers, she untied her apron and tossed it on the table. "Have you seen my husband this morning?"

Ernest frowned but didn't answer.

"If you see him, would you please send him over to the sheriff's office?"

Ernest nodded briefly, then hesitated.

"Is something wrong?" She didn't have time for this right now. Colin had news and, good or bad, she needed to hear it.

Oh sweet heaven, what if it was bad?

Rhea swallowed hard. Perhaps she'd take a few minutes to sort out whatever was bothering Ernest.

"If you'll beg my pardon, Miss Rhea, it ain't right the way your husband carries on."

"I'm sorry?"

"I know it ain't my business," he said, seeming to age

right before her eyes, "but he left here this morning with . . . that woman."

That woman.

"The one who bought him the suit?"

Ernest's eyes widened. "You knew."

"Of course."

"Then you know—"

"It's okay." She patted his arm gently. "That woman is his sister."

"His sister?" Ernest shook his head slowly. "I don't think so. She's so . . . and he's so . . ."

"I know." Rhea laughed lightly. "It's hard to imagine, but it's true."

"Well I'll be durned." He slapped his hand over his mouth, a look of horror falling over his face. "I apologize, Miss Rhea. I shouldn't—"

"It's fine," she said, still smiling. "I thought something similar at first."

"His sister." Ernest held the curtain open until Rhea stepped through. "Can't say I'd let any sister of mine prance around in men's . . . *sit-down-upons.*"

Rhea forced a chuckle. "It's 1882, Ernest, and most women do not appreciate being told what they can and cannot do. How would you like it if a woman ordered you around?"

"That's different." He shrugged as if the discussion was over. Silly, silly boy.

"Why would it be any different?"

"The man is the head of the household," he argued. "And the womenfolk need to abide by his rules."

Rhea stopped at the door and turned to look at him. It was beliefs like those that made her appreciate Deacon all the more. He might have teased her about not wearing trousers, but if she decided that was what she was going to do, he wouldn't try to stop her.

"If that's the case, Ernest, then you must agree with Mr. Hale sending Polly away, even if it means you'll never see her again and she'll no doubt up and marry another man."

His face went from flushed to a deep scarlet in less than two seconds. "You know I don't think that's right. Polly's my girl, and I woulda made her my wife eventually."

"But Mr. Hale's the head of that household, and the womenfolk need to abide by his rules."

"It ain't the same. I just meant—"

She raised her hand. "I know what you meant, Ernest. And while I'm sure you don't mean to insinuate we *womenfolk* are dimwitted, you do make it seem as though we are incapable of making our own decisions."

He couldn't seem to decide whether it was safer to agree with her or not.

"Women are a lot smarter than men usually give them credit for. We think, we plan, we dream, just like the menfolk." She sighed, then smiled at the poor young man's tortured expression. "Polly is a beautiful, smart girl, and any man would be lucky to have her as his wife."

Outside, two men crossed the street, heading toward the store.

"If you let her father send her away, you're inasmuch saying Polly shouldn't have a say in what she does with her own life."

"I ain't sayin' that!" He frowned. "But what can I do?"

"Talk to Mr. Hale. Tell him how you feel about his daughter." The men were getting closer. "He's a reasonable man, and if you take the time to discuss the situation with him, you'll go a long way in proving your own worth to both him and Polly."

Before he could answer, the door opened and the two men stepped inside.

"Good morning, gentlemen."

"Miss Rhea." Both pulled their hats off and bobbed nods in her direction.

"Ernest will help with anything you need." With a final smile, she left the store and headed to see Colin at the sheriff's office. A fine example she was to poor Ernest. Here she was preaching about women making their own decisions, yet her entire life had been ruled by her men. Her father made the rules she grew up with, Colin had been all set to sell the store out from under her until she married, and even Deacon held power over her most vulnerable side.

Where was Deacon? She hadn't seen him since she left the lake yesterday, and he hadn't been in the room when she woke up this morning.

Maybe it was too late. Maybe Kit took him back yesterday.

She'd barely closed Colin's door behind her when he looked up and scowled. "Where's Deacon?" he demanded.

"I don't know." Her voice trembled, but not nearly as much as her legs did. If Deacon was gone . . .

Colin dragged his chair out from behind his desk and pointed her toward it. This man before her was not the same man she'd lived with her whole life. He'd bathed, shaved and dressed in clean clothes. She couldn't even detect a hint of whiskey on him.

Something wasn't right.

"You look very nice," she said. "Is something—"

"Sit." His sharp word brought her situation crashing back. She would have dropped to the floor right then if it meant she could stop teetering on her shaky legs.

"What is it?" She almost crumpled into the chair.

Before he could answer, the door blew open and in came Deacon, walking a little crooked.

"Nice of you to join us," Colin grumbled as he leaned back against the edge of his desk. Deacon kicked the door shut and stood behind Rhea, his hands resting on her shoulders. She felt she should shrug them off, but her muscles wouldn't move. Instead, she tried to soak in the comfort his touch provided. If the look on Colin's face was any indication, she was going to need all the comfort she could get.

"Would you care to explain why I got a wire from Judge Hicks this afternoon?" Colin asked, seeming to struggle to keep his voice even.

"How would I know?" she answered, struggling for her own calm.

"Because he was responding to a wire you sent him this morning!"

"Then why did he send it to you?"

"Rhea!" Colin roared.

Deacon leaned close to Rhea's ear. "Who's Hicks?"

"A friend of our family's," Rhea hastened to explain. "He's the circuit judge here."

The vein in Colin's forehead throbbed disturbingly hard. "He's no friend of ours."

"What did the judge say?" Rhea asked.

Colin dragged a piece of paper across his desk and held it out for her to take. "He'll be here the end of the week."

Rhea skimmed the missive once quickly, then read it a second time. "Good. Thank you."

Colin kicked the back of his boot against his desk. "Do you even know what you're doing, Rhea?"

"Watch yourself," Deacon warned, stepping out from behind Rhea.

Colin snorted softly and laughed, but there was no

humor in it. "You stupid, sorry son of a bitch. You don't even know what she's up to, do you?"

"Whatever it is, I'm sure she had her reasons."

Another snort. "In case you haven't noticed, my sister's reasons for doing things usually make everything worse."

"Not this time." A look of calm fell over Deacon's face as he glanced Rhea's way. "I know why she asked him to come, and she was right to do it."

Rhea caught her jaw just before it fell open. She hadn't told Deacon anything about what she'd done, and by the look on Colin's face, he suspected as much.

But Deacon went on completely unruffled. "I've said right from the start that the easiest way to protect Rhea would be for the two of us to marry for real."

"And she made it pretty clear that she wasn't interested in that idea," Colin snapped. "So unless something's happened that makes it necessary for you two to be married for real . . ."

"Colin!"

"What else am I supposed to think, Rhea?" He pulled open the top drawer of his desk and took out a bottle. Empty. He clicked his tongue in disgust. "Not so many days ago, you were adamant that you didn't want to marry him, and now, suddenly, we have a judge coming?"

Rhea swallowed hard. She was going to be in debt to Deacon for a long time over this.

"It's for the best, Colin."

"That remains to be seen, doesn't it?" He scrubbed his palms over his face and sighed. "On top of this disaster, we have another problem."

"What problem?" Deacon asked. He hadn't moved from where he stood, but the frown on his face deepened.

"To start with, there seems to be a slightly more colorful version of Deacon's 'death' floating around." The vein in Colin's forehead continued to pulse as he glared at Deacon. "I assume we have you to thank for that."

Deacon shot Rhea a quick grin and snorted softly. "I wouldn't assume anything if I were you."

"I'm glad you find this so amusing," Colin growled at Deacon. Then he turned to Rhea. "But in case you've both forgotten, we have enough people talking about you as it is. It might be nice if we kept things quiet for a while."

"Of course." Rhea's breath hitched. She should never have told the Dietrich girls anything, but once again, a fit of impulsiveness had taken control. "What else?"

Colin's angry glare moved to Deacon and stayed there. If it was a challenge he was hoping for, Deacon appeared willing to take him up on it. Neither man blinked. It didn't seem as though either was even breathing.

Finally Colin stepped toward Deacon, his eyes narrowed, his jaw tight. "Who's the redhead?"

Rhea pushed to her feet and moved between the men. "That's Kit," she explained. "She's Deacon's sister."

"His sister?" Sarcasm oozed from Colin's voice. "I'm sure she is."

"She is," Rhea insisted.

"Don't be stupid," he said, never taking his eyes off Deacon. "You've seen her, Rhea. They're nothing alike."

"So what? That doesn't mean anything."

"Yes, it does." He spat onto the floor, then wiped his mouth. "It ain't the first time he's done something like this to you, and I don't expect it'll be the last."

Deacon moved forward just as Colin did, squishing Rhea between them.

"Stop it!" she cried, pushing against their chests. Deacon's muscles flinched beneath her hand, and his breath hissed sharply, but his face gave nothing away.

"Tell him, Deacon," Rhea begged. "Tell him about

Kit and . . . and the other one. Lucille." It would be much easier to speak if she wasn't expending all her energy trying to push the two of them apart.

Deacon made no attempt to explain anything. Instead, he pushed closer to Colin, who immediately did the same.

"Oh, for the love of God." Why were men such yacks? Why did they think everything had to be settled with violence?

She ducked out from between them and waved her hand in the air. "Go on, then. Beat each other senseless and get it over with."

The words were still reverberating through the room when Colin pulled back and swung just as Deacon dodged to the right. The punch caught the edge of Deacon's chin and knocked him back a step, but when he found his balance, he came back swinging. He slammed his fist into Colin's jaw with the force of a freight train. Colin fell back into the desk, righted himself and charged.

Deacon's breath whooshed out as both men lost their balance, tried to correct it and crashed sideways into Rhea.

She hit the floor hard, pinned beneath Deacon's weight and a flurry of swinging punches.

"Get off me!" she bellowed, landing a few punches of her own.

Colin scrambled to his feet, followed by Deacon, who immediately whipped her up beside him.

"Are you hurt?" Even as he grimaced through his own pain, Deacon's hands were touching her everywhere—her head, neck and shoulders—before Colin shoved him away.

"Don't touch her." Then it was Colin's turn to ask, "Are you hurt?"

"Stop it!" She slapped both of their hands away. "Just stop."

Her new skirt had a large rip down the front, where it must have snagged on something, and the white shirt-waist she'd managed to wash and dry overnight was now even dirtier than yesterday.

"Ugh," she grunted. Deacon stepped toward her again, but she shoved him away and glared both men down.

"Now you listen to me," she said through gritted teeth. "Both of you."

At least they had the decency to look remorseful. Blood oozed from the corner of Deacon's mouth, and he seemed to be favoring his right side a little. If she hadn't been so angry, she might have offered him a little sympathy.

"I don't care one single continental if you believe it or not, Colin, but Kit is in fact Deacon's sister."

Her brother's mouth opened, but slammed shut when she darkened her glare.

"I don't need you to remind me of Deacon's past," she ground out. "Believe me, I'm well aware of what he's done. I'm not quite as stupid as you seem to think."

Her glare shifted to Deacon, who looked as though she'd just slapped him. It took her a second to find her voice again. "He's never promised me anything, and he never will. It's just not in him, and I've known that since the day I met him."

"Then why do you l—"

"B-because," she stumbled, then huffed out a breath. It wasn't just one thing that made her love him. It was a million little things. It was the way he looked at her, the way he let her say whatever she wanted to say without worry of being reprimanded or scolded. It was the way he let her be who she was without trying to change her or make her more proper, the way he mocked her when she was being too serious, the way he laughed with her when she was being silly and, of course, it was the way he touched her.

Rhea inhaled a long breath before turning her attention to Colin.

"He offered to do this and I took him up on his offer. That's all that matters."

"Rhea." Deacon's one word ripped a jagged hole through her heart.

Damn him.

"No." She held up her hand and stared at her boot for a second, fighting back the lump that lodged halfway up her throat. "Don't. I'm fine."

He took her hand and pulled it to his chest. "You're not fine."

"I *will* be fine—once this is over."

"And just when the hell d'you think that's going to be?" Colin scowled. "Once you're married for real, Rhea, you're married. That's it. There's no turning back, and the only person you'll have to blame is yourself."

Deacon squeezed her hand gently, but she wouldn't look at him. Even when he tipped her chin up, she kept her eyes cast down. She'd be damned if she'd let him see her tears. Not this time.

"This is the easiest solution, Rhea."

"Easy?" Rhea choked on a sob. "For whom? Me?"

"Well, yes."

She yanked her hand away and swiped at her eyes. "You think it's going to be easy for me to be married to a man who isn't capable of loving me? A man who comes and goes as he pleases, without so much as a good-bye? A man—" She swallowed back a sob. "Do you really think I want to be married to a man who frequents the . . . whores . . . at the saloon?"

A deep frown creased Deacon's forehead. "But you've been pretending to be married to me for months now." He reached for her again, but she twisted away. "So what difference—"

"The difference," she cut in, "is that with the exception of the last few days, I've been pretending to be widowed, not married. It was easier."

"Rhea."

"Leave her be," Colin warned, but Deacon advanced anyway.

At least he didn't touch her. Thank God for small mercies. She wanted to scream at him, to make him go away—but if she opened her mouth, she'd never stop crying. Instead, she kept her back to him, crossed her arms over her stomach and stared out the small grimy window.

When he next spoke, his voice was so close, she could feel his breath against her neck.

"Look at me, Rhea," Deacon said softly.

She shook her head.

"Please." He set his hands on her shoulders and turned her slowly. "Look at me."

Why was she so weak? After all this time, she shouldn't hurt so much.

Deacon took her chin between his thumb and forefinger and held her face up to his until she finally blinked up at him. By marrying Deacon, she would at least save her reputation. The only thing left to do would be to concoct a believable story about why he was leaving again.

He looked straight into her eyes as he stroked his thumb over her bottom lip, his touch so tender, so slow.

How could he look at her like that—with so much desire, so much heartache—when he knew it was killing her?

"Nothing happened between me and Salma."

"Oh, for Christ's sake." Colin slammed his hands flat on his desk.

Rhea closed her eyes, swallowed once, then again and pushed Deacon's hand away. And she'd thought it couldn't hurt any worse.

"I'm telling you the truth," he said.

"I have to get back to the store."

Before he could stop her, she yanked open the door and ran outside. She caught a flash of red hair from the corner of her eye, but kept running until she was safely out of his reach.

Damn Deacon.

Damn him, damn the store and, most importantly, damn herself.

Colin lifted the chair and walked it around the desk. "Get out."

"With pleasure." Deacon straightened his jacket and headed for the door. His shoulder throbbed from being slammed against the floor, and the new wounds stretched across his back screamed in agony, but he wouldn't let Colin know that.

"I mean *go*." Colin slammed the chair down but didn't release it. Instead, his fingers gripped the armrests with a fierceness that threatened to snap them off. "Leave town. Me and Rhea'll figure this out on our own."

"I can't do that."

"Of course you can." Colin laughed bitterly. "You've done it before."

"Then let me rephrase. I *won't* do it. Rhea needs me."

"No," Colin howled. "What she needs is to have someone knock some sense into her."

Fire blazed inside Deacon, hotter than anything in Hell. "If you so much as touch her—"

Colin pushed up from the chair, giving Deacon a clear view of his battered face. A purple bruise had already started along his swollen jaw up to his eye. "I didn't mean *I'd* knock her around, you stupid ass."

"You better not."

"Why? Because you're going to protect her?"

"Yes." If Deacon hadn't been so furious just then, he might have admired Colin's concern for Rhea.

"You don't get it, do you?" Colin fell into his chair and buried his face in his hands. "The only thing she needs protection from is you!"

The bruise on Colin's cheek was no match for the one growing inside Deacon. He pushed it down deep, crushing it on top of every other regret he had for what he'd done to Rhea. But no matter how hard he tried to compress them, the pile was getting awfully big, awfully fast.

"I don't mean to—"

"I don't give a good goddamn if you mean to hurt her or not," Colin said, his voice sounding as tired as Deacon felt. "The fact is you *do*. So why the hell don't you just leave—just go away and stay away."

Deacon gripped the lapels of his jacket and swallowed hard. "I . . . the thing is . . . Rhea—"

"Do you love her?" Though asked in a calm, even tone, Colin's question screamed through Deacon's head, echoing off his skull until it finally buried itself on top of every other regret.

When Deacon didn't answer, Colin folded his hands on his desk and sighed wearily.

"Do us all a favor and just leave. Pack up yourself and your *sister*, and go. Give Rhea at least that much respect."

"I'm not going anywhere." Each word was an effort. In all his life, he'd never defended himself to a human of any sort, and it wasn't something he was especially enjoying now. "I have done nothing wrong, and I told Rhea I'd see her through this."

"And then you'll leave."

Deacon stared back at him in cold silence. It was probably a very good thing he didn't have any powers just then, or Colin would never draw another breath.

"If there's nothing else." He didn't wait for Colin to excuse him, but stepped outside and slammed the door shut behind him.

Yesterday morning, everything had seemed to be working out pretty well. In fact, for a couple of minutes there, he'd almost believed he and Rhea could have a future

And then Kit had appeared out at the lake, and everything he'd tried to build had collapsed into a massive crater that just kept getting deeper.

Damn Kit.

Damn her, damn their father and, most importantly, damn himself.

CHAPTER NINE

"I can't believe you're walking upright after what happened this morning." Kit swooped down on him the minute his boots hit the sidewalk.

"Go away." Deacon kept walking, hoping against hope his sister would give up and go away. Of course she didn't.

She skipped ahead of him and turned to walk backward. Several people stopped to stare, but Deacon kept moving. Nosy humans.

"What are you going to do?"

"First thing I'm going to do is find some clean bandages."

"I meant about the woman. She's not making this very easy on you, is she?"

For the first time all morning, Deacon felt a genuine smile tug at his mouth. Rhea had never been one to make his life easy. She challenged him, not to be difficult, but simply because she knew he needed it.

Kit's voice continued to grate in his ears. "You'd be better off just giving up and coming back with me now."

Deacon grabbed her by the elbow and half dragged her down a narrow alley between the feed store and the bank. When they were safely out of earshot of anyone walking by, he jabbed his finger toward her face.

"I came here for a purpose, Kit, and you being here is not helping."

"I'm not here to help." She stood toe to toe with him, her hands fisted on her hips and her green eyes shooting fire. "I'm here to make sure you remember where you belong."

"Believe me, Kit, I know perfectly well where I belong, and once I'm done here, I'll go back." Deacon sighed. "Did you ever consider that I might be finished sooner if you'd stop interfering?"

"And did you ever consider that today's turn with the whip was only a taste of what you're bringing down on yourself?"

Of course he'd considered it; did she think he was a complete imbecile? From the moment Kit took him into the old feed store, he knew what to expect, and his father was nothing if not consistent. Those twenty lashes across Deacon's back were merely a warning of what was to come if he prolonged his time with Rhea.

Kit's fiery glare cooled slightly, and her fists relaxed.

"Your punishment this morning must have left him feeling charitable," she said quietly. "He's giving you until the end of the week to finish this—not a minute more."

The end of the week; the same time Judge Hicks was expected. Without another word, he left Kit standing in the alley and hurried toward the store. He needed to find Rhea, needed to ease the frown from her mouth and wipe the tears from her eyes.

How was he ever going to win her trust and soothe her heart if he kept making her cry?

One step inside the store, he was met with the full force of Ernest's hostility.

"Miss Rhea's been crying," he said, blocking Deacon from moving any further. "And nobody makes Miss Rhea cry."

"Where is she?" He tried to brush by, but Ernest grabbed his jacket and held on. Deacon stopped, looking at the bunched edge of his new garment clutched in Ernest's fist and then up into the boy's face.

What looked back at him was no longer a boy; Ernest seemed to have grown from boy to man in the fifteen seconds since Deacon walked in.

"I know somethin' ain't right with you and her," Ernest said, his voice calm, yet bordering a little too close on threatening. "But if you ever make her cry again, you and me are gonna have words. D'you hear me?"

There was something oddly familiar about that glare and the way he held himself so straight.

"Ernest," Deacon said slowly. "Let go of me."

After another few seconds of glaring, Ernest released his jacket and shook his fist out a bit.

"Thank you." Deacon pressed his palm over the creases. "While I'm sure Rhea appreciates how protective you are toward her, I am her husband, not you. Whatever happens between us is none of your concern."

Ernest's expression held. "If you're gonna keep upsettin' her this way, then I'm gonna make it my concern."

"I appreciate the warning," Deacon said, reining in his frustration. "Now if you'll excuse me . . ."

They stared each other down for a few more seconds before Deacon pushed past him and headed to the back. As far as humans went, Ernest seemed to be one of the more likeable ones—if there was such a category—and if he was looking to protect Rhea, then Deacon would let him win that round.

He mounted the steps to their room two at a time

and pushed the door open so fast, it banged against the slanted ceiling.

Empty. Her clothes still hung on the pegs and her hairbrush lay on the table next to the washbasin, so at least she hadn't moved out.

Where would she be? He hurried back downstairs and marched right up to Ernest, who was helping a woman at the counter.

"How will you be paying?" he asked.

"On account." The woman looked up, and Deacon almost groaned. Mrs. Hale. There was more money Rhea would never see.

He stepped right up to Ernest. "Where did she go?"

"Good day to you, Mr. . . . um . . . Deacon." Mrs. Hale frowned a little as she tripped over his name, then took up her parcel and scurried out of the store.

Ernest finished writing up her purchase as though Deacon wasn't even there.

"Where did she go?" If Ernest didn't answer him this time, he was going to clean that boy's plow but good.

"I don't know." Ernest closed the account book and slid it back in place on the shelf beneath the counter. "And even if I did, I wouldn't tell you."

"She wouldn't just leave without telling you where she was going or how long she'd be."

"She never has before." The look Ernest leveled at him was one of ice-cold anger. "Which just goes to show how much she don't want to be found."

The door jangled open and in walked Mrs. Foster, her white hair covered by a truly awful brown-and-green plaid bonnet, and wearing an equally horrid dress of the same pattern.

Deacon cursed under his breath and made for the door.

"Hello," Mrs. Foster called out. "It's so nice to see you again."

"Yes," he hurried to answer. "Thank you."

She started toward him, but Deacon ducked down a different aisle.

"I'm taking some fabric, Ernest," he said, "and I'll pay for it when I get back."

Mrs. Foster went right on talking. "I saw you coming out of the old feed store earlier. Are you planning—"

"My apologies," he offered, grabbing a large folded piece of white cotton fabric. "I'm in a terrible hurry. Another time, perhaps?"

"But—"

Without giving her time to finish, Deacon yanked open the door and stepped out onto the walk. Of all the people to have seen him this morning, it had to be her. Did the old bat ever stay home?

He needed to find Rhea. She was all that mattered. If he could just—

"I see you found something to bandage yourself with." Kit stepped up beside him, looking as innocent as she could, which wasn't saying much. "Need some help?"

He tried to ignore her, but Kit was nothing if not persistent. Her hair blew around her head in wild chaos, and her hands were wrapped around her suspenders as if she were a common farmhand.

"In case you haven't noticed, Deacon, your plan isn't working." She skipped a few steps to keep up. "Telling her the truth isn't making her feel better, and it's not doing you a whole lot of good, either."

Deacon ground his teeth together. He knew it wasn't working; the last thing he needed was someone—especially Kit—pointing it out to him.

But why wasn't it working? Why couldn't Rhea just

believe what he'd told her about Salma? It would sure make things easier.

"Do you have any idea where you're going, or are you just hoping she'll pop out of one of these buildings and surprise you?"

He knew exactly where he was going and couldn't believe he hadn't thought of it right away.

"Don't you have some poor downtrodden soul to drag back to Hell or something?"

"No," she answered airily. "It's kind of slow today."

On the other side of the street, Colin stepped out of the sheriff's office and stood there, his thumbs hooked into his gun belt, watching Deacon and Kit with narrowed eyes.

The urge to kick something was almost too strong to ignore. Didn't anyone have anything better to do than watch his every move?

"You have that look," Kit said cautiously.

"What look?"

"The one you get when you're up to something."

He kept walking, lengthening his stride with each step. "I am," he said, not bothering to hide his irritation. "That's no secret."

She didn't look convinced. "There's something else."

"The only other thing going on right now, Kit, is you getting in my way and making everything harder than it needs to be."

"Who, me?"

For a split second, as they neared the livery, Deacon considered renting a buggy again. But there was no way Travis would rent him anything after the way he'd returned the buggy and horses yesterday.

When Rhea walked away from the lake, she'd left him to harness the animals alone, and he didn't have the first idea what he was supposed to do. It stood to reason that harnessing the animals would simply be the direct opposite of releasing the harnesses, as he'd done with Rhea. But no matter what he tried, the straps didn't want to fit the way he thought they should, and the horses, sensing his unease, had been less than accommodating about the whole thing.

He ended up walking the horses back and leaving Travis to go fetch the buggy.

No, Deacon was going to have to walk all the way to Colin's. It was only a couple of miles, but it also meant a couple miles worth of dust covering his boots, and step after step of stretching his wounds open.

"Are you going to tell me where you're going?"

"No," he answered as he jammed the cloth inside his pocket. "But if you keep following me, you'll end up there about the same time I do."

She seemed to think on that a second. "Is it far?"

"Seems like a million miles away right now," he groused.

Kit walked along beside him for a long time, keeping pace with him even though it meant she often had to jog a bit to do so. When they rounded the bend about three quarters of the way out, she disappeared without a word.

He tried not to wish he could still do that and tried even harder not to think about where she'd gone or what she would do once she got there.

All he could do was hope Rhea was strong enough to withstand it until he arrived.

"Hello, Rhea." Even before Kit stepped up beside the coop, the chickens scattered in a frenzy of clucking and flying feathers.

"Hello, Kit." Rhea spread the rest of the chicken feed

around the pen, then set the bucket upside down near the gate. "What do you want?"

"Can't a girl stop by to say hello to her sister-in-law?"

"I'm sure under normal circumstances that would be perfectly acceptable." Part of Rhea's brain chastised her. She had no reason to be cross with Kit—she hadn't done anything to Rhea. But the other part of her brain, the louder and more judgmental part, continued to fire anger at the woman. She was, after all, only there to take Deacon away again.

She stepped out of the pen, closed the gate behind her and moved toward the barn. Colin had at least milked the poor cow regularly, but that was all he'd done. The second the poor beast sensed Kit's presence, its eyes widened and it pulled against its tether and tried repeatedly to sidestep away.

"Beautiful day, isn't it?" Kit moved airily behind Rhea, as though she didn't have a care in the world, but Rhea knew Kit's kind didn't hang about dirty barns unless they had a good reason. And, obviously, Rhea was part of that reason.

"You can't come in here," Rhea said flatly. "So if you're not going to tell me what you want, either get out of my way or take that pitchfork and get to work— in the farthest stall."

While Rhea positioned herself on the milking stool beside the twitchy cow, Kit picked up the pitchfork and moved to the far end of the barn, but made no attempt to use it. Instead, she leaned against it, watching as Rhea set to milking the bawling beast.

"You're really not afraid of me, are you?"

"Should I be?"

"Most humans are." The pitchfork scraped against the

floor. "Do you have any idea what I could do to you? Or what our father could do to you?"

Rhea snorted. "I have spent twenty-four years of Sundays down on my knees in Reverend Goodwin's church," she said. "So yes, I have a pretty good idea of what your kind is capable of."

Another scrape, then the smell of dirty straw filled the air. "And that doesn't frighten you?"

Rhea's hands paused on the udder for a moment, then resumed their pumping. "No."

It was Kit's turn to snort. "Deacon was right—you are a firecracker."

"The way I look at it," Rhea said, "your kind works on fear. Everything you do and everything you know is built on what you're afraid of and what you can make others afraid of. Am I right?"

"Partly." Kit came around the corner of the stall and leaned on the pitchfork again, just inside Rhea's peripheral vision.

"You prey on the weak and the lonely because they're easy. And when others see what you've done to these poor souls, they become more afraid themselves. Fear leads to weakness, which leads to more fear, which leads back to—"

"Okay," Kit interrupted. "You made your point. But that doesn't explain why you're not afraid."

"Simple." Rhea released the cow and lifted the pail into her arms. "I'm not weak."

At least not in the way Kit was looking for.

Kit's eyes narrowed suspiciously. "No, you're certainly not, but being lonely is a whole 'nother thing, isn't it?"

The reply Rhea started to fire back died on her tongue. There was no reason for her to be lonely. She had Colin, she had her store and she had plenty of folks who cared enough to stop by to say hello every day.

It was more than a lot of people had. And yet, buried deep in her heart, in the place she'd never shared with anyone, was a profound longing no one but Deacon had ever been able to satisfy.

For a while, she'd tried to believe any husband and children could fill that void, and she could have had both easily enough.

But it would have meant marrying a man she didn't love, and that simply wasn't an option. The only man she would ever love could not be hers; even if Judge Hicks married them, Deacon wouldn't be hers like a real husband. Because of that, the gaping hole of loneliness remained.

In short order, Deacon would be gone again and she would have to push that ache down deeper, until she could muffle it beneath the other aches she'd silenced.

"He's got you tied up in knots, doesn't he?" Kit's voice held a touch of awe. "You know you can't have him, yet you refuse to let go of that fragile thread of hope."

When Rhea didn't answer right away, Kit shrugged. "You humans are a strange lot. Why don't you just give up on him?"

Rhea sniffed softly. "What I do is none of your concern."

She walked out of the barn and headed for the cabin, with the milk pail clutched tightly in her arms.

Kit hurried behind her. "But it just doesn't make sense," she said. "You're a smart girl, and you know he's going to leave you again."

Of course she knew, but that didn't mean she was going to discuss any of this with the likes of Kit.

Rhea sighed and pushed open the door. "Would you like some coffee?"

"You want to make me coffee?" Kit's perfectly arched brow furrowed.

"No," Rhea answered. "I'm making myself coffee, but you're welcome to have some if you like."

Inside the dingy little room, Rhea set to work on the coffee while Kit wandered slowly, seeming to study every inch of the four walls.

"Did you and your brother live here with your parents?" she asked. "It seems awfully small."

"No." Rhea tried to stall the sadness from her voice. "We used to have a house a ways out behind the barn, but it burned."

"Your parents?"

"Y-yes." With shaking hands, she poured water into the coffeepot and set it on the stove to boil.

"That must have been horrible for you." If Rhea didn't know who Kit was, she's almost think the woman was being sympathetic. "You and your brother survived, though."

The grinder slipped from Rhea's hands. She lunged, caught it, then juggled it two or three times before she finally slammed it down on the table.

"Pa went back for Ma. Neither one made it out."

Kit stopped moving and tipped her head toward Rhea without actually looking at her. "That's rather curious, don't you think?"

"Stop it." Rhea pressed her hands flat on the table. "I'm not going to discuss this with you. My parents are dead, and while that doesn't mean anything to you, it means a great deal to me."

"I'm sorry."

"No, you're not." It was an extreme effort to keep her voice low and even, but somehow she managed.

The door banged open, and in walked Deacon. Sweat trickled down his forehead, and his fine black suit was covered in a thin layer of Texas dust.

"Took you long enough," Kit said with a cheeky grin.

Deacon ignored her and moved straight to Rhea, his face twisted into a tight grimace. For a fraction of a second, she felt herself reach toward him, needing to ease whatever it was that pained him so much.

That moment passed when she caught sight of Kit again.

"Are you all right?" Deacon asked. "Did she—"

"Come now, Deacon," Kit sighed with feigned offense. "I'm not that horrible. In fact, I quite enjoy your new wife."

"I'm fine." Rhea dashed the back of her hand across her cheek and forced herself to meet his gaze. "What do you want?"

"I was worried."

"Awww," Kit drawled. "That's so sweet. What a good husband you are."

Gripping the back of a nearby chair, Deacon closed his eyes, clenched his jaw and turned on his sister. "Get out."

"I've been invited to stay for coffee."

"Now!" His roar rattled the windows, but Kit didn't seem the least bit distressed.

Instead, her smirk widened. "All right, then, I'll go and leave you two lovebirds alone." She waggled her brow toward the tick in the corner. "I'm sure you'll find some way to spend the time. Maybe she can help with that bandage."

"What bandage?" Rhea frowned; it was only then she noticed the white cloth hanging out of Deacon's pocket.

"Kit." Deacon's growing growl dragged her name out into two separate syllables. By the time he was done, she was already making her way to the door.

"I'm going." With a final waggle of her brow, she stepped outside and closed the door behind her. Rhea watched out the window, but never caught another glimpse of that all-too-familiar red hair.

Kit had disappeared, just as Deacon had done so many times before. All that remained was the pit of despair in Rhea's stomach.

She slumped onto a chair and buried her face in her hands.

"Rhea." The other chair scraped against the floor and a moment later, Deacon eased her hands away from her face.

"How did you know where I was?"

He tried to smile, but it didn't reach his eyes; it barely reached his mouth for that matter. "If you were a man, I would've found you in the saloon. If you were any other woman—a sane woman—you would have gone to a friend's house or locked yourself in your room to cry."

"I did lock myself in our room."

"Not for long," he said. "You can't sit still for more than five minutes, no matter how upset you are. And since you'd rather be doing anything than wallowing in misery, it wasn't terribly difficult to find you."

His thumb moved in circles over her palm as it always did; his voice was low, quiet. "I've been half expecting you to bring these damned animals into town so you could look after them properly."

Rhea shrugged. Caring for the animals helped her think of something else besides her pathetic self.

"Are you all right?" Deacon's blue eyes searched her own, looking for what? Rhea didn't know, and she didn't care; at least, she didn't want to care.

"No," she finally choked. "I'm not."

"Tell me what to do. Let me help."

"Help?" She shook off his hands and pushed away from the table. "How do you think you can help when you're the problem?"

He followed her across the room. "But we're going to make this better," he said. "Once the judge arrives, and we make it legal—"

"God, Deacon, why don't you understand?" She turned to face him, but warned him off from reaching for her. One touch from him would do her in at this point. "It's not just about our *marriage*."

"Then what?" His hands twitched at his sides until he tucked them under his armpits. The movement made him wince again. "D'you mean Salma?"

"No," she sighed. "Yes. It's Salma, it's everything."

"I told you the truth back there. Nothing happened between Salma and me."

She shook her head. "Even if that's true, what difference does it make now? You're still going to leave, aren't you?"

She'd never seen a person crumple before, but that was the only way she could think to describe what Deacon did. His shoulders sagged, and he wouldn't look at her.

"You asked me to trust you, and Lord knows I want to." Rhea dashed her hand across her cheeks again and sniffed back another round of tears. "But it's not that simple."

"It *is* that simple!" He raked his fingers through his hair and exhaled a long whoosh of air. "I hurt you, Rhea, and I just want to make it up to you. I want to help your heart heal so you can stop being so sad and go on with your life." He paused, swallowed hard and looked as though he had more to say.

She waited a minute, but when he didn't finish, she brushed by him and yanked the pot of heated water off the stove.

"I've been gone too long," she said. "I need to get back to the store."

"Dammit, Rhea!" He was across the room before she could catch her next breath. His hands gripped her upper arms and shook her, gently, but enough to get her attention. "I just don't want to hurt you anymore. Why can't you believe that?"

"I want to."

She let him pull her closer, but turned her face away from his.

"I came back because I missed you, and I wanted to earn your trust again." His fingers tightened around her arms. "So help me, I couldn't stand being away from you for another minute."

"It hasn't been a lot of fun for me, either," she retorted. "But it is what it is. I can't help what I feel for you any more than you can help what you *don't* feel for me."

"You have to know—"

She pressed her hand against his mouth. "Don't. I'm too tired to fight about this anymore. Let's just leave it alone, okay?"

His mouth opened beneath her hand, but she shook her head.

"You didn't come back to stay, and every day you're here makes it harder for me to remember that."

His only answer was to tighten his lips.

"I'm trying my best to accept what this is." She choked over a small sob. "Or what it isn't. But all it's doing is turning me into a half-crazed lunatic."

She covered the milk pail with a cloth and reached for the door, but he reached past her and pushed it shut. He was so close she could feel the rise and fall of his chest against her back.

"Before you go," he said, his voice full of regret, "I need your help."

"With what?" She slumped against the door and waited. All she wanted to do was go back to the store.

At least there she could concentrate on something, even if it was only a bowl of mismatched buttons.

He pulled a large piece of white cloth from his pocket and set it on the table.

"It's not as bad as it looks," he said as he stepped back, easing his jacket down one arm, then the other.

Guilt flooded Rhea. "Is it your shoulder?"

He chuckled quietly but shook his head.

"Was it the fight with Colin?"

He didn't answer, just began unbuttoning his shirt. Rhea blinked hard. What were those stains? And why was he grimacing so much?

Her mouth tasted of dust. Deacon never took off his shirt in front of her. And now that he'd pulled it open, she wished he'd put it back on.

Wrapped around his torso was the nastiest piece of cloth she'd ever seen. Caked in blood and God only knew what else, the filthy rag looked as though it would need to be scraped away from his skin. And if that didn't kill him, the infection probably would.

"What the—" Rhea gasped. Colin couldn't have done that to him.

"I need you to clean it and rewrap it with the other bandage." He slipped the shirt off and stood facing her. "Can you do that?"

"I, um . . . oh, Deacon." She set the milk down and inhaled a shaky breath. She could do this; she might need to vomit, but she had to help him.

Pinching the end of the rag between her fingers, she began to ease it away from his stomach as gently as she could. The first time it stuck, he sucked in a sharp breath; the second time, he pressed his hand over hers to stop her from pulling it any further.

The third time, he pushed her hands out of the way and with a gut-wrenching howl, ripped the rest of the cloth from around his body and let it fall to the floor. Rhea stumbled back in absolute horror.

Ragged, angry slash marks crisscrossed his rib cage, but there was no doubt those marks were simply the ends of the real wounds. "What happened?"

Once he'd caught his breath, he tried to shrug it off, but even that made him wince.

"Let me see your back."

"It's worse," he muttered, stepping away from her.

"All the more reason to see it." When he hesitated, she looked up at him. "I've seen it before, remember?"

"Yes, but that was when they were healed over. It's different when they're fresh."

She had no answer for that. All she could do was swallow hard and nod. "Turn."

Very slowly, Deacon turned in a half circle. As ghastly as his sides were, it hadn't prepared her for the shock of his back. She swallowed the gasp that started in her throat and blinked past the tears that sprang to her eyes. Regardless of what he'd done to her, she didn't need to shame him with her horrified fear.

It was impossible to tell how many lashes had sliced into his back, but it looked as though each one had curled around his body, which would explain the gaping wounds along his ribs.

She pulled a strand of dirty string out of the gaping wound, causing him to jump as if she'd shot him again. "Sorry," she muttered. "They need to be cleaned out."

"I know," he said through gritted teeth. "Just do it quickly."

Rhea twisted the chair around and motioned for him to sit. "Where's the whiskey when you really need it?"

"Still swooshing around in my shoulder." Deacon's grin was just short of pathetic.

"What happened?"

He straddled the chair and leaned his arms over the back. "Don't ask."

"I'm asking." She used the warmed water from the coffeepot, wet a cloth and set to cleaning each slash as gently as she could. What could make someone do this to another person? Her hand froze in midair as Deacon spoke.

"My father stopped by for a visit this morning."

She forced in a breath, then swallowed. "Your . . . he was *here*?"

"He's only interested in me."

The devil himself had come to Penance. Breathe. Focus. Deacon needed help.

"You'll be lucky if you don't get infection from that filthy rag." She tsked, forcing another breath. The devil had come to Penance, and she was cleaning his son's wounds. She squeezed her eyes shut for a second and tried to push the madness of the whole thing out of her mind. "Why didn't you say something earlier?"

He turned his head a little and flashed her a quick wink. "It was a little difficult to get a word in between you and your brother, especially once he started swinging."

"That's not funny." She flicked the back of his ear. "Stand up."

He pushed up from the chair and straightened, but not before she saw him wince again.

The cuts across his ribs had stopped bleeding, but they were still oozing and raw. With every touch of the cloth, he flinched, which in turn made her start.

"I-I don't even know what to say about this," she murmured.

"Don't say anything."

He'd been sliced open over and over again, and she wasn't supposed to say anything?

"But this is just so—"

He covered her hand with his and left it there until she looked at him. "Please."

The words she couldn't find a moment ago danced across her tongue, pushing to be set free, but that look on his face—part weariness, part humiliation—made her stop. She cleaned the rest of them in silence, keeping her head bowed so he wouldn't see her tears.

So much pain . . .

She had no idea how much time passed. As long as it seemed to her, it must have been a hundred times worse for Deacon. When she'd finished, she dashed her hand across both eyes and stood.

"You should leave these open to the air for a while so they can heal."

"I can't do that," he said, his voice flat. "Just wrap it."

After a moment, she nodded briefly and unfolded the cloth to one long, wide strip. She held the end out to him, but instead of taking it, he circled her wrist with his long fingers and held her still.

"Rhea."

She looked up at him, blinking past the pain she felt for him and his poor beaten body. But she must not have blinked hard enough.

Deacon swiped the pad of his thumb beneath her eye, catching the tear before it fell. "Don't waste these on me," he murmured. "I'm not worth it."

He took the end of the cloth and held it against his stomach, but it took her a moment before she was able to move. Holding the cloth firmly, she walked in a slow circle around him, making sure she covered each gash as much as possible.

When she was done, she fastened the end to the top layer with a pin and stepped back. She didn't know where to look or what to do now.

"Thank you." Deacon reached past her and retrieved his stained shirt from the table.

"You're welcome." She scooted out of the way and retrieved the bucket of milk. "I need to get back."

"Rhea, wait."

She closed her eyes and dropped her chin to her chest.

Deacon's breath whispered across her neck, sending goose bumps racing down her arms.

"Kit's going to keep on pestering you," he said, his voice laced with regret. "But no matter what she says or does, you need to stay strong. Don't give her anything she can use against you, and if you can figure out a way, try to block her from seeing . . . inside. Keep your guard up around her."

"I will," she said quietly. "I have enough problems without either one of you being able to use my feelings against me."

He lifted a strand of her hair and twirled it between his fingers. "I would never do that to you."

Trembling, she pulled his hand away and pressed it against his own chest. "You do it every time you touch me."

CHAPTER TEN

By the time Rhea made it back to the store, Ernest had locked up and gone home. Just as well; the last thing she needed was him asking questions or hovering.

She walked straight up the stairs, changed into her nightgown and climbed into bed. The sun hadn't even set, but she didn't care. All she wanted was sleep, and if she didn't wake up for three days, that would be just fine.

Minutes ticked by, but sleep would not come. Her eyes were closed, her blanket tucked all around her and her pillow fluffed. Nothing helped. Instead of settling down, her brain continued to flash images at lightning speed until it seemed the whole room was spinning around her.

This past week had been more than just a little overwhelming. There'd been so much confusion and frustration, but in between, there'd been a few moments where everything seemed perfect. Funny how those moments only occurred when there was no one else around except her and Deacon.

She'd tried so hard to put him out of her mind these past months, to forget his crooked smile, how he always smelled of sunshine and the way his arms made her feel warm, secure and safe.

A single tear slid out the corner of her eye. Oh, who was she kidding? She would never get him out of her mind, because doing that meant shutting him out of her heart and no matter how hard she tried not to, she still loved him.

It was just her luck that the only man she had ever loved would be the one man who couldn't love her back. How much more pathetic could she get?

Pathetic or not, crying never solved problems. Thinking solved problems.

Instead of focusing on what she *hoped* to be true, she needed to focus on what she *knew* to be true.

"Think with your head," she muttered, "not with your heart."

Deacon couldn't help who he was. He hadn't chosen his parents any more than she had. He'd been raised to know nothing but darkness and fear, and while he wasn't terribly keen on people in general, he'd never been cruel to her.

Until he took up with Salma. The pain of that night was as sharp today as it had been when she'd first found out.

Now he was trying to convince her that he'd done nothing wrong with Salma. Why would he make her think something so horrible, then turn around and deny it? Once again, it was a battle between her head and her heart.

Rhea frowned. Deacon made her feel things she'd never imagined and had certainly never heard any other women in town whisper about. His simple smile made her pulse quicken, the touch of his hand sent tremors racing through her body, and when he kissed her . . .

Rhea squeezed her eyes tighter and groaned. God help her, but when he kissed her, it was pure heaven.

Time stopped, the earth spun faster and it was as though they were the only two beings in the universe.

Out the window, the sun began its surrender to the pull of the moon, leaving the room filled with shifting shadows. And there, in the growing darkness, her brain and her heart finally came to a compromise: if she couldn't stop loving Deacon, then she needed to stop fighting it and start accepting it.

She knew what to expect this time. She knew he wasn't going to stay, and she knew she would probably never see him again once he left.

Knowing this, could she love him, freely and without expectation, and still have the strength to keep on going after he left? Her heart was going to be broken again, no matter what. So long as she knew it, and prepared herself for it this time, maybe it wouldn't be so bad. Her sensible side would simply have to protect her other side.

It wasn't going to be easy, but then, what ever was?

The scuffing of boots sounded a warning on the stairs. Rhea pulled her hand off Deacon's pillow and buried it beneath her own. Her heart thundered against her ribs, and her stomach flipped over twice. Maybe she should pretend to be asleep.

The door creaked open, then shut with a click.

"Rhea?" His whisper floated over the air and settled against her skin.

Don't say anything. Pretend to sleep. Close your eyes.

"Mm-hmm." *Idiot.*

"I brought supper. Have you eaten?"

Say yes. "No."

He moved toward the bed and set the basket down beside her. "Do you mind if I light the lamp?"

Say yes. "No."

Brilliant. Now he was going to see her puffy eyes,

messy hair and blotchy complexion. If that didn't send him screaming back to Hell, nothing would.

He struck a match to the wick, but kept the light low. Then he toed off his boots, slipped out of his jacket and climbed up onto the bed, sitting Indian-style at the foot.

Each movement seemed to be a cautious and slow decision, but he never winced or complained. As he began pulling things from the basket, Rhea pushed herself up to sit, too.

The slant of the ceiling prevented her from leaning up against the wall, so she moved up to the head of the bed and adopted Deacon's position, setting her pillow on her lap to use as a table of sorts. She didn't bother trying to wrap the blanket around her this time; there wasn't enough light in the room to cause either one of them any embarrassment anyway.

Besides, Deacon seemed fairly intent on keeping his eyes fixed on anything but her, so what did it matter?

That was fine, because it gave Rhea the opportunity to watch him without being discovered.

His face was smudged with dirt, and the blood stains on his shirt had darkened almost to black. His hair was all mussed and looking very unlike him. In fact, Rhea hadn't seen his hat since yesterday at the lake. That was odd. Just because she didn't like it, didn't mean she expected him to stop wearing it.

"Where've you been?" she asked quietly.

"Stayed out at Colin's for a while," he answered. "Thought you might want some time alone."

"Thank you. How are your . . . cuts?"

"Sore." Still, he wouldn't look at her.

The savory aroma of thick beef stew drifted out of the basket, mixed with the warm scent of fresh bread and sour apple pie. If her stomach hadn't chosen that exact moment to growl like a bear, she would have protested at how much food there was.

Instead, she accepted the bowl Deacon filled for her and dug in.

Five swallows later, she couldn't stand the silence anymore.

"I'm sorry," she said, sticking her fork through a piece of meat. "I have no right to be angry with you, when all you've done since you got back is try to help me."

Deacon's fork froze over his bowl. He bounced it a few times, then set it down, wiped his mouth and looked up at her. Finally.

"*I'm* sorry." He sighed slowly. "Sometimes I think it would have been better if we'd never met."

"Oh." Rhea fought to swallow the pain his words inflicted. "I've never thought that, not for a second."

"Rhea." His Adam's apple bobbed hard. "I don't mean to hurt you."

"I know that," she said. "And I don't mean to let you." She shook her head, trying desperately to keep the tremble from her voice. "It's okay. I've been doing a lot of thinking this afternoon, and it seems to have helped."

"How's that?"

"Well," she said, wishing she didn't sound as foolish as she did. "The sensible side of my brain has always known this wasn't a fairy tale and that there would never be a happily-ever-after for us."

He twirled his fork in his bowl. "What about the other side of your brain?"

She choked out a half laugh, half sob. "That would be the not-so-sensible side."

"Yeah, that side." His voice was quiet as he watched his fork twirl.

"Oh, it believes there's hope for us yet." She scooped

up a forkful of potato and stuffed it in her mouth, but she could have been eating the bowl itself for all the taste it had.

Regardless, she had to project the image of sensible control; otherwise she was going to lose herself in those endless blue eyes of his.

"Now that my sensible side has finally stepped forward again," she said, "I think I know what I need to do."

"Yeah?" He pushed his bowl away and leaned sideways so his bent elbow rested on the bed and his head rested in his hand. "Maybe you better explain it to me, because I'm stumped."

"You won't poke fun at me?"

His only answer was a smile of regret, and before Rhea could stop her tongue from moving, she'd already started talking. "Here's the thing."

She shifted again, fighting against her nightgown, and then moved back to her original position, each repositioning making her more uncomfortable, more nervous and more uncertain.

"What's the thing?"

She could do this. She just had to stop staring at him, stop imagining herself wrapped in his arms and force her sensible side to stand up and be heard.

If she kept it matter-of-fact, it would be easier to explain. *Stop being such a ninny, and just say it.* It couldn't possibly mean anything to him, anyway, so what difference did it make if she admitted it out loud?

"Right." Could he see her blushing in the dim light? Lord, she hoped not. "It's no secret I, um, well, surely you must know—"

"Say it." His voice was like velvet. Gone was any sense of mirth or teasing, and the way he looked at her . . . even in the low lamp light, his gaze burned right through her.

Rhea shuddered. Don't look at him. Don't look . . .

She lifted her chin, locked her gaze on his and exhaled.

"I love you." There, she'd said it. She'd never said it out loud to him before, and now all she wanted to do was throw up. Or cry. Both, maybe. And for the love of God, why was he smiling at her that way? If he made one joke at her expense, one teasing word, she'd finish the job she'd started with that blasted Winchester.

Lucky for him, he didn't make a single sound. He didn't even move, just lay there with that stupid smile on his face.

"Anyway," she hurried to add, willing her voice to hold steady and not crack the way it did in her mind. "What you did with Salma was . . . well, that's something I don't think I will ever forget, but considering I've roped you into a marriage you don't want, Salma is something I'll have to learn to live with."

"I told you—"

She shook her head and charged ahead, leaving the rest of his words unspoken.

"Aside from my own daydreams, I never had any reason to believe we would have a life together, especially given where you come from. You never once said anything to me that would indicate it's what you wanted, and I know . . . I know the time we've spent together, before and now, is not the same for you as it is for me."

He pushed up from his elbow and sat straight across from her, his smile faded but not gone.

"No matter what's happened between us, Deacon, you don't owe me anything, and yet you've stepped in and are pretending to be my husband when you could have just as easily left me to face the consequences of my lie alone."

As she rambled on, he gathered their still-full bowls and tucked them back inside the basket.

She shuffled closer to the wall, feeling suddenly very self-conscious. "Now that I've had time to think on this, it's helped me see how wrong I've been about everything. I've known since the first day that there would never be a lifetime commitment between us, but still, I've been acting like a silly little girl, and I'm sorry." She took a deep breath. "From now on, I will do my very best to stop carrying on like a lunatic where you're concerned."

Bending over beside the bed, he set the basket on the floor, winced slightly, then straightened.

"A lunatic?"

"Yes." *Nod. Nod again. Make him believe you mean what you're saying.* "I tend to let my emotions get the better of me when it comes to you, so I'm going to try very hard to stop that."

"But you said you couldn't help how you feel about me."

"I can't." *Nod again.* "But if I would just let my head rule my heart, instead of the other way around, then at least I might be able to make some sense of all this."

She wasn't making any sense at all.

"What I mean is that I can't stop myself from feeling . . . what I feel, but I *can* stop myself from hoping for more than what this is."

His eyes opened in wide confusion, so Rhea plunged on.

"We're here, together, and no matter what's happened in the past, I'm going to try and make the best of this situation until you leave again. Or until Judge Hicks has me sent to prison for forging our marriage certificate." She tried to laugh, but failed miserably.

"You're not going to prison." As she watched in stunned silence, he set to work on unfastening his trousers.

The heat from her embarrassment instantly tripled. She flopped down on the bed and twisted over on her side to face the wall.

"Y-you don't know that," she managed to stutter.

A few seconds later, he blew out the lamp and crawled in beside her. The bed creaked beneath his weight, then creaked again as he shifted closer.

She held her breath, waiting for him to settle, but he didn't. Instead, he pushed one arm beneath her, the other around her, and eased her back against his chest.

Rhea's whole body stiffened. This wasn't what she'd planned, and it sure as shootin' wasn't going to help her sensible side stay in control.

Deacon sighed softly into her hair. "Say it again."

"Say what?" Why did he have to hold her this way? And why was her traitorous body melting against his instead of staying rigid, as she wanted it to?

"Say it," he repeated.

His scent tickled her nose, his arms easing every worry from her muscles. Rhea couldn't help herself. She snuggled deeper into his arms until it was impossible to get any closer. Heaven itself couldn't be better than this.

"Rhea." Barely a whisper.

It meant ripping another piece of her heart out, but that was a small price to pay to have him hold her that way.

She whispered it softly, barely loud enough for her own ears to hear. "I love you."

He breathed a smile against her hair, and within moments, his arms relaxed as he drifted off to sleep.

Wrapped in his warmth, it didn't take long for Rhea's mind to finally settle into that wonderful pre-sleep fog where everything is the way it should be. As her body finally gave in to sleep, one last thought slipped through like a thief in the night.

Deacon felt anger, amusement, pain and regret. All human emotions.

"Hmmm." The thought was gone as quickly as it came, and all that was left was sleep; glorious, deep and dreamless sleep.

Deacon fingered Rhea's hair back from her forehead and gazed down into her beautiful face. What a difference a few hours could make.

Yesterday afternoon, he was sure he'd lost her forever. She'd never forgive him, and her heart would never heal. This morning, he had a whole new perspective.

"It's time to wake up," he said quietly. If he believed such nonsense, it would seem Rhea's fairy tale was happening right there. She was Sleeping Beauty and would only wake if kissed by a handsome prince.

He might not be handsome, and he might not be the typical fairy-tale prince, but if Sleeping Beauty didn't wake up soon, she was going to be late for work.

Leaning closer, he breathed a kiss across her brow, and then one on the tip of her nose. Her mouth opened slightly, but her eyes stayed closed. It was a tough job, this prince business, but duty called.

He pressed a kiss against her lips, then pulled back just enough to see her face again. Her hand moved toward him and rested against his shirt-covered chest, sending jolts of fire racing through every inch of his body.

He kissed her again, longer this time, pulling her awake one sleepy sigh after another. She was like water to his parched body, and he couldn't seem to soak up enough of her.

He nibbled her bottom lip, running his tongue along its edge with tentative strokes. His whole body ached to touch her, to feel her pressed against him, skin to skin, but he held back, using nothing but his mouth.

She whimpered softly, her mouth moved beneath his, and then she was kissing him back. Her eyes might not be open, but there was no question Rhea was wide awake.

Her fingers fisted around his shirt, her body arched toward him. She opened fully to him, welcoming his kisses, asking for more and giving back as much as he gave. Maybe more.

His breathing came in labored gasps, his heart thrashed and though it probably shouldn't have mattered, it made him smile to discover Rhea's body was reacting the exact same way.

"Good morning." He smiled against her lips, amazed at how she could be so beautiful when she was such a mess.

Her cheeks turned pink as she slowly opened her eyes. "Good morning."

"I'm going to hanker a guess," he murmured between the quick kisses to her chin and cheek, "that your sensible side hasn't quite figured out what your other side has been up to this morning."

She slapped her hands over her face and moaned, but he pulled her hands away and smiled down at her.

"Don't be embarrassed," he said. "It's nice to have this side of you wake up first, and besides, I started it."

Her lips quivered against a smile. "Yes, you did, but I didn't exactly put up an argument, did I?"

"Nice change," he said, kissing her one more time.

"Hey!" She made to shove him away, but he took her wrists in his hands and held her still. He wasn't done with her yet, and by the look on her face, she wasn't going to argue this time, either.

They reached for each other at the same time, her hands sliding through his hair and holding him close. He moved over her, grimacing against the pain shooting up his arm, and then rolled on to his back, pulling her on top of him. The ache in his arm gave way to the burning pain screaming across his back, but he struggled through it.

Rhea was in his bed, in his arms, and he was going to enjoy every second of it. He cupped her face in his palms, savoring each kiss, each taste, never able to get enough.

She inched her hands down his neck, over his shoulders and across his chest until they found their way beneath his shirt. Her fingers moved over his skin like a second layer of silk, turning him into a mass of trembling muscle.

If she wanted to play that way, he'd be only too happy to go along. It wasn't easy to maneuver, but he managed to work his hands between their bodies, searching for her buttons. He fumbled with the top one, then the second, while he tasted her lips over and over again. She overwhelmed his senses, until he couldn't decide which one to satisfy first.

A door slammed. Deacon's hands froze against Rhea's buttons, his lips against hers. Brown eyes stared down at him, first in shock, then embarrassment, and finally laughing.

"Damn that kid," Deacon growled. "Is he ever late?"

"Not once," she giggled.

He let his arms fall to his sides and groaned up at the ceiling. "And I don't suppose you'd consider being late?"

"How would that look if the boss was late?" she asked coyly, pressing a kiss to his chest. She crawled off him, none too steady on her feet, he was happy to note, and reached for her yellow dress. "Will you give me some privacy?"

He stared back at her, his mouth hanging open. "You're suddenly shy?"

"Deacon, please." Her face was near to scarlet.

"Sorry, Rhea, I can't leave this room."

"Why ever not?"

He grinned back at her, standing there in all her indignation. "Because there are some things I'd rather not have Ernest see, and I'm afraid it's, uh, too hard for him not to notice."

"What are you talking about?" Even as she spoke, understanding dawned over her face. "Oh my . . . that's just . . . you're horrible."

"You're the one who said a person couldn't help how he felt," he laughed. She was even more beautiful when she was flustered. "I could hide under the blanket."

She pondered that for a moment. "Do you promise not to look?"

Without a word, he pulled the blanket up over his head and lay there perfectly still while she scurried about.

With deft fingers, he eased the blanket down, bit by bit, until his left eye barely peeked over the edge. If it was torture he was looking for, he'd just found it in spades.

Rhea's nightgown lay in a heap on the floor. She'd propped her right foot on the end of the bed and was bent over her leg, tugging a gray stocking up over her knee.

She didn't have another stitch of clothing on.

Deacon clamped his teeth down on his bottom lip until he tasted blood. After a few seconds, she changed legs and set to work on the other stocking, then reached for her chemise and drawers. As she turned back, their eyes locked, and she let out a small scream.

Deacon jumped, sat up, and let the blanket fall from his face.

"You promised you wouldn't look!" She clutched the

underthings to her body as if that would erase everything he'd already seen.

"I never promised anything," he laughed. "You asked if I promised, and I didn't answer."

"Deacon!"

"What?" He scooted back on the bed until his back rested against the narrow headboard. "You're a beautiful woman, Rhea. I can't help if I want to look."

"Oooh, you're such a . . ."

"I know, I know." He crossed his arms over his chest and tipped his head to the right. "You better hurry, or Ernest is going to wonder what happened to you."

Her glare might have appeared fiercer if she wasn't flushed pink and fighting a smile. After a moment, she resigned herself to the fact he wasn't going to stop looking, dropped the shift to her feet and stumbled into her drawers.

As much as he hated to see her cover up that luscious body, it was probably best she did. But now that he'd been through that sweet torture, he'd be counting the minutes until he could suffer through it again.

After much fussing and fretting, and a few more glares his way, she was dressed, her hair braided and her boots buttoned.

As she walked by the bed, Deacon grabbed her around the waist and pulled her back down on his lap.

"It's only proper for a wife to kiss her husband good-bye, you know."

"Is that right?" She pursed her lips and frowned over her smile. "Well, goodness knows we've been the epitome of propriety up 'til now, haven't we?"

"Absolutely," he said, pulling her closer.

She kissed him softly, just the once, then pushed up from the bed, her fingers still twined in his.

"Rhea?"

"Hmm?" She was studying their fingers and obviously avoiding his eyes.

"Say it again."

Color raced over her face, and her fingers trembled against his. "I don't think—"

Her tongue darted out over her bottom lip, and she was quiet for a long time. Easing his fingers from hers, he used both hands to turn her toward the door.

"You don't want to keep Ernest waiting." He had meant for that to sound more good-humored than it actually did.

Instead of leaving, though, she stood at the door, with her back to the room. After a moment, she half turned and looked straight at him. Going by her expression, there was no doubt how much it pained her to say it, but she did.

"I love you."

With that she was gone, leaving Deacon to stare after her, sharing her pain, but grinning like a fool nonetheless.

She loved him.

Despite who he was, and what he'd led her to believe, she still loved him. Humans really were a crazy lot—Rhea more than most.

A small shiver ran through his body, starting at the very tips of his toes and moving steadily upward until it touched every hair on his head.

Power.

The familiar feeling was back, not as strong as it had been, and certainly not encompassing all the powers he'd once had, but it was something. Perhaps having his powers back would make him want to return to his real life instead of lying there in Rhea's bed playing at being human.

Deacon propped one arm under his head and stared

up at the ceiling. Despite the obvious downsides to being human, if it meant he could stay right there for the
rest of time, it might be worth the effort.

What the . . . when had he ever been one to think of
what could be? His life was what it was, and he'd be
stupid to hope for anything more.

Ever since he met Rhea, he'd discovered his ability to
feel many human emotions, including anger, amusement
and regret. Maybe it was possible for him to feel other
emotions, too.

Deacon gave himself a sharp mental kick. Maybe it
was possible for the sun to rise in the west, too.

CHAPTER ELEVEN

"Is that boy here today?" Mrs. Hale stormed through the door, dragging Polly behind her. The poor girl's face was blotchy from crying, and every second breath tripped over a hiccup.

"Mrs. Hale." Rhea looked up, startled. The fierceness in the woman's eyes surprised her even more. "I–I'm afraid Ernest has already gone home."

If Polly didn't look so completely miserable, Rhea might have thought she was relieved. Hard to tell at that point.

"Fine." Mrs. Hale nodded sharply. "I'll deal with him later. But you—"

"I'm sorry, Miss Rhea," Polly choked out. "I tried to stop her."

Mrs. Hale advanced toward Rhea until the only thing separating them was the counter. "Who do you think you are?"

Rhea's mouth fell open, but it took a few more seconds before she could push the words from her tongue. "I beg your pardon?"

"I told you Polly was going to go live with my aunt. In Houston she can learn about the world, different cultures, and have a life away from all this." More spittle formed in the corners of her mouth the angrier she got. "And the first thing you do is run and tell that *boy* you have working for you."

"Mrs. Hale, I assure you—"

"Do you deny that you told him to talk to Polly?"

"No."

"Do you deny telling him Polly should have a choice in the matter? That he could perhaps sway her to stay here?"

"I—"

"Thanks to you and your meddling, that fool has it in his head that he's going to marry Polly and keep her tied down here—in Penance!"

Polly hiccupped again, standing beside her mother, with her hands clenched at her waist and her head bowed. Rhea wanted to grab her up and hide her in the backroom until the woman stopped yelling.

"Mrs. Hale," Rhea said quietly, "if you'll remember, Ernest was standing right over there when you told me about sending Polly to Houston, so it would have been impossible for him *not* to hear."

"Is that supposed to make me feel better?" The woman's face was a deepening shade of red, and her hands vibrated against her small bag.

"I-I'm sorry. What would you like me to do?"

"Do?" Mrs. Hale was almost screeching. "I want you to tell her how foolish it is. Tell her that one day she'll come to regret marrying him and staying in this horrible little town; that her life will be full of nothing but heartache and hard work."

"I'm sorry, I can't do that."

"You can, and you will!" Mrs. Hale shook Polly's sleeve until she looked up at Rhea. "Now tell her."

"Mrs. Hale, please."

"You, of all people, know it's true. If it hadn't been

for your family's store, what choices would you have had?"

"I hardly think—"

"Please." Mrs. Hale's screeching turned to pleading. "Don't you think my Polly deserves a chance at something better? A life where she won't have to work from sunup to sundown? Where she'll have choices and . . ."

"Of course she should have choices," Rhea said. "And one of those should be deciding whether she wants to go to Houston."

"She's seventeen, for goodness sake—she can't begin to know what she wants."

"I'll be eighteen next week, and I want to stay here and marry Ernest." Polly's voice, cracked and choking, strained against each word. "I love him."

"Love?" Mrs. Hale spat out. "You're too young to know what love is."

"You married Pa when you were sixteen!" Polly cried. "How is that any different?"

The look on Mrs. Hale's face made the difference crystal clear.

"Polly." Rhea took the girl's hand and smiled. "Your mother loves you very much, and she only wants what's best for you."

"But she's lived here her whole life. Why can't I?"

With a glance at Mrs. Hale's grim face, Rhea plunged on. "It was a different time back when your folks got married. Women didn't have as many options as we do today."

"What do you mean?"

Oh, Lord, what was she getting herself into here?

"Back then, women were expected to marry young and start a family. And sadly, love was not often a consideration for many of those girls." Another glance at Mrs.

Hale confirmed her last statement. "Imagine how hard it would be to be married to a man you didn't love."

"But I do love Ernest."

"I'm sure you do." Rhea smiled at Polly, whose face glowed with hope, dreams and expectations. "But you must understand that love isn't always enough to make a hard life easier, is it, Mrs. Hale?"

"No, it's not." Thankfully, the woman didn't expound further.

"No mother in the world wants her child to go through the same hardships she has, and I'm sure your mother is just afraid that is what will happen if you stay here."

"But I don't care! I'm not afraid of hard work. I love Ernest and I want to marry him."

Good Lord—what was worse: the howling mother or the sobbing child?

"Polly, please." Mrs. Hale's eyes welled with tears. "You have to trust me on this."

"Miss Rhea, you've only been married a little while," Polly hurried on, her voice growing stronger. "And you've had a horrible time of it already."

Rhea laughed. "It's certainly not been easy."

"But you love Mr. Deacon, don't you?"

"That's different, Polly."

"No, it's not. You love him and that's all that matters. You survived even after you thought he died, and surely there's no worse hardship than that."

"I . . . well, yes, but . . ."

Footsteps behind her warned of Deacon's approach.

"Mrs. Hale, Polly." He bobbed his head in a brief hello to both women. "I hope you'll pardon my intrusion, but I couldn't help overhearing."

As mother and daughter stared back at him in silence,

Rhea offered up a silent prayer of thanks he'd taken a clean shirt from the rack.

"You're right, Polly," he said. "There is no worse hardship than what my Rhea went through, and as it was my fault entirely, I will spend the rest of our time together trying to make it up to her."

It was Rhea's turn to stare at him, completely speechless. What was he doing?

Deacon's eyes warmed, but he kept talking to Polly. "She's a strong woman, my Rhea. Are you ready to be that strong, too? You have to be willing to make sacrifices, even when you don't want to."

"Ernest is almost twenty. He can decide what's best for both of us."

Luckily for Deacon, he covered his smirk with his hand before Polly noticed it. But Rhea noticed and responded with a quick poke to his ribs.

"Don't do that, Polly," she said, trying not to sound like she was lecturing. "You have a perfectly good mind of your own, and it's up to you to decide what *you* want. Don't ever let anyone turn your life into something they want. In the end, it'll only make you both miserable."

Deacon coughed twice, then quickly recovered. "If it's any consolation, Mrs. Hale, I've come to know the young man, and he seems to be a levelheaded sort. Hard worker, by all accounts, too."

"Yes." Rhea nodded.

"And so handsome." Polly sighed over a smile, then realized what she'd said and blushed furiously.

"Enough of this nonsense," Mrs. Hale said, her breathing sharp. "You are going to Houston, and that's the end of it."

Mrs. Hale dragged Polly back down the aisle and shoved past Kit, who was just coming in the door.

"That was not a happy customer," Kit said, staring

after the woman and her daughter. "You didn't let Deacon wait on them, did you?"

"What do you want, Kit?" Deacon's smile, so easy and free a moment ago, vanished.

Kit didn't answer him, just continued to watch the Hales hurry down the boardwalk.

"Just think, Rhea," she muttered loudly. "If that girl gets her way and marries Ernest, you'll have to invite her horrid mother to all your family gatherings."

Rhea clicked her tongue and made to go back to the counter, but something made her stop.

"Get out of here, Kit." Deacon's warning came low and dark.

"No, wait." Rhea shook her head. "Why would I invite the Hales to family gatherings?"

Kit shrugged indifferently. "Good question. I know I wouldn't, even if she was part of the family. Who'd want to eat with that woman?"

"Kit . . ." Deacon's warning went unheeded.

"I understand why you don't invite crazy old lady Miller to your family dinners. I mean, after all that's happened—"

"Mrs. Miller isn't family."

"I know *she's* not," Kit said, "but that doesn't mean—"

"Kit!" Deacon started toward his sister, but she ducked out the door before he reached her.

"Colin knows the truth," she called through the crack before shutting the door and hurrying away.

A slow tremble began in Rhea's ankles and worked its way up her legs until she was helpless to stop it. Her heart quivered and goose bumps raced over her arms as the icy fingers of fear wound through her blood.

"What did she mean, Deacon? What does Colin know?"

He shook his head slowly, his mouth set in a grim line. "I don't know, sweetheart."

"But what she said . . . do you think she meant . . . ?" Her thoughts ran in a hundred different directions at once.

"I need to talk to Colin." She was already at the door before Deacon caught up with her.

"Wait," he said. "Just wait. You can't go over there all fired up like this. For all we know Kit was just talking in circles like she usually does."

"But why would she do that?"

"Because she can!"

Rhea pulled open the door, then turned back to Deacon. "Are you coming with me?"

He didn't move, and Rhea wasn't about to wait for him. She started down the walk but only made it half a dozen paces before he stopped her.

"Rhea, wait."

She pulled the key out of her skirt pocket, tossed it to Deacon and waited impatiently while he locked the store.

A moment later they were inside the sheriff's office with the door shut behind them.

The fear she'd begun to feel earlier now crept into her throat. Whatever Kit had been talking about, Rhea had a feeling it wasn't going to be good.

Colin looked up as they walked in, his expression flipping from hopeful to impatient in less than a heartbeat. But a moment later, it changed again.

Without Rhea saying a word, she could see by Colin's expression that he knew something was wrong. Horribly wrong.

He licked his lips, swallowed, then folded his hands on top of his desk and sighed. "What?"

Deacon stood next to Rhea and wrapped his arm

around her waist. She chewed her bottom lip for a moment, then charged ahead. There was no point in being anything but direct.

"What do you know about the Millers?"

"What?" Every bit of color faded from Colin's face. Not a good sign.

"Are they somehow related to us?"

He unfolded his hands, twisted them in his lap, then folded them on top of the desk again. "How did you . . . I mean, where did you . . . ?"

"It's true?" She stepped closer to his desk, but stopped when he pulled his hands back into his lap and stared down at them. "How?"

"It doesn't make a lick of difference anymore, Rhea."

"Then why won't you look at me?"

He released an annoyed sigh, rolled his eyes at her and immediately looked away again.

"I know it's not Mrs. Miller," Rhea pressed. "Was it Mr. Miller?"

Colin's jaw clenched, but when he looked up, he looked straight past her to Deacon.

"Oh my Lord," she gasped. "It's not Mr. Miller, is it?"

Colin shook his head slowly.

"Ernest?" Suddenly, she didn't want to look at her brother, didn't want to see the truth in his eyes, the truth he'd kept from her for God only knew how long.

"Shit." Colin's voice sounded a hundred miles away.

"Oh, for—" Deacon wrapped his arm around her shoulders and ushered her toward Colin's chair. He scrambled to get out of it a moment before Rhea sank down on it in a heap.

"Ernest?" she repeated. "But how?"

"It's complicated," he said, his voice subdued, his face a sickly shade of gray.

"Does he know?"

"Yes." He pulled a half-full bottle from his drawer and set it on top of the desk.

She made to lunge at him, but Deacon held her back. "And neither one of you thought to tell me?"

"Rhea, please."

"No." Her throat felt raw, her voice not her own. "He's our . . . and you knew!"

The door opened and Donnelda Dietrich breezed in, looking more like spring than nature itself. Her blonde curls sat pinned beneath a soft pink bonnet, which tied beneath her chin with a huge satin bow.

Her dress, matching pink of course, was a simple yet elegant affair, with its modest neckline and fitted bodice. Lace trimmed the hem and wrists, and tiny bows adorned each shoulder.

A large basket, balanced carefully on her hip, slid from her grasp and would have hit the floor had Deacon not moved so quickly.

"Oh," she gasped. "I'm sorry, Col . . . er, Sheriff. I didn't know you were busy."

"Excuse me." Colin grabbed the basket away from Deacon and ushered Donnelda back outside. A moment later, he was back looking none-too-pleased, yet it took him a long time before he sighed and nodded.

"I knew," he said slowly. "But it was so long ago . . ."

"Sweet mother of God, Colin," Rhea cried. "I don't care if it was yesterday afternoon—you should have told me!"

He didn't say anything.

She twisted her fingers together as she paced the floor in front of him. "How did this happen?"

"Come on, Rhea." He let out an exasperated sigh. "You know how babies are made."

"Don't you dare take that tone with me! If anyone

has the right to be angry here, it's me. And if you don't start telling me the truth, I swear to God—"

Deacon took her hand in his and squeezed gently.

"What's to explain?" Colin cracked his knuckles and leaned back against the wall, his gaze fixed straight down at the floor. "Pa took up with Mrs. Miller, and now we have Ernest."

"Pa . . . and Mrs. . . ." Rhea shook her head. No. This couldn't be. "But he loved Ma. He would never do that to her."

Colin snorted. His shoulders shook, whether with rage or sadness, Rhea couldn't be sure because he didn't look up. "Well, he did."

She sagged against Deacon for a moment, then forced herself upright. "Did . . . did Ma know?"

Silence. A long tortuous moment of silence that ended with a sharp, brief nod of his head.

"She knew?" Rhea cried. "But she never said anything . . . she never . . . she must have been devastated."

Colin cracked his knuckles again, but at least she didn't have to prod him for more information.

"Ma wasn't exactly a saint either," he muttered.

"No!" She would have collapsed right there if Deacon hadn't grabbed her. "Ma?"

Pain ripped through Rhea's heart. Not her mother . . . no. It couldn't be true.

Colin cleared his throat quietly. "Why do you think Pa's 'good friend' Judge Hicks came around so often?"

"No. Oh no." He had to be lying. It just couldn't be true. "Not him."

"Him."

Rhea leaned over, resting her elbows on her knees.

"How long have you known?" she asked, pushing each syllable from her tongue.

Colin uncorked the bottle, stared longingly at the amber liquid, then sighed and set it back down.

"Tell me." She shouldn't want the details; it was bad enough knowing the outcome. "How long?"

He pursed his lips for a second. "Long time."

"Why didn't you say something?" she cried.

"For God's sake, Rhea, you were five! What was I supposed to say?"

Each breath was like swallowing a giant rock. "Five? But that means you were . . . you—"

"Ten," he ground out. "Ten years old and I walked in on Pa and that woman, naked as jaybirds, and going at each other like—"

"Colin!" Deacon's voice snapped like a whip.

"You should have told me." It was all she could do not to reach for the whiskey herself.

"Why? What good would that have done?"

She was out of the chair in a heartbeat and standing right up in front of him.

"They were my parents, too." Her throat burned with a pent-up sob. "And I should have been told. I don't need you to protect me from the truth."

"No? You prefer knowing Ernest is our father's bastard son? Or that Ma lifted her skirts for the judge and God knows who else?"

"That's enough," Deacon warned, but Rhea ignored him. She didn't need him protecting her from the truth, either.

"Don't be ridiculous," she said. "Of course I don't *want* to know that, but it would have been better than living this lie, wouldn't it?"

Anger this deep was new to her. She didn't know what do, where to look.

"I can still see Pa's face when I found them." Colin spat on the floor at his feet.

"Oh dear God." The room began to spin around her, the light narrowing to a single point in front. She slumped back in the chair, bent over at the waist and hung her head down in front of her knees. "Did y–you say anything to them?"

She must have looked like a crazy woman bent over that way, but did it matter at this point?

"Hell no!" Colin barked. He slammed his fists down on the desk. "Wasn't my place."

None of this made sense. There must be some mis-understanding.

"But how did they . . . I mean . . . Ma and Pa spent all their time together, at the store during the day and home at night. When would they have time . . . oh my Lord."

Colin shook his head. "You don't want to know."

No, she certainly didn't. She didn't want to know any of this, but she couldn't get past this last question. Something told her it was the answer for more than just this question.

"Please, Colin," she said quietly. "You have to tell me."

Deacon crouched next to the chair and wrapped his arms around her.

"Rhea," he murmured. "Are you sure you don't want to go lie down for a while? You know the truth now; does anything else matter?"

"Y–yes," she stammered. "Of course it matters. Every last detail matters."

She rested her head in the crook of his shoulder but even the warmth of his embrace couldn't stop her trem-bling.

Everything she'd believed about her parents was a lie. Which meant everything she'd been raised to believe was also a lie.

"Tell me," she whispered, pushing up from Deacon's shoulder.

Colin exhaled a loud breath. "I don't think—"

"Just tell me."

Deacon laid both his hands on her shoulders and squeezed gently. If only she could climb inside him and hide from everything Colin was saying—or trying *not* to say, as the case may be. But she needed to know.

Colin lifted the bottle, but again didn't drink. Instead, he rolled it between his hands, watching the amber liquid slosh around inside.

At long last, he looked up at Rhea with eyes that had seen too much, his face looking more like the boy she grew up with than the man he'd turned into.

"Think about it, Rhea," he muttered. "What did you think that room above the store was used for? Storage rooms don't normally have beds and washbowls set up in them."

"You son of a bitch." Anger surged through Deacon with such force that it took a long time to gain control over it. "And you let her stay up there?"

"I couldn't tell her," Colin mumbled, shaking his head. "Look at her. I just couldn't."

He sounded weary, but Deacon didn't care. All that mattered was Rhea. Her body continued to quake uncontrollably, and he had no idea how to help her. He took her back in his arms, but the trembling didn't stop. It didn't even slow down.

He lifted his chin off Rhea's head and fixed his glare on Colin. He could feel the burden in Colin's soul, could almost see the darkness clouding it.

No.

He couldn't let that power come out yet. If he used it once, it would be too easy to use again, and then his father would have control over him again. Deacon wasn't ready for that yet. He closed his mind to it and stared at Colin until the other man finally dragged his vacant gaze from the floor and looked back at him.

Keeping this secret had taken its toll on Colin. Rhea might not see it and she might not understand it, but her brother had done right by not telling her. It had obviously crippled him, and by keeping the secret, he'd saved Rhea from a similar fate.

With his eyes still fixed on Colin, Deacon pressed his lips to the top of Rhea's head and tightened his hold on her. Her breath shuddered another tremor up her spine, but she didn't make any other sound.

"Hey," he whispered. "Do you think you can walk?"

She sniffed against his neck and nodded, but didn't release her grip on his shirt.

"Okay." He eased her up to stand, but couldn't bear to watch her tremble that way. Ignoring her cries of protest, he scooped her up in his arms and turned toward the door.

Without so much as a word, Colin shuffled over, opened the door and clicked it shut behind them.

"Please put me down," she whispered. "People will stare."

"What else is new?"

A dozen paces away, the man from the newspaper stepped out onto the sidewalk, but Deacon strode right past him, and then past two women who pointed and whispered but made no attempt to get out of the way. He didn't even pause as he passed the store, and hoped Rhea's eyes were closed so she didn't have to look at it. When they reached the hotel, he used the tips of his fingers to pull open the door.

"Now will you put me down?"

"No."

There was no one behind the desk, so he shifted Rhea into his left arm and snagged a room key off the board on the wall.

He headed for the stairs, but only made it to the second step before a woman cleared her throat nervously behind him.

"Excuse me, sir . . ."

Deacon didn't slow down. "I took the key to room four," he called over his shoulder. "I'll be down shortly to settle up."

"But—"

A few steps later, he was shifting Rhea in his arms again so he could unlock the door. Inside, he nudged it closed with his foot and walked straight to the bed. It was at least twice as big as the one they'd spent the last week in, with clean blankets and two thick pillows.

He tucked her under the quilt, then sat on the edge, fingering her hair back from her face.

She was too pale. And far too quiet.

"How are you doing?" he asked.

Rhea rolled over on her side and curled up into a tight ball. "I-I think I need to be alone for a while."

Her voice shook almost as hard as the rest of her body.

"Can I get you some water?" He took a quick sweep of the room, cursing the lack of a water pitcher. "Something to eat, maybe?"

"No, thank you."

"I'm not leaving you like this."

"Please, Deacon," she mumbled over a sob. "I-I can't think with you sitting there."

He reached out to touch her, but she shook her head against the pillow.

"Rhea—"

"I'll be fine," she sniffed. "Please."

She damn well wouldn't be fine. But how could he refuse her when she was so upset?

"I'm going downstairs for a minute," he said, "but then I'll be back. If you need anything, I'll be right outside that door."

She shook her head again, but still didn't look at him.

At the door, he stopped. "We'll get through this, Rhea," he said. "Might not seem like it now, but we will."

No answer. The only sounds were those of her sniffing and trying to cover up the quiet sobs that continued to rack her body.

He stepped out into the hall and locked the door, but it was a long time before he could finally bring himself to walk away from the room. On feet of lead, he made his way to the lobby, where he was met by a woman in a dark green dress and circular spectacles.

"I beg your pardon, sir," she said, her voice as ghastly thin as herself. "But guests are not permitted to help themselves to whichever room they like without checking in first."

"Forgive me," he said, doing his best to look contrite. "But my wife is feeling poorly and needed to rest."

"I'm sorry to hear that," she sniffed. "Would you like me to send for the doctor?"

"Thank you, but I don't think that's necessary. She just needs to rest."

"Very well. Perhaps now you can take a moment to fill in the register."

"Of course." He lifted the quill from the desk and scrawled his and Rhea's names on the line she indicated. As he reached into his pocket for payment, the woman spun the book back to her, licked her lips and sputtered.

"*You're* Deacon? Miss Rhea's husband?"

"Yes."

"And she's ill?" The woman's entire demeanor changed. "I'll have someone fetch Doc Jamieson straightaway."

"No, thank you," he said. "She'll be fine."

"But—"

"We appreciate your concern," he said, forcing a congenial smile. "But she has asked only for some time to rest and regain her strength."

"Yes, of course."

"Now, if you'd be so good as to tell me what we owe you for the room . . ." He hesitated, the wad of bills clutched in his hand. How long would they be staying there? Everything was such a mess. Besides this, they still had to deal with the impending visit of Judge Hicks. "Perhaps I should pay for the first week now. If we need it longer, we'll make arrangements then."

"You're welcome to stay here as long as you need." The woman looked more and more motherly by the moment. "But don't concern yourself with payment."

Deacon frowned. "We don't need charity, Miss . . ."

"Fillion. Emily Fillion." She extended her hand, which Deacon shook, still frowning. "And I didn't mean to offend you, Mr . . . er . . . Deacon. I simply meant that we will settle the bill when you're ready to leave."

"That's very kind of you." The suspicion Deacon expected to feel never materialized.

A smile twisted the woman's mouth up in a small curve. "Your wife has helped most every family in this town at one time or another," she said. "And mine is no different. I'm happy to be able to help her this time."

"I'm sure she'll appreciate it." He made to leave, then stopped. "Would you please have some food sent up to our room?"

"Yes, sir, right away."

"Thank you." He started back toward the stairs, even though she kept right on talking.

"Please tell Miss Rhea I hope she's feeling better soon. And if you change your mind, I can have the doctor here in matter of minutes."

Deacon nodded silently and continued on to their room, but didn't go in. Instead, he pressed his ear to the door, wishing he could go in and take this pain from her. Each one of her sobs was another slash to his heart; and each slash to his heart ripped another rash of prickles across his scars.

But it wasn't the pain of his father's lashings that weakened him, or even the constant reminders that prickled his old scars. It was this new pain, the one that felt like an ever-expanding crater inside him.

There was no way to close this wound, no way to cover it with fancy shirts and silk jackets. It was a pain he'd feel every day for the rest of his life.

Rhea had weakened him beyond repair.

He sat on the floor next to the door, his arms resting on his bent knees. How long before he could go in there? How long before she'd let him hold her again?

And how long before he'd have to walk away from her for the last time?

So many questions battered around in Rhea's head, she didn't know what to think first. She'd wanted Deacon to stay with her, but she knew it wouldn't help. This was something she needed to sort out herself.

Colin had known for almost twenty years what their parents had done; twenty years of keeping that horrible secret to himself, of trying to protect her from the ugly truth so she could continue to live her life in ignorant bliss.

Who did he think he was, keeping this from her?

Instead of giving her the chance to deal with it, he'd taken that from her and used the excuse of wanting to protect her.

It certainly explained why Colin could barely speak a civil word to Ernest, why he avoided the store as much as possible and why he flat-out refused to set foot inside the upstairs room.

That room . . . no. She wouldn't think about it yet. First thing she needed to do was calm down. Inhaling long, slow breaths, she kept her eyes closed and tried to ease the chaos in her head.

As strange as it seemed, the fact that Ernest was her half brother didn't disturb her as much as she expected it to. He was a sweet young man who'd done his best work for her at the store.

No, it wasn't that tying her stomach in knots until she curled up in pain. It was the realization that everything she believed in had been a lie. It was bad enough when she'd learned about Deacon and Salma—but her own parents?

If the two people she trusted most in her life couldn't honor their vows, how could she expect anyone else to?

Maybe it was a foolish thing to believe in the first place. Maybe men and women simply weren't capable of finding a lifetime of happiness with one person.

Deacon had been very kind to her in the past few days, had even been affectionate and considerate, but she'd lived her whole life watching her father treat her mother the same way.

It didn't mean anything.

She hadn't moved since Deacon left. Night crept in, filling the room with its hollow loneliness, but still she didn't move. Long after Deacon's footsteps stopped outside the door, long after she heard him slump to the floor in the hall, she stayed just as she was.

It was going to take a long time to push the pain down far enough that it didn't choke her anymore.

Muted voices sounded in the hall, followed by the sound of someone walking away, but it wasn't Deacon. His footsteps were unmistakable, and besides, he'd told her he'd be outside the door. No doubt that was exactly where he'd stay.

She squeezed her eyes shut and tried to ignore the little voice in her head that wouldn't be quiet. It wasn't right for her to leave him out there in the hall. He'd supported her at the jail when she needed him, and he'd carried her all the way here, without so much as slowing down to consider taking her back to their room above the store.

He didn't deserve to be treated this way.

She shuffled off the bed and opened the door to find him standing on the other side, jacket bunched under his arm, his expression one of apprehension and concern.

"Are you all right?"

She shook her head and left the door open as she shuffled back to the bed. Deacon lifted a tray of food from the floor and stepped inside the room, quietly closing the door behind him.

He dropped his jacket on the end of the bed, set the tray on the wide window ledge and turned back to her, his fingers fisting and flexing at his sides.

"What can I do?" he asked.

"Nothing." She unbuttoned her boots, let them fall to the floor and tried to smile. "But you can't very well sit out there all night."

"Yes, I can."

He was halfway to the door before she realized he was serious.

"Deacon, don't be silly."

"If you don't want me in here with you, I'll go," he

said, "but I'm not going any farther than right outside that door."

"I don't want you to leave," she whispered.

He nodded toward the basket. "Are you hungry?"

"Not terribly." She rolled back onto the bed and pulled the blanket up to her neck. "I just want to sleep."

"Okay." Several minutes later, he hadn't moved.

"Are you going to stand there 'til morning, or are you going to come and lie down?"

He certainly took his sweet time making up his mind, but eventually, his boots landed beside hers and he crawled in next to her.

"Deacon?"

"Yes." Even through the darkness, she could see his eyes were wide open.

"Why do men think they need to rule women's lives?" She leaned up on her elbow. "I have more education than most men in this town, I own a business and I've survived both my parents' deaths."

"As well as your husband's." He flashed a toothy smile as he mirrored her position so they lay face-to-face in the dark.

"So why would Colin think he needs to shield me from something like this?"

Deacon's smile faded as he lifted his shoulder in a shrug. "He was only doing what he thought was best for you."

"That's exactly what I mean," she said. "I don't need him doing what he thinks is best for me. I'm perfectly capable of taking care of myself."

"Rhea, you're his sister. He loves you."

"I love him, too," she argued. "But I don't go around treating him like a child, do I?"

Deacon looked like he was going to say something,

then changed his mind. She huffed out a breath and frowned at him.

"And that whole business with you carrying me over here from the jail . . . I could have walked just fine."

Again, he looked like he was holding back whatever it was he wanted to say. She reached for his hand and pressed a kiss against the palm.

"But thank you for not taking me back to the store."

He nodded quietly, and after a moment of silence, Rhea let his hand fall. She rolled onto her back and lay staring up at the ceiling.

Torn between what was bouncing around in her head and the exhaustion that begged to be sated, Rhea finally gave in to both sides.

"Would you mind . . . what I mean is . . ."

He was reaching for her before she stumbled over her last word. Lying on his back, he pulled her right up beside him and wrapped his arm around her. She rested her cheek on his silk-covered chest and her hand against his stomach.

He flinched slightly, but when she made to move, he covered her hand with his own and squeezed.

"Doesn't it hurt? You might be more comfortable if you were on your side."

"I'm fine," he said quietly.

"No, you're not, you big liar."

His only response was a small grin and a kiss to her forehead. She snuggled deeper into his embrace and closed her eyes.

"Thank you," she whispered.

"You're welcome." He kissed the top of her head and sighed into her hair. "Now go to sleep."

Sleep. Yes. That was what she'd do. She'd go to sleep and when she woke up, this would all have been a bad dream—a bad dream that felt far too real for her liking.

She shifted her body so her entire length pressed against Deacon, right down to their feet. Bad dream or not, she wouldn't have been anywhere else in the world at that moment.

CHAPTER TWELVE

Deacon didn't sleep. Kit was down on the street, staring up at their window. He'd seen her when he brought the tray in, but if he'd told Rhea about it, she never would have fallen asleep.

So he lay on the bed with Rhea curled up against him, as each laceration burned lines of fire across his skin. He welcomed the pain; it kept him focused and helped him remember to block everything Kit represented. A challenge at the best of times—now it was going to be a full-on battle.

He understood it now; he understood why Lucille had fought so hard to keep her human safe. And he understood why the consequences didn't matter.

All that mattered was Rhea. Deacon ground his teeth together and forced his mind to focus. If his father knew for even a second that Deacon felt this deeply for Rhea, there'd be no telling what would happen. It was one thing for his father to drag him back to Hell, but Deacon wasn't about to let anything happen to Rhea.

Although . . . Deacon grinned. If anyone could give his father what-for, it would be Rhea.

Maybe she was just what Hell needed.

Rhea murmured in her sleep and pressed her arm

tighter around his middle. He sucked in a breath, but didn't move for fear of waking her.

The air shifted, Rhea whimpered softly and before Deacon could catch his breath, Kit appeared at the foot of the bed.

"What are you doing?" he whispered through gritted teeth.

"Don't fret," she said airily, waving his question away. "She won't wake up until I'm gone."

He twisted his neck until he could see Rhea's face. Sure enough, Kit had frozen her while she slept.

"You need to stop this nonsense." She leaned against the rail of the footboard and waved her hand between him and Rhea. "Come home, Deacon. Come back to where you belong."

Deacon eased away from Rhea and climbed out of bed. "I'm not ready."

"This isn't about you anymore." She stepped away from the footboard and pointed at his stomach. "If you're not careful, he's liable to turn his anger on her, instead."

"He can't do that."

"Oh, for . . ." She threw her hands up in the air and laughed out a choking snort. "Of course he can! There are no rules for something like this. He'll do whatever he wants, and there's nothing you can do to stop him."

"You don't know what you're talking about." He crossed his arms over his chest and stood taller, doing his best to intimidate her with his size if nothing else.

Typical Kit, she was completely unimpressed. "If you know what's good for you, you'll start using the powers he's given back," she said with a decisive nod.

"No."

Her mouth opened, then slammed shut as her green eyes blazed fire. "What do you mean 'no'?"

"No, I won't use any of his powers." He laughed, though neither thought it was funny. "Just because he gave them back doesn't mean I have to use them."

And Deacon wouldn't, not unless he absolutely had to. For a moment, he thought Kit was going to topple sideways.

She fisted her hands in her hair and scrunched it until her knuckles turned completely white. "He's going to come after you, Deacon, and he won't show mercy, no matter how much you beg for it."

"I've never begged."

"Not yet." The air shifted again and she was gone.

A second later, Rhea blinked her eyes open and sat up.

"Deacon?"

"Yeah," he answered. "I'm here."

She turned toward his voice, her face illuminated by the veiled moonlight coming in through the slits in the curtain.

"What happened?" she asked.

He took a tentative step toward her. "What d'you mean?"

"Just now," she said over a deep frown.

"You were sleeping."

"But it was like I wasn't really here. You were over there, talking to someone—Kit, I think. But I felt like I was . . ." She shook her head.

"Like what?" One more step took him to the side of the bed.

"It sounds crazy," she said, "but it was almost like I was a ghost, hovering in the air, and you couldn't see me. I've never had a dream like that before."

"Doesn't sound crazy at all." Before climbing back into bed, he unfastened his trousers and threw them on top of his jacket.

Even in the dark of the room, he could see the color flood her cheeks.

"Sorry," he muttered. "D'you want me to put them back on?"

"No," she answered rather hastily. "That's how you've slept all week."

There was something else she was itching to say, but didn't. Her eyes darted from him to his trousers and back again.

"Feel free to do the same." He grinned. "It can't be comfortable trying to sleep in that getup."

She laughed softly, but made no effort to remove her dress.

"I promise not to look."

"Haven't we been down this road before?" she asked.

"Not quite." He stepped over to the far corner of the room and kept his forehead pressed against the wall. "If you'll recall, I made no promises last time."

From the amount of scurrying going on behind him, she must have been frantically undoing buttons and shuffling blankets. A minute later, the commotion stopped.

"I'm ready."

He waited another few seconds before turning around. Had it really only been this morning when he'd watched her stretch that stocking up her leg? Felt like an eternity had passed since then, even though the image of her standing there, with her leg bent at the knee, her body bowed over it . . .

There was nothing his father could do to him that was worse torture than reliving that memory over and over.

"Right, then." He climbed in beside her and held out his arm, waiting for her to resume the position she'd been in before Kit showed up.

"You don't have to, you know."

Deacon let his arm fall to the bed and looked up at her, sitting there in her white cotton chemise, her hair spilling over her shoulders and her teeth worrying her bottom lip.

"I'm not doing it because you want me to," he said. "And I'm not doing it because I think you need to be taken care of."

She didn't look convinced.

"It's probably not wise to admit," he said, waggling his brow and lifting his arm again to wave her over. "But I'm doing it for me, so get over here and make yourself comfortable."

"You're such a liar." She laughed softly, but scooted over and snuggled against his side as she'd done before.

Once again, he was telling her the truth and she was refusing to believe it. Maybe a tiny part of him wanted to comfort her, but mostly he just wanted to touch her, and more than that, he wanted to have her touch him.

But now that she was pressing the entire length of her body against him, he wasn't sure he could stand torture this sweet.

He ground his teeth together and managed not to groan too loud when her hand slid between the buttons on his shirt and settled against his chest, but when her fingers curled and uncurled, scraping her nails against his skin, he almost exploded. Her hair smelled faintly of roses, and her lips, so soft, tickled his neck with every breath she took.

Didn't she realize who he was? Temptation wasn't something he'd ever been good at avoiding, and she was more temptation than he'd ever faced.

He lay perfectly still, gritting his teeth and wishing she would go to sleep—soon.

"Deacon?" Her lips fluttered against his neck.

"Mm-hmm." It was hard to talk with his jaw clenched

so tight, and when she wiggled against him like that, it only made him clench it tighter.

"You smell good." If she hadn't whispered the words so close to his ear, he probably wouldn't have heard her.

Couldn't she just go back to sleep? As difficult as it might be, he was fairly certain he could manage to hold her all night, so long as she was asleep.

But knowing she was awake, murmuring against his neck and moving against him that way . . .

A growl began to build, starting from the soles of his feet, and crescendoing until it threatened to burst from his throat. There was nothing he wanted more than to let it go, to press Rhea into that mattress and do whatever it took to pull a desperate growl from her throat, too.

But he couldn't. Not until she asked him to.

"Deacon?" Like everything else about her, Rhea's voice was as soft as down.

And dammit, he was rock hard lying there beside her. He didn't dare open his mouth to answer her, but instead turned his head just enough to press his lips against the top of her head.

Big mistake.

She tipped her face up to look at him, and even in the darkness, Deacon could see her every emotion, her every desire, staring back at him.

The growl ripped from his throat as he rolled over and pinned her beneath him, fisting his hands in the pillow on either side of her head.

She slipped her hand up under his shirt and raked her fingers along his belly, just under the bandage. Her other hand snaked out and grabbed the opening at the top of his shirt. With one quick yank, his face was but a breath away from hers. She watched his mouth for a long moment, smiled when he licked his lips and then pulled him in for a heart-stuttering kiss.

Her lips were velvet beneath his, her hands fire against his skin. If he ever considered what Heaven might be like, this would be it. He nudged her legs apart and knelt between them, never once breaking their kiss.

Inch by inch, he kissed his way down her neck, beneath each ear and over the spot that pulsed as hard as he did. Her breathing turned to gasps as he inched lower, nudging her chemise out of the way so he could taste the top of each breast. Her hands were in his hair, holding him close, all the while purring low in her throat.

It was a sound unlike any other; soft, feminine and full of raw desire.

She opened to him and arched upward as he pressed against her, gently at first, until she moved, rubbing herself against his hard length.

He didn't know who moaned that time, and he didn't care. All he knew was that he was going to explode any minute, and when he did, he didn't want to have their drawers between them.

He eased away, sliding his fingers beneath the bottom edge of her chemise and across her belly.

"Oh," she breathed. "I . . . oh."

Lower, lower, until he felt the band of her drawers. Pinching it between his fingers, he began to tug them down, slowly, slowly, without sending either one of them off the edge. She lifted off the bed and shoved them down herself, scrambling to keep him close at the same time.

Without that barrier, Deacon took a second to enjoy her bare skin. He kissed one knee, then the other, dancing his fingers across her thighs.

She whimpered, moving into his touch, but he just smiled and kissed her again, below her navel, then above it.

"Patience, sweetheart."

Even as he said it, he walked his fingers across her thigh, then higher. She gasped and squeezed her legs together for a second, but when he slid his tongue over the fabric covering her breast, she spread wider, not only welcoming his touch, but seeking it.

He inched upward again, marveling at her quick response to his touch. She was ready, *more than ready*, and so was he. He slipped his finger barely inside, then out again. Rhea's mouth opened, her tongue pressed between her teeth as he did it again, then again.

She wriggled beneath his hand, cried out and pressed her own hand on top, pushing his finger deeper, then deeper still. He kissed her hard and deep, his tongue mimicking his finger as she held him there, crying out with release.

He needed the rest of her clothes off, and he needed it soon. As they fumbled with each other's strings and buttons, he couldn't help wondering at this woman. After everything she'd been through today—

Deacon froze.

After everything she'd been through, all he cared about was getting inside her drawers. Hell, he *was* inside her drawers.

What kind of a fool was he?

Dammit.

Double dammit.

"Deacon?" His name shook off her lips, her hands scrambling to reach for him again.

"I'm sorry," he muttered. "I shouldn't be doing this."

"Yes, you should," she cried, grabbing the front of his shirt and pulling him down again. Her lips moved over his, silently pleading for him to kiss her back.

This was beyond torture.

"Rhea." Still kneeling between her legs, he took her hands in his and kissed each knuckle. "You know I want to, but you've been through so much today . . . it wouldn't be right."

"It wouldn't be right?" she cried, her voice full of blatant anger and frustration. "Get off me." She shoved both her hands against his chest and pushed as hard as she could, sending him back down on the bed. She pulled her legs out from under him and moved over to the other side of the bed.

"I'm only trying to do what's right," he said, pulling himself back up. His cuts screamed against the exertion, and if he wasn't mistaken, he'd just split open the ones along his right side again.

"For whom?" Rhea snapped. "You? Or me?"

"Why are you mad?" He reached for her hand, but she snapped it away before he got anywhere near it.

"Why? Oh, for—"

It was almost funny how mad she was, but Deacon wasn't completely stupid. Laughing at her right then was tantamount to suicide.

"I. Don't. Need. You. To. Protect. Me." As she spoke, she slapped her pillow to emphasize each word. "Was that clear enough for you?"

He couldn't help it. He battled it back for as long as he could, but the second he opened his mouth to answer her, he laughed in her face.

Judging by her color and the fierceness of her fists, Deacon half expected smoke to come pouring out her ears. She grabbed up her pillow and smashed him in the side of the head before flopping down on the bed with her back to him.

"Rhea," he laughed. "Don't be mad at me. Come on." He knelt closer, resting his hand on her hip. She promptly slapped it away. "You have to admit it's a little funny."

"No, not even a tiny bit." She yanked the blanket up until it reached just below her earlobe.

"Of course it is. I mean, look at us. You're the good Christian woman and I'm the son of the devil, for crying out loud. Of the two of us, it really shouldn't be me doing the right thing."

"Fine time for you to grow a conscience," she snapped.

Deacon chuckled as he slid down to lie beside her. "I'm not overly excited about the timing myself."

Stiff as a board, Rhea stayed tucked under her blanket, without so much as twitching a muscle.

"Come on," he murmured. "Are you really going to sleep that way all night?"

"Yes." She twisted her head around and smiled sweetly. "I'm sure your new conscience will be happy to keep you warm tonight."

So much for that idea.

"You can't stay mad at me forever."

"Watch me."

"But you know I'm right." Was that his voice sounding so weak? So desperate? "If we had made love tonight, it would have been one more thing you'd be worrying over in the morning."

"And how, exactly, does that concern you?"

He wrapped his arm around her, blanket and all, and rolled her back to face him. "Because when we make love, Rhea—and you can be certain we *will* make love—it's not going to be something either of us regrets or has to worry about the next morning."

Her mouth opened to argue, but he was quicker this time. He pressed a kiss against her lips and smiled down at her frustrated frown.

"I'm right and you know it."

Her eyes narrowed for a fraction of a second before her body relaxed against the bed. Deacon lay next to her, lifted his arm and waited.

As the seconds ticked by, his confidence wavered

slightly, but he continued to hold his arm where it was until finally, *finally*, she resigned herself to what they both wanted.

Once she was pressed up against his side again, with her head tucked under his chin and her fingers grazing his chest, he let himself relax.

Damn conscience could get a fellow into trouble.

Rhea curled tighter against Deacon as the sun inched its way higher. A new day, something she usually welcomed, but not this morning. This new day shone its glaring light on what she'd learned about her parents, until all she wanted to do was bury her head under the blanket and hide there all day.

She wouldn't, but she'd sure like to.

In hindsight, Deacon had been right about last night. So now, to add to her anger and confusion, she was half naked, with her drawers on the floor somewhere and her dress kicked off the edge of the bed.

"Good morning." His voice was full of sleep, but that didn't stop him from kissing the top of her head or wrapping his arm tighter around her shoulder.

"Morning."

"How are you feeling?"

Better with his fingers dancing up and down her arm like that, but after last night, she couldn't very well tell him that. She buried her face in his neck and laughed.

"I think mortified is probably the best way to describe it."

"Don't be silly." But he was laughing, too. "If anyone should be mortified, it should be me. I don't know what I was thinking last night . . ."

"Seemed to me we were thinking the same thing," she answered dryly. "For a while, anyway."

"Hey." He tipped her chin up and stared down at her with those deep blue eyes. "It wasn't the right time."

Rhea sighed and shrugged in resignation.

"Believe me," he murmured, "when the time is right, it's going to be amazing."

Her whole body flamed in embarrassment.

"What?" he laughed. "After what you did last night, you're embarrassed by that?"

"After what *I* did?" she cried, pulling out of his hold. "You're the one who—"

He tipped his head, grinned and gave her that "tell-the-truth" look.

"Okay, maybe it wasn't just you," she conceded before moving back into his embrace. "But I never would have carried on that way with anyone else, so you're not entirely innocent, either."

His chest expanded beneath her ear. "When you put it *that* way, I'm happy to accept the blame."

All the anger and frustration from yesterday seemed to fade when she was wrapped up next to him this way. She inched closer, sliding her leg on top of his and wrapping her arm around his body, careful of his bandage.

"You're being so good to me," she whispered. "I'm not sure why, and I'm even less sure I deserve it, but I *am* sure it feels good."

"Rhea?" His voice sounded tight, gravelly.

"Hmm?" She slid her foot lower, so her toes touched his. The warmth of his skin, the beat of his heart beneath her ear and the feel of his kiss against her head; it all added up to one thing—a sense of home.

"I'm pretty new at this whole 'doing-the-right-thing' business," he said.

"Mm-hmm."

"So you'd be helping me out a lot," he hissed, "if you'd stop doing that."

Rhea froze. "I'm sorry."

"Don't be sorry." He pulled his leg out from under hers, then nudged her over a bit. "Just save it for . . . later . . . when I'll be free to . . ."

"Okay, okay." She laughed and rolled onto her back. "I have to get up anyway."

"What for?" He was already reaching for her, but she ducked out the other side of the bed and scrambled to find her drawers.

"I have a business to run."

Deacon sat bolt up in bed, sucked in a breath and stared straight at her, his hand resting across his bandage.

"You're not seriously going to open the store today?"

"Of course." She snapped her dress up off the floor, shook it out and slipped it over her head.

"But what about—"

She sat down on the edge of the bed next to him and took his hand in hers.

"It's not going to get any easier by hiding out here." Weak as it was, she smiled at him. "Not that I wouldn't like to, though."

Deacon sighed and shook his head at her. "You're amazing."

"Why?" she snorted. "Because I can't seem to get out of one mess before falling headfirst into the next one?"

"Well, that too." He laughed for a moment, then stopped and looked at her with eyes as blue as a July sky. "You just don't know how to quit, do you?"

"Oh, I know *how* to quit," she said. "I've just never been very good at knowing *when* to quit."

"And you don't think now's a good time?"

"Not a chance."

He grinned a slow grin and shook his head again. "Stubborn to the core."

"So I've been told."

She pushed up from the bed and continued buttoning her dress. Without her brush, she could only imagine what her hair must look like, but she fumbled it into a braid, using her fingers as a comb, and fastened it with yesterday's ribbon.

Deacon was climbing out of bed as she finished.

"Give me a minute," he muttered.

"You don't have to come with me," she said. "In fact, you should stay in bed and rest—those wounds aren't going to heal easily."

But Deacon was already doing up his trousers. "No wife of mine is going to go to work and face the vultures of this town while I lounge around in bed. It's not right."

Rhea started to argue, then stopped. She didn't need Deacon to hold her hand through this, but it would certainly make it easier.

Chapter Thirteen

"Good morning, Ernest." Rhea spoke quietly, moving into the store ahead of Deacon. Without a word, he locked the door behind them and they made their way toward the counter side-by-side, Deacon's hand resting lightly on the small of her back.

It was an odd feeling being back at the store; it seemed she'd been away from it for years, when in fact it had been less than a full day. But everything was different now.

Ernest fidgeted with the jars of candy on the counter, moving the cinnamon-flavored sticks in front of the peppermint, then back again. He neither spoke nor looked up from the candy.

"Back there." Deacon moved behind the counter and held the curtain back for the others to pass through.

Head down and shoulders slumped, Ernest was barely behind the curtain before he started.

"I'm real sorry, Miss Rhea, but it weren't my place to tell you."

"Please." She motioned for him to sit, but he refused, choosing instead to pace the short length of the room, jamming his fingers through his hair every few steps.

Deacon followed them into the room and snapped

the curtain closed. If he was trying to intimidate the boy, it was working. Rhea flashed him a warning look, then turned back to Ernest, who continued to pace and ramble on.

"The sheriff told me you was some upset when you found out, and I can't say as I blame you, but I gotta know, Miss Rhea . . ." He stopped and looked right at her, his fingers twisting at his waist. "Are you going to fire me? I would if I was you, but there ain't no other job anyone's gonna give me."

"Ernest." Looking at him now, she began to see similarities between him and the rest of her family. Different colored hair and eyes, but there was something in the way he tipped his head, something in his stance that was suddenly so much like Colin.

So much like their father.

"I'm gonna have to move Ma to another town somewhere, I guess." He didn't seem to be speaking to either Rhea or Deacon anymore, but more to the walls. "Prob'ly should've done that before now, but . . ."

Ernest slumped back against the wall and moaned. "Polly."

Deacon leaned close to Rhea. "You better say something or the boy's going to have a heart seizure."

With a quick nod and a smile, she stepped toward the fretting young man—her brother—and reached out her hand.

"Ernest," she said. "I'm not going to fire you, for goodness sake."

He looked up at her and frowned. "You're not?"

"Have you done anything that would give me reason to?"

"Well, no, ma'am, but the sheriff said—"

"Yes, I know what he said, and he's right. I was upset." She squeezed his hand between her own. "And

I'm going to be upset for a long time to come, but that has nothing to do with your job here at the store."

"What about . . . I mean . . ." He stared at their hands and chewed his bottom lip. "I just figured what with it bein' my ma and all . . ."

Rhea stiffened until Deacon eased up behind her and set his hand on her hip.

"What they did was wrong, Ernest, but you're not any more to blame than I am."

He didn't look convinced.

"I'm angry with you," she said, "but only because you didn't tell me the truth."

"It weren't my place."

"Whose place was it, then?" The frustration she'd been trying to rein in came bubbling out all at once. "If it wasn't yours and it wasn't Colin's, then who do you think should have told me? *Your mother?*"

"Rhea." At the sound of Deacon's voice, she froze, mortified at what she'd just said.

"I'm sorry."

A loud tapping sounded on the glass window out front. Rhea's body moved on instinct, but Deacon stood between her and the curtain, his arms crossed over his chest.

"They can wait."

The tapping came again, louder this time, but Deacon just shook his head and remained where he was. This would be the second time in a week she'd opened late; she could only imagine what people were saying about that.

"Ernest." Rhea pulled the chair toward her and sank down on it. "I'm sorry. This can't have been easy for you, either. Have you always known?"

He shook his head slowly. "Ma told me after my pa . . . after he died."

Rhea's stomach sank like a stone. She'd never understood why Mr. Miller shot himself, but now it made a bit more sense. It also explained why Mrs. Miller never left their farm.

"I'm so sorry."

"Weren't your fault. Ma done what she done."

Deacon's boots scuffed the floor behind her. "You've done well by her, Ernest," he said. "Lots of boys would have taken off running by now, but you stayed."

Finally Ernest raised his head. Red streaks stained his eyes and he was a ghastly shade of gray, but he didn't cry. Thank goodness.

"No matter what she done, Mr. Deacon, she's still my ma."

The tapping on the glass came again, more insistent. Rhea didn't even turn her head this time.

He twisted his mouth to the side. "You sure you ain't gonna fire me?"

"Never." She forced a bright smile. "You sure you don't want to quit?"

"No, ma'am." He shrugged slowly. "Just don't know what to say to people now."

"Easy." She pushed up from her chair and reached for the aprons. "If they should ask me, I'm simply going to tell them how happy I am to discover I have a new brother, especially one who cares about the people in his life, who has already proven himself to be a hard worker and who is a fine young man."

Color raced up Ernest's face and settled on his scalp.

"You don't gotta say that stuff," he mumbled.

"Why not?" she asked. "It's the truth."

"But w-what if they ask you about my ma?"

Deacon stepped closer, but didn't touch her.

"I-I . . ." Rhea stopped and took in a long breath. "I don't know if I'll ever be able to forgive our parents for what they did to our families. But that doesn't mean I have any interest in speaking ill of your mother to anyone—she's been through enough, don't you think?"

The boy nodded and accepted the apron she held out to him.

"Can we open now?" Her question was directed more toward Deacon, in jest, but Ernest was the one who nodded.

He sniffed a few times as he tied his apron, then breathed deeply and stepped through the curtain. Rhea turned to follow, but Deacon blocked her again.

"You really are an amazing woman." He cupped her face in his palm and smiled down at her. "He's lucky to have you for a sister."

She chuckled quietly. "Somehow I doubt Colin would say the same thing."

"Colin's an imbecile."

"Miss Rhea?" Ernest's voice beckoned from the front of the store. "The sheriff's here to see you."

"Speak of the devil." Deacon grinned wickedly, but Rhea didn't smile back.

"I don't know if I can talk to him right now," she said, taking a few steps backward. "It's too soon."

Deacon caught her hand and pulled her back to him. "How much worse can it get at this point?"

She didn't answer.

"I'll stay right beside you."

She still didn't speak, but she nodded briefly and let him lead her out front. Ernest was taking stock of the tools, his back to the room, and Colin stood just inside the door, as though taking one more step would be too much for him.

"Colin." Deacon dipped a nod at him, but Colin didn't respond.

He looked about as grim as Rhea had ever seen and

for a moment, she considered running, but the only way out was through the backroom to the upstairs room, and she wasn't nearly ready to go back up there yet.

"I've got news."

"About what?" Deacon's hand squeezed hers tighter.

Though he answered Deacon's question, Colin kept his gaze fixed solely on Rhea. "The judge."

"What's the news?" Again, Deacon's question.

Colin frowned, flashed a pointed look at Ernest's back, then cleared his throat.

"Ernest, would you mind giving us the room for a minute?"

The boy made no sound, just turned and hurried into the backroom, pulling the curtain behind him as he went.

Colin watched him go, then swallowed hard. "He expects to arrive tomorrow."

"Tomorrow?" Rhea gasped.

Colin nodded grimly. "He'll be on the afternoon stage."

"There's no chance he'll be delayed?" Deacon wrapped his arm around her waist and pulled her close.

"Not unless the stage tips over."

Rhea looked up at Deacon, whose eyes widened as his brow shot up.

"No." Colin glared at both of them. "Don't even think about it."

"How can I even look at that man now?" What started as a small tremble in Rhea's knees quickly turned into a rumble up her spine.

Without another word, Colin yanked open the door and was gone.

"Tomorrow." How could a single word, one she'd used a million times in her life, suddenly sound so daunting? She stood staring after her brother long after he'd disappeared from her line of vision.

"Rhea."

She turned at the sound of her name and blinked up into Deacon's face. It was his face she saw in her dreams. It was his face she loved, even after she learned the truth about him. And it was his face she could look at and see through to who he really was.

More than just the devil's son, Deacon was his own man. The confidence and arrogance he put on view for everyone else was nothing more than a distraction so they wouldn't see his insecurities.

But Rhea saw them. And standing there looking at Deacon now, the answer suddenly became clear.

If he could overcome those insecurities, it might just save them both.

Deacon inhaled slowly and drew Rhea close. He seemed to do that a lot lately, but since she no longer objected, he was going to keep on doing it.

Mr. and Mrs. Worth started past the window, both openly staring inside with looks of utter disapproval.

Rhea stiffened in his arms, but he wouldn't release her. Instead, he tucked her head under his chin and held her tighter.

"Let's get naked and give them something good to stare at," he murmured against her hair.

Rhea snorted, choked, then buried her face in his shirt and laughed 'til she shook. Didn't take long to realize her shaking wasn't caused by laughter anymore; the whole front of his shirt was damp and wrinkled.

"Come on," he said once the town criers had passed. "I'm giving you the day off."

"I-I can't." She sniffed again, but didn't pull out of his arms.

"Of course you can." Pressing a kiss against the top of her head, he took her by the hand and led her toward the back, where Ernest was still hiding. He left her standing at the counter and ducked behind the curtain.

"Rhea's taking the day off," he said. "Can you manage the store by yourself?"

"No, I'm not." Rhea's voice called from the front of the store, but there was no strength behind it.

Deacon rolled his eyes and lowered his voice. "Yes, she is. Can you manage?"

Ernest nodded silently, his eyes round.

"Good. There's one other thing . . ."

"Is she all right?" Ernest asked. "She don't look very good."

"She's fine, or she will be." He could hope, anyway. "I need you to do something for her. For us."

Ernest nodded eagerly.

"Have someone pack our things upstairs and send them over to the hotel. Room four."

Another nod. " 'Course."

"And make sure it's someone who's not going to go whispering about this to everyone on the street."

"No, sir. I'll ask Polly to do it."

Deacon frowned, but before he could argue, Ernest said solemnly, "Polly would never say anything against Miss Rhea."

"Fine, then. I appreciate your help."

"And I appreciate being able to give it," Ernest said. "Don't expect anyone else in this town woulda kept me on after what's happened."

"No," Deacon agreed. "You're probably right on that."

Without another word, Deacon pushed through the curtain and headed straight for Rhea. She was standing over the button table again, sorting colors and doing a horrible job of it; reds mixed with the pink and greens in with the blue.

If it wasn't so sad to see, it'd almost be funny.

He pressed his hands over hers, easing them open until the buttons she was holding fell back to the table.

"Let's go."

"I can't." She didn't try to pull her hands away, but she didn't look at him, either.

"I know these buttons are making you crazy," he said, "but I think they can wait one more day."

"I—" After a moment's hesitation, she curled her fingers around his and smiled up at him. Fear and desperation shone through her unshed tears. "Okay."

Without giving her a second to change her mind, Deacon started tugging her toward the door.

"What about—"

"Ernest can manage."

"But—"

"He'll be fine, Rhea." Deacon stopped at the door and, though it pained him, he released her hand and let it fall to her side. "If you honestly want to stay here today, we'll stay."

She worried her bottom lip for a long moment, glancing back at Ernest, who'd made his way out front again, and then at Deacon, who stood as stoic as he possibly could.

It didn't take as long as he thought it would for her to decide. Taking one of his hands back in hers, she smiled one of her forced and painful smiles and nodded.

"Where will we go?"

"Anywhere but here."

"What will we do?"

He shrugged. "Anything. Everything."

"Don't you worry none, Miss Rhea," Ernest said. "I'll manage your store just fine."

"Yes," she answered quietly. "You've proven that enough this week, haven't you?"

Before she had a sudden attack of second thoughts, Deacon pulled open the door and led her outside, but he had no idea what to do next. Where should they go?

"Let's walk." He slipped her hand beneath his elbow and started down the street as though they were simply out for their daily stroll. No one need know it was likely their last.

Halfway down the boardwalk, Rhea pulled her hand from his arm and laced her fingers through his instead. Her thin fingers were cold between his, even after he wrapped his other hand over top.

The silence was next to unbearable. There was so much he wanted to tell her. But coward that he was, he didn't say anything. And neither did she, which was what worried him the most. When had Rhea not had something to say?

On they went, past the newspaper, the restaurant and the bank, looking for all the world as though everything was as right as rain.

Their feet moved in sync, same pace and same direction. Neither was leading, yet both knew where they were going.

Colin's animals needed tending.

Thick gray clouds rolled in from the east, bringing with them a warm breeze and the threat of a spring storm. As it grew darker, so did Deacon's mood. It was almost as if the storm were inside him, building, pushing, and there was no telling when it would let loose.

If only Rhea would say something.

"Everything will be fine tomorrow," he said quietly.

Facing forward, she nodded—barely—and pushed her mouth up into a smile, but still she didn't speak. It was the longest two-mile walk of Deacon's life.

Without so much as a pause, Rhea released Deacon's

hand and walked straight into the barn. He, on the other hand, hesitated before following her inside.

The cow's eyes grew wide as they rolled in Deacon's direction. It jerked against its tether and kicked the bucket over twice before Rhea spoke.

"Are you able to make coffee?" she asked.

Deacon shrugged and half nodded. "I think so."

"Maybe you better go do that while I get this done. Otherwise I'm likely to take a kick in the head." She tried to laugh it off, but Deacon couldn't even bring himself to grin.

The animals recognized his powers had returned and it could only be all the other distractions that kept Rhea from truly recognizing it, too. It would only be a matter of time. He'd not used them yet, but a tiny voice in his brain told him that didn't matter. He should have told Rhea about what was happening to him.

He left her alone and went to start the coffee. All he knew for sure and certain was that water needed to be boiled. After that . . .

He stood in the middle of the room, staring at nothing and seeing only her. He'd been wrong to come back and simply expect her to forgive him. He'd been wrong to let her believe the story about him and Salma. And he'd been horribly, horribly wrong to bring her into his life to start with.

She deserved so much better than him.

Learning what her parents had done only reinforced her belief that he must have done the same with Salma. And even though he'd told her different, she didn't believe him.

How could she?

Somehow he'd have to prove to Rhea that he and

Salma had never so much as held hands. It had all been a ruse, one that worked well.

Too well.

It would mean Rhea would have to speak to Salma directly, and that wasn't something any respectable lady should be asked to do. And he'd have to tell her about Lucille. He had no reason to hope she could ever see her way past what he'd done, but he hoped nonetheless.

He hoped.

He'd never seriously hoped for anything in his life, but he did so now. He was still standing there, staring at nothing, when Rhea came in and closed the door. The air crackled inside the cabin as the first snap of lightning shot across the sky.

"Coffee?"

"Oh, r-right," he stammered. "Got a little distracted." He lifted the coffeepot off the stove and filled it with water from the big bucket, the ladle shaking in his hand. When he reached for the bag of beans, Rhea stopped him.

"Don't bother." She smiled guiltily. "I don't really want any—it was just something for you to do."

"Just as well"—he grinned back—"because I have no idea what happens after the water boils."

She stepped up to the stove and pulled open the door. "Here's a hint," she said. "The water boils faster if there's a fire lit beneath it."

"Wha—"

Rhea laughed at his embarrassment as she stuffed some kindling inside the oven and lit it. The fire crackled slowly, then gained strength as she fed it bigger pieces of wood.

"We'll use the water to clean your wounds," she said, leaving the stove door open just a crack. "Sit."

"We can do it later," he said. "We need to talk—"

"No." The sound of her voice made him sit. His bandage could have waited, but Rhea couldn't. She needed something to do, someone to look after.

He slipped out of his jacket and started to work on his shirt buttons while she searched her sewing basket for another strip of cloth.

Lightning blazed outside the window, followed immediately by a low rumble of thunder.

When he started to pull the bandage away, Rhea stopped him. "I can't watch you do that again," she said quietly. "Let me."

How was he supposed to explain that the feel of her fingers against his skin was a thousand times more painful than the bandage being ripped off?

He ground his teeth and nodded, but it took her a while before she began to slowly peel the cloth away. The first layer wasn't too bad, but the bottom one had sealed almost completely to the wounds. Unlike his way of tearing it off in one quick rip, Rhea took her time, easing the cloth away slowly, using one hand to hold the cloth while the other hand pressed against his skin.

His heart slammed against his rib cage, and his lungs threatened to explode if he didn't release the breath he'd been holding.

"Sorry," she murmured, "but I don't want to open them again."

Deacon expelled the breath in a long whoosh. "It's fine."

"Liar." Her whisper breathed against his back, but though it nearly killed him, he didn't allow himself to shiver.

An eternity later, the last of the bandage came free and he sat there bare to the waist, once again dreading her reaction.

"How much do they hurt?" It wasn't pity he heard in her voice, but worry.

"They'll be fine," he said, hoping he sounded more confident than he felt.

She felt around the top shelf in the room until she found the bottle of laudanum and handed it to him. The water in the pot hadn't boiled, but it was warm enough, so she poured some into a small bowl and went to work cleaning the areas around the slash marks. It was slow work, and it seemed so much slower in the silence.

Deacon studied her face as she cleaned his sides. Her bottom lip was clamped between her teeth; she rarely blinked, but when she did, it was three or four times in rapid succession, and then nothing for a long time. Her fingers, moving gently across his skin, barely touched him, yet still managed to drive him half mad.

And everything was made twice as hard by how much her cheeks pinked each time their eyes met. At least he wasn't the only one suffering.

She couldn't finish fast enough for him. And at the same time, he would have happily sat there forever, listening to the rain splatter against the glass pane and feeling the whole cabin shudder with each slap of thunder.

"That should do it," she murmured. "But we should leave them open for a while before we bandage them again."

"I'd rather—"

The look she gave him, half warning, half pleading, froze the protest on his tongue.

"Fine," he grumbled.

She collected up the old bandage and the rest of the supplies and set them on the table. Using the same bowl of water, she took a bar of soap and scrubbed the old bandage until the stains were all but gone.

"They'll need to be changed again in a few days," she

said quietly as she wrung it out and draped it over the other chair. "You should go see Kwan at the bathhouse. He's good with healing, or you could go straight to Doc Jamieson."

Her spine was too rigid, her words too brittle. Deacon was behind her in a heartbeat, his arms around her, his chin resting on her head.

"What are we going to do?" He hadn't meant to give voice to his question, but there it was.

Rhea wrapped her hands around his arms and laughed quietly. "You're the expert on getting in and out of trouble," she said. "Don't suppose there's anyone you can summon to help delay the judge? Or better yet, take us back a year?"

He tightened his hold on her. "That's not funny, Rhea."

"I know." She leaned her head back on his chest and sighed. "I'm sorry."

"We have the rest of today and half of tomorrow," he said. "There are things I need to tell you—"

"Deacon."

"But now's the perfect time," he said. "There's no one here to distract us, or bother you with helping them find the perfect blue button."

Rhea turned in his arms, careful of his wounds, and flattened her hands against his chest.

"You're right," she said. "Now *is* the perfect time. For us."

Deacon's mouth went dry as dust. He couldn't have spoken if he tried, and Rhea used his silence to her advantage.

"We can't do anything about tomorrow," she said quietly, snaking her fingers around his neck. "But we can use the time we have now to—"

"Rhea." Her name came out as a raw plea.

"We don't know how many nights we have left, Deacon. Even if Judge Hicks agrees to marry us tomorrow, how much longer can you stay here with me?" She pulled him closer, her lips whispering against his. "Make love to me."

He shouldn't . . . it wasn't the right time, it certainly wasn't the right place, and she would probably regret it in the end.

But her fingers tickled the back of his neck, her body was pressed up against his and her lips were a breath away, waiting for him to kiss her.

She didn't have to wait long.

CHAPTER FOURTEEN

It couldn't have been more than a second, but it felt like an eternity before Deacon kissed her. This was what she needed. Talking about tomorrow wouldn't solve anything, worrying about what was to come would only make the waiting worse and doing nothing would drive her stark raving mad.

But this . . .

This was the only thing that mattered.

His body thrummed beneath her fingers, his skin warm and tempting. Leaning into him, she drew his kiss deeper and his body closer, though it was never close enough.

Rhea stretched up on her toes, but dropped just as fast when Deacon sucked in a breath.

"I'm sorry," she said. "Did I hurt you?"

"No," he ground out. "It's just the . . ."

"I'm sorry," she repeated. "I wasn't thinking." Every little movement must pain him, yet she'd been only thinking of herself. She made to step away, but before her foot hit the floor, Deacon was pulling her back.

"Take off the dress," he said, his voice harsh and strained against her cheek.

Heat rushed up her neck and across her face. She

would have had to get undressed at some point, but this wasn't how she'd thought it would happen. In her dreams, Deacon had undressed her, taking his time over each button and—oh!—just like he did with that one.

Rhea's pulse pounded in her ears as he reached for the second button, then the third. With each button he released, he pressed a kiss to the skin beneath it. By the fourth button, her chemise prevented him from reaching her skin. Not to be deterred, Deacon kissed the fabric instead, drawing his tongue down between her breasts as she gasped for breath.

He moved lower, button by button, until he was kissing her belly—once, twice. Rhea's legs threatened to buckle. She stumbled back into the table, grasping for something, anything to help her find some sort of balance.

When the last button had opened and he'd pressed his last kiss against her belly, he splayed his hands against her spine and slowly kissed his way back up to her throat.

"Oh my . . ." Her body responded on impulse, arching into his touch. She let her head fall back, savoring the sensation of his lips against her neck.

With one hand still pressed against her back, he used the other to slide one side of her dress down her arm and then the other until it slipped down her body and pooled at her feet.

Lightning crashed again, illuminating the room with its sharp fleeting white light.

Rhea wasted little time on her chemise; it was on the floor beside her dress in short order, leaving her bare from the waist up. She felt a moment of embarrassment, a moment when she wished the room was completely dark so he couldn't see her uncertainty or the way her hips jutted out like that.

That moment vanished the second Deacon's lips

found hers in a long, slow and all-consuming kiss. He eased her upright, tight against his chest. This time, there was no wincing, just long contented sighs as bare skin met bare skin for the first time and Rhea's soul melted into a pool of love.

She slid her fingers through his hair and smiled when he moaned.

"Like that?" she whispered.

He pressed another long kiss against her throat and moaned again.

"I'll take that as a yes." Her teasing was short-lived when Deacon's fingers danced up her rib cage and over her breast.

"Oh," she gasped, pushing herself deeper into his palm.

"Like that?" he teased.

She pressed her own hand on top of his as she gasped again. His hand was warm and gentle against her breast, his fingers like magic.

"I'll take that as a yes."

He caressed her with gentle strokes as his lips left a burning trail across her collar bone, then lower. His teeth grazed her other breast before the tip of his tongue sizzled against her skin. She couldn't breathe; all she could do was slide her fingers through his hair and hold on.

Thunder exploded outside. The window rattled and the dishes clattered on the shelf.

Something was threatening to explode inside Rhea, too. A strange heat rippled deep within her, radiating to every nerve, every cell of her body.

Deacon kissed his way across each breast, then down to her navel, dipping his tongue inside until she cried out.

"Deacon." Her voice was not her own; it was ragged, harsh, desperate and nearly impossible to hear over the storm outside.

"Mmm?"

"I can't stand—"

She was instantly swooped up in his arms, then settled on top of her quilt. Deacon leaned over her for a long minute, staring into her eyes as his fingers toyed with her hair.

"Damn, you're beautiful."

If she hadn't already been burning hot, Rhea was certain she would have ignited right there.

"You are," he said. "Let me look at you for a minute."

"N-no," she said, trying to sit up.

"Why not?" His voice was painfully quiet.

"Because it makes me feel . . . I don't know . . ." How could she speak clearly when he insisted on trailing his finger between her breasts that way? Didn't he know . . .

"Oh." Rhea lay back on the quilt and gave in to the shivers he created with such a simple touch.

A wicked smile lifted his lips. "You don't want me looking, but you don't mind me touching?"

"No," she murmured, half wishing he'd stop looking at her that way, and half wishing he'd *never* stop looking at her that way. "I don't mind that at all."

His kiss was hard and hungry, demanding and delicious, giving her no chance to catch her breath until she was reaching for him, scrambling to pull him closer again.

He hooked his fingers into the waistband of her drawers and kissed her right earlobe. "Lift," he whispered.

Before she could draw her next breath, he'd tossed her drawers on the floor and ripped two buttons from her boots in his haste to get them off. All that was left were her stockings.

"Pull them off," he whispered.

Rhea hooked her fingers into the first one and started pushing them down her leg, but Deacon stopped her.

"No," he said, sitting up. "Do it slowly, just like the way you put them on the other morning."

"What?" She started to protest, but the look on his face—one of deep and unfulfilled hunger—made her stop. She pulled it back up her leg, then scooted off the bed.

Swallowing her embarrassment, she bent her right leg, set her foot on the edge of the mattress and began to roll the stocking down her leg, making each new turn last longer than the last.

Deacon's Adam's apple bobbed hard. By the time she reached her knee, his mouth was open slightly and he'd all but stopped blinking.

Who knew she had so much power over him? Rhea continued to roll it down, stretching over her knee and trying not to laugh at him. Halfway down her calf, Deacon finally blinked and swallowed. It was then his gaze locked on hers and she was caught.

He'd seen her laughing at him, and the look that came over his face was a mix of embarrassment and revenge.

"You think that's funny?" Before she could move, his hand wrapped around her wrist and dragged her back down to the bed. She squealed and laughed, but he didn't release her. "It's not wise to torment me, Rhea."

He straddled her hips and grinned down at her with the most wicked grin she'd ever seen.

"But you told me to," she cried.

"You didn't have to enjoy it so much," he growled over a grin, pressing her wrists to the sides of her head. He lowered his head slowly, keeping his gaze fixed on hers. Lower, lower, until he was a mere whisper away from her breast.

His breath tickled her sensitized skin, torturing a long groan from her throat. Rhea gave up struggling against his grip and tried to give him what he wanted, arching toward him, but he just laughed, low in his throat.

"Oh, no. Not yet." He blew a soft breath over the tip of one breast, then the other. His tongue moved in slow, agonizing circles all around it, barely touching, yet somehow leaving a trail of fire in his wake.

"Ohhh."

Again and again, he teased her, touching but not touching, tasting but not tasting, until he'd driven them both to the brink of insanity. Then, with a long moan, he gave in to what they were both desperate for and took her full in his mouth.

She dragged her hands out of his grip and fisted them in his hair. God help her if he tried to move . . . but move he did, right over to her other breast.

A long building rumble thundered outside, then another.

Burning hot and unable to lie still, Rhea's hands were everywhere: in his hair, on his shoulders, bunching the blanket beside her. Deacon was a man starved, and she was the feast he'd been waiting for. Not an inch of her face went unkissed; not a hair on her head went untouched.

Still, she needed more. The heat inside her burned out of control, the ache deepened and her body quivered beneath his touch, begging for more.

But how much more could she take?

Deacon lifted one of his legs and nudged it between hers until he could kneel between her thighs.

"But you're still—" Her breathing came in sharp gasps, so instead, she gripped the waistband of his trousers and tugged in a futile attempt to push them off.

He didn't hesitate. In one fluid motion, he'd shucked his trousers, as well as his boots, until he was as naked as she. The sight of him should have given her concern, but all she could do was hold her arms out to him and welcome him back.

His kisses were slow, tender strokes that matched his touch against her hip. The ache inside her moved lower, making her shift beneath him, seeking the relief only he could give. Deacon slipped his hand beneath her and lifted, just enough to press her against the length of his desire.

It wasn't enough. She needed more, but he wouldn't give it to her. Not yet.

He caressed the inside of her thighs, easing them wider. She squirmed against his touch, her moaned pleas swallowed by his kiss until he slipped his finger deep inside her.

Rhea gasped so hard it startled both of them, but he soothed her with another kiss and another touch. His finger was thick and hard, but no matter what she did, she couldn't take him deep enough to satisfy the ache.

He withdrew his finger slowly, but she arched up again, urging him back. He pressed two fingers against her, eased in, stretching her, and then eased out again.

"Dea—" She couldn't finish.

He smiled against her lips, dipping his tongue inside her mouth as his fingers dipped in the same rhythm. It was agony—sweet, delirious agony.

Nudging her wider, he lifted her hips a little and teased her with the tip of his hard length. Rhea just about came off the bed, but Deacon eased her back with a tender kiss.

Again he slid inside her, just barely, and then waited. Rhea writhed beneath him, clinging to him for fear she'd crash into something she had no idea about. Her breath was ragged, her hips thrust forward, taking him deeper, yet not nearly deep enough.

Deacon leaned over her, took her breast in his mouth and stroked it relentlessly with his tongue.

"I . . . please."

He held her hips in his hands, slipped his length almost completely out, and then in one long stroke, buried himself deep inside her.

She cried out, but held on. Her breath wouldn't come, and her heart threatened to explode out of her chest. He moved inside her, harder, deeper, pushing her to the edge of something she'd never imagined. And all she could do was wrap her legs around his waist and lift her hips higher, taking the full length of him again and again.

He buried his face into the side of her neck and let out a low growl that only spurred her on further. Moving in slow circles, she rubbed against him. The ache inside her pushed deeper, fuller, until with one final thrust, she exploded into a world of exquisite frenzy.

Deacon gasped, his whole body went rigid, and then he collapsed on top of her. She couldn't breathe, and she didn't care. All she cared about was him, buried deep inside her, and how she wished she could keep him there forever.

When he raised his head a minute later, she thought he was going to end it, but he didn't. He kissed her again, full on the lips, and then rolled to his side, pulling her with him.

"Don't—" she started to protest, but he must have read her thoughts.

"I'm staying right where I am, sweetheart," he murmured. "I just didn't want to hurt you."

"What about your wounds?"

"What wounds?" He kissed her again, held her hips

firmly between his hands and pushed into her one more time.

They lay there, wrapped only in each other's arms, long afterward. By the time the storm outside subsided, leaving the room awash in the light from the full moon, Deacon had eased the deep ache inside Rhea twice more.

"Are you all right?" Even now, fully dressed and getting ready to walk back to town, Deacon's need to touch her was overwhelming.

"I'm fine." Rhea's face pinked again as she struggled to rebraid her hair.

"Leave it down." He brushed her hands away and ran his fingers through the length of her hair, sending it cascading down her back and over her shoulders. It drove him half mad seeing it that way, with its streaks of gold making it an impossibly amazing color.

He expected her to argue, but she didn't. She simply kissed his cheek and left her hair as it was.

"Shall we go?" Her voice was too bright, her smile too forced.

"Don't do that," he said, cupping her face in his hands. "Don't pretend with me."

The smile faded until all that was left were trembling lips and scared brown eyes sparkling with unshed tears. "Sorry."

Deacon pressed his forehead against hers. "Whatever happens tomorrow . . ."

He wanted to say something comforting, something to ease the worry from her brow, but words wouldn't come. The only thing he could think to do was kiss her. He pressed his lips to hers, finding his own comfort when she kissed him back so readily.

If only her lips weren't flavored with the salt from her tears.

"We can stay here tonight if you want."

"No." She shook her head. "It's better if we don't."

"Better for whom?"

She smiled again, but at least it wasn't forced this time. She reached for his hand, and they stood for a moment in the quiet of the room.

A feeling he could only attribute as panic began to grow in Deacon's stomach. His time with Rhea was coming to an end, regardless of what happened with the judge tomorrow. Kit hadn't popped in for more than a day, and that could only mean one thing.

Trouble.

"Don't worry," Rhea said, her voice quiet. "Whatever happens, happens, and it's my fault entirely."

"You say that like it should make me feel better."

"It should." She pulled open the door and stepped outside, waiting for him to follow. "You've done nothing except try to help, Deacon, and that means everything to me."

"A lot of good it did," he muttered. "You would have been better off if I hadn't come back to town in the first place."

She tucked her hand in his, and they started for town.

"A week ago, I would have agreed wholeheartedly," she said, squeezing his hand lightly. "Not now."

Deacon forced a breath past the knot in his lungs and grinned down at her. "You only say that because you've just experienced the most amazing afternoon of your life. Tomorrow you'll be dancing a different jig."

He fully expected her to make a jest at his expense, maybe comment on how it hadn't been *that* amazing, but she didn't. She kept walking, her back ramrod straight and her chin lifted high.

"It's more than that," she said. "And yours is the only 'jig' I'll ever dance."

Now what was he supposed to say to that? Jesting he could respond to, but when she spoke words like these, with her voice so certain and so strong, all he could do was grind his teeth into his tongue to stop it from blathering.

Rhea didn't need a man to speak words of love and affection to her. She didn't need him to be all sentimental and soft.

She needed a man who was strong, who would love her and look after her without suffocating her, who would listen to what she had to say even if he disagreed. And who would love her more with each new breath.

If only he weren't the devil's son, he could be that man for her. If only.

The moon bathed Rhea in its pale yellow light, making her seem almost angelic. The thought had barely registered in his mind when a rip of pain sliced across the still tender wounds on his back.

He stumbled, swallowed the gasp that jumped to his tongue and forced a quick grin for Rhea.

"Two left feet," he said. And a father who didn't appreciate him thinking of angels. The pain eased slowly, until it was nothing more than another bad memory, pushed down on top of all the others just like it.

Her hand tightened around his and they kept going, walking in silence until the lights of town came into view. She still didn't speak, but she seemed to be breathing harder and if she chewed the side of her cheek any harder, she'd soon gnaw right through it.

He bent his head closer so as not to disturb the quiet around them. "We need to do something before going back to the hotel."

"What?"

It was his turn to chew his cheek. "You're not going to like it."

"Deacon." It wasn't a warning, more of a command.

He stopped walking and took both her hands in his, forcing her to turn and look at him.

"We need to stop at the . . . saloon." There, he'd said it. And she was already shaking her head. "Rhea, listen."

She yanked hard, trying to pull her hands away, but he wouldn't let go.

"I need you to talk to Salma. Ask her anything you like."

"No." Her eyes, wild with nerves already, blazed with a whole new kind of hurt. "How can you even think to ask such a thing?"

"I'm not asking." He pulled her hands to his chest and held her firm. "I need you to know the truth, and the only way you're going to believe it is if you hear it from her directly."

She shook her head again, harder this time. "I can't go in there," she said, obviously horrified.

"You don't have to go in," he said. "I'll have her come down."

Still, she shook her head. "Don't do this, Deacon. Just let it go."

"No." He released her hands so he could wrap his hands around her upper arms; then he had to force his grip to relax, or he'd bruise her arms. "We don't know what the judge is going to say tomorrow, but . . ."

"But what?"

He let his chin fall to his chest, wishing he didn't have to tell her, wishing he could be the coward he was before and just leave.

"I'm leaving tomorrow."

"You're leaving?" she squeaked. "Already? But I thought—"

"Rhea." Why did his throat burn so much? "We both knew this was only a temporary thing."

"Yes, but—" she sputtered, stopped, and then let her shoulders slump.

"Please," he begged, "talk to Salma. She'll tell you the truth about what happened that night. And then tomorrow . . ."

Her bottom lip trembled, and she dropped her chin to her chest. Deacon released one of her arms and eased her chin back up.

He brushed the pad of his thumb across her cheek, wishing it wasn't the last time he'd be able to do it.

She stared back at him for a long minute, the moonlight illuminating the confusion and pain in her eyes.

"Okay, I'll talk with her." Her voice was low, her tone one of uncertainty. "But I am *not* going inside that saloon."

Deacon expelled the breath he'd been holding. Finally—she'd know the truth, her heart would heal and everything would go back to the way it should be.

Well, almost everything, anyway.

"Thank you," he murmured, pressing a kiss to her forehead.

They walked the rest of the way in silence, Rhea keeping half a step behind him as though that would prevent her from getting where they were going.

He led her around the back of the saloon and stopped in the shadow of the building.

"Wait here," he said. "I'll go get her." Before she could argue with him, he ducked inside the back door and went in search of Salma.

Rhea stayed where Deacon had left her, but with each passing minute, the urge to run became stronger and stronger until she couldn't stand it anymore.

Three steps out, the back door creaked open, and Deacon stepped into the moonlight with Salma.

It was little wonder the men wanted her. With a clear, olive complexion most women would kill for, eyes the color of pitch and hair to match, she was one of the most beautiful women Rhea had ever seen. The gaudy red dress she wore, however, left little to be desired.

Her ample bosom bulged over the feather-strewn neckline and though there were laces to hold the garment over each shoulder, she hadn't bothered to tie either one.

"Lemme go." Salma batted Deacon's hand away and pulled out of his reach. "What d'you want?"

Rhea didn't move; she could hardly breathe. How could she talk to this woman about something so personal? It was unthinkable! And it was incomprehensible that Deacon would even ask her to.

Thankfully, she didn't have to ask at all.

"Salma," Deacon's voice was low in the darkness. "I need you to tell Rhea what happened the last time you saw me here."

The woman snorted in very unladylike fashion. "What for?"

"Just do it. Please."

The other woman squinted toward Rhea in the shadows. "She don't look like she wants to hear anything I've got to say."

When Rhea didn't respond right away, Salma turned on her heel and started back for the door. "I got customers."

"Wait." Rhea had to say it twice before Salma heard her. She took one tentative step toward the woman, then another. "I-I'm listening."

Salma cocked a brow at her and sighed. "What d'you want to know?"

"Tell her what happ—" Deacon huffed, but Rhea stopped him in midsentence.

She took one more step, then stopped right in front of Salma. "Did you and he ever . . ."

She couldn't say it. Just the idea of it was making her sick to her stomach again.

"Oh, honey," Salma chuckled. "This man here was the easiest money I ever made."

Rhea stumbled backward, but Deacon was beside her in a heartbeat. She shook out of his embrace, not knowing what to do first—hit him or kick him.

"Salma." Deacon's growl was fiercer than anything Rhea had ever heard.

"Not that way," Salma said. "Just the opposite."

Rhea blinked hard, stepping out of Deacon's reach. "What do you mean?"

"Your fella had been in a few times, mostly with the sheriff, of course, but all they done was play cards and drink. Didn't hardly speak to anyone except themselves."

Rhea cast a quick glance at Deacon, who seemed to be standing straighter, his head nodding along with Salma's explanation.

"But the last time he came in, something was different." Salma seemed to drift back in time for a second. "Was almost like something was diggin' at him. He couldn't sit still, he wasn't drinkin' and he didn't pay no never mind to any of the games goin' on."

Rhea neither spoke nor moved. The woman was a prostitute, for goodness sake; certainly not someone she should put any stock in, yet there was something in the woman's voice that unsettled Rhea.

She was telling the truth. So far, anyway.

"Next thing I knew," Salma went on, leaning against the stair rail, "your man wants to go upstairs with me."

Sharp pain shot through Rhea's heart, but she stayed right where she was.

"He never done that before," Salma said. "But I'm always up to try new things, so we went upstairs."

She didn't mean to, but Rhea found herself stepping forward again. "What happened?"

"It was the damnedest thing." Salma shook her head and chuckled again. "He gives me a piss-pot full of money an' then ducks out the back door."

Rhea stared at her in stunned silence.

"That's the same look I had on my face," Salma laughed.

"But why . . ." Rhea turned to stare at Deacon, his face full of righteous determination. She turned back to Salma and studied the woman for a minute. "This happened months ago," she said. "How do you remember it so clearly?"

"Oh, honey," Salma fluffed her black hair and nodded. "A girl don't forget the man who pays her ten dollars to *pretend* she had sex with him."

"*Ten dollars?*" Rhea gaped. "To *pretend* you had—"

"I know!" The other woman shook her head as though still bewildered by the whole thing. "All he said was I needed to stay upstairs for a while to make it seem like we'd done it."

"But you didn't?" Rhea's mouth hung open in shock.

"Nope. Didn't even take his boots off."

"Why didn't you say something before now?" Rhea cried. "Do you have any idea what I've been thinking all this time?"

"I'm guessin' you were probably thinkin' what he wanted you to think." Salma lifted her chin indignantly. "'Sides, you never asked, did you?"

"I-I—" Rhea didn't even know what to say to that. A second later, Salma clicked her tongue impatiently and disappeared back inside, leaving Rhea to stare after her in shocked silence.

Deacon had paid this woman to pretend she'd had sex with him? The relief she wanted to feel, she expected to feel, didn't come. Instead, she was left with the gnawing question that remained unanswered: why?

CHAPTER FIFTEEN

They walked the rest of the way to the hotel in silence.

The room was dark, but someone had obviously been there. Her dresses hung on the hooks by the door, and her nightgown was folded neatly at the foot of the bed.

She didn't bother with the lamp, nor did she wait for Deacon to give her any privacy. She simply undressed in the dark, pulled her nightgown over her head and climbed into bed without so much as a word to Deacon.

It had hurt enough when she thought he'd betrayed her, but now that she knew the real truth—that he'd gone out of his way to make her believe such a horrible, horrible lie—the pain was immeasurable.

Rhea pulled the blanket up to her ear and curled up as tight as she could. For a long time afterward, the only sound was the constant tapping of Deacon's boot heels as he prowled back and forth in front of the window.

Twice he stopped, inhaled as though he was going to speak, and then didn't. The third time he stopped pacing, he finally pulled his boots off altogether. A minute later, the bed creaked beneath his weight and again as he rolled toward her. Rhea didn't move. After the day they'd spent together, the things they'd shared, she couldn't believe it was going to end this way.

But it was. She loved him, he knew it, and he intentionally set out to break her heart. And she couldn't even blame him completely because she knew it was going to happen and didn't guard against it.

From the second he'd stepped foot in her yard, she knew he'd leave again, but instead of letting her brain control her emotions, she'd given her heart full rein.

She had no one to blame but herself.

"Rhea." Her name was a plea, to forgive him, to try to understand.

She rolled away from him, hoping the meager distance would help. It didn't. It was hours later before Deacon finally fell asleep, and Rhea was able to breathe normally again.

By the time morning broke, she felt as though someone had wrung her out like a sheet on wash day, but she had to get up and out of that room before he woke up. Such was her hurry that she didn't even button her boots until she was safely locked inside the store.

Standing behind the counter, she stared out over the store she'd spent her whole life in. She'd deceived everyone in order to keep it for herself, but now, as she let her gaze roam over each section, she had to wonder why.

Her parents had deceived not only each other, but their children as well. Her brothers had helped cover up the deceit, and despite her anger, Rhea knew she was no better. She'd deceived everyone by pretending to be married. She'd used Deacon's name as her own these past months, but it had never really been hers. And now it never would be.

Deacon told her he hadn't meant to hurt her, but that was a lie. What he'd done with Salma was an intentional attempt to cause her more pain than she'd ever experienced.

Rhea sighed. After today, it wouldn't make any difference. Deacon was leaving, and even if the judge agreed to marry them this afternoon, she wouldn't go through with it. She refused to live with any more lies. And she refused to take vows with a man who wouldn't keep them.

The door opened and Ernest stepped inside, a brilliant smile across his face right up until his eyes met Rhea's.

"'Mornin', Miss Rhea," he said. "How are you feeling today?"

She almost laughed at the question. Should she tell him the truth—that she felt as though her heart had been carved out with a dull spoon?

"I'm fine, thank you, but I do think it's time you stopped calling me 'miss.'"

His face flushed and he didn't seem to know where to look. After a moment, he nodded briefly and made his way to the back for his apron. Rhea followed him.

"You're awfully happy this morning," she said warily. "What's going on?"

Ernest handed her an apron and waited for her to tie it before he spoke.

"It's Polly." He looked as though he was about to burst wide open. "I asked her to marry me, and she said yes."

It took a full two seconds for his words to settle in Rhea's brain.

"That's wonderful!" She threw her arms around him. "Congratulations!"

Ernest edged out of her hug. "Mrs. Hale's insisting on a big church weddin', so we gotta wait for Reverend Goodwin to get back before we can even set a date," he said. "But we're hopin' he's back soon, because neither one of us wants to wait another minute."

Of course they didn't. They were young and in love; everything was perfect. She beat back the cynical voice that wanted to laugh in his face and explain how imperfect love was, how easy it was to hurt each other and how easily vows could be broken.

Instead, she forced a brighter smile.

"What about Houston?"

The boy's face positively glowed. "I told her pa there weren't no man in Houston—or the great state of Texas, for that matter—who'd love his daughter more than me, and that's all he needed to hear."

"I always knew he was a reasonable man," she said. "Let's hope the reverend's back very soon."

She hugged him again and then shooed him out front so he wouldn't have to see her cry.

The more she tried to stop, the faster the tears flowed, until she finally gave up and let them run out. By the time she had regained her composure, Ernest was helping Mr. Worth find something in one of the catalogs, so Rhea was left to wander aimlessly around the store. There was always something to do, stock that needed to be tended or refilled, but her mind wouldn't focus on any of that.

All she could do was stare out the window and wait for the stage to pull up across the street.

Just after Mr. Worth left, Rhea caught sight of Deacon walking toward the store. He looked about as grim as she felt, but his stride was long and determined. As he neared the newspaper office, a small orange tabby cat crossed the boardwalk in front of him. It froze, arched its back and stalked away, hissing at Deacon.

"No." She pressed her hand over her mouth to keep from crying out. It couldn't be . . . he would have told her, wouldn't he?

Rhea fought back another sob. Of course he wouldn't. It was just one more thing he'd kept from her.

Deacon had his powers back.

When they'd gone for the ride out to the lake, the horses hadn't sensed anything because he didn't have any powers. But yesterday, out at Colin's, the cow wouldn't settle until Deacon went into the house. And now, this cat . . .

Stumbling back into the display of canned goods, she righted a few that fell, then ran straight to the backroom. She grabbed up an old metal bucket and bent over it as her empty stomach revolted against the bile, causing her to heave again and again.

Her spine ached, her throat screamed, but she couldn't stop. Ernest begged her to let him fetch the doctor, but she shook her head. She didn't want to see anyone, especially not Deacon, who strode in seconds later and immediately knelt at her side, rubbing her back.

"Don't. Touch. Me." Her voice shook more than her legs. She wiped her face with the apron, then yanked it off and threw it in the corner. "I can't believe I was stupid enough to trust you again."

"Rhea, please, Salma was telling the truth," he said, his voice sounding as shocked and desperate as hers was angry. "What can I do to make you believe me?"

"Salma?" she cried. "She might be a whore, but at least I can trust her. You—"

"What?" He actually had the audacity to look confused. "What did I do?"

"You didn't do anything, did you?" She moved slowly but steadily toward the curtain, keeping her voice to a harsh whisper. "You let me believe you'd had relations with that woman instead of just telling me the truth."

"The truth?"

"Yes, Deacon, the truth. Believe it or not, I'd rather

hear you tell me you didn't love me than leave me thinking those things about you and Salma."

"*Not love you?*" he gaped. "Why would I—"

Her heart was beating so hard, she actually thought it might beat its way up her throat.

"Because you're a coward! It's easier for you to run away than it is to stand up and tell the truth."

"I've told you the truth."

"Oh really?" She set the bucket on the floor and stood to face him. "When did you get your powers back?"

"My what?" This time he did move closer. Too close.

"Your powers." She backed up a bit more and reached for the broom. Not exactly the best weapon, but she'd use it if she had to. "You told me he'd taken them away from you."

"He did."

Rhea forced each word from her tongue with infuriated precision. "When did you get them back?"

He stopped, blinked hard and exhaled. "The cow."

"I wasn't thinking clearly yesterday," she spat, "so the stupid cow didn't mean anything to me. But the cat . . ." Rhea stopped, gulped a breath. "Were you ever going to tell me? Or was it going to be just one more of those things you needed to protect me from?"

"It was better for you if you didn't know." He looked as though he was going to topple sideways, but Rhea didn't care. Let him fall. Let him hurt.

God knew she had.

"Um, Miss . . . er . . . Rhea."

She whipped the curtain back to find Ernest standing on the other side, looking decidedly uncomfortable.

"The sheriff's here." He gestured toward the front door. "Says to tell you the stage is in."

Rhea's stomach plummeted straight to her feet. "Oh . . . I, um . . . oh."

It didn't seem possible she had more tears, yet they continued to pour down her face, so fast she couldn't wipe them away before more fell.

"Thank you, Ernest." She forced a smile through her sniffles, knowing darn well it would do nothing to ease the distress from his face. "I'm afraid I need you to mind the store again this afternoon. C-can you do that for me?"

"Of course." She'd never heard his voice so tight, and she'd certainly never seen him look at someone with as much hatred as he shot toward Deacon. "I'll be fine, Miss Rhea. Don't you worry."

"Thank you." She whirled at the sound of Deacon's footsteps and jabbed the end of the broomstick into his chest. "You can go to hell."

Inhaling a steadying breath, she pushed the broom into Ernest's hand and walked straight through the store toward Colin, who paced outside on the walk. The last thing she heard as she closed the door behind her was the sound of bones crunching, someone grunting, and then a loud crash.

She didn't look back.

All the way to the jail, neither Rhea nor Colin spoke. She had no idea what she was going to say to Judge Hicks, the man who'd helped to ruin her mother's good name; the man who held her own future in his hands.

A sob lodged in her throat. What future?

Before she could answer her own question, Colin ushered her inside and closed the door.

Judge Hicks pushed to his feet and stood awkwardly behind Deacon's desk. His black suit was covered in a thin layer of dust, and his string tie looked as though it had been loosened and retightened several times. Time had been kind to the man, leaving him with enough gray hair to look distinguished, but not old. The lines on his face were no doubt the result of his easy laughter, which had always been one of the things her family had found so charming.

Or so she'd thought.

Rhea didn't speak. She simply moved farther into the room, using all her strength to stay upright.

"Rhea," Judge Hicks said. "Well, aren't you a sight for sore eyes." His smile was uneasy, made worse by the way he plucked at the buttons on his vest.

"Judge."

He offered her the chair, which she immediately took, leaving the judge to lean his backside against the corner of the desk and Colin to stand against the adjacent wall.

"How are you?" Judge Hicks asked.

"I've had better days."

"I'm sure." The judge blinked slowly. "Obviously we have a marriage issue to discuss, but before we get into that," he said, "we should discuss your mother."

Rhea's hackles instantly shot up. "I have no intention of sitting here and discussing my moth—"

"I loved her, Rhea." The pain etched across his face as he spoke would almost have broken Rhea's heart—if there'd been anything left to break. "I know that doesn't excuse what we did, but I don't want you to think it was anything less than what it was."

"Oh, I know full well what it was," Rhea snapped. "It was both of you dishonoring my father."

The judge nodded solemnly. "As he had dishonored her so many times."

"That doesn't make it right." Fresh waves of anger and pain washed through her with such force she couldn't hold on to either one for any length of time.

"No, it doesn't." Despite how much she hated him at the moment, she had to admire the courage he had to sit there and endure her anger. "If it's any consolation,

I wanted to marry her. I begged her to leave your father, but she wouldn't. She wouldn't shame him that way."

"So instead she takes up with the first man to walk through the door?"

"Rhea." Colin's rebuke went ignored.

"It wasn't like that," the judge said slowly. "I loved your mother from the first day I met her. She loved me, too, but even after she found out about your father and the Miller woman, your mother continued to honor her vows."

"Until you convinced her differently."

"Yes," he confirmed. "I did. I pushed her until she couldn't resist anymore, and once your father's child was born . . ."

The mention of Ernest drained all the remaining strength from Rhea's body.

"I don't expect you or your brother to understand or to forgive me for what I did," the judge said. "But I will never regret one minute I spent with your mother. And to this day, I feel her loss as if she'd been my wife instead of your father's."

It took her a long time, but eventually Rhea had to offer him a grudging nod. At least he'd loved her mother. That made it a little easier to accept. Not much, but a little.

"Okay," Judge Hicks breathed, crossing his arms over his chest. "Tell me what's going on."

Rhea clamped her mouth shut until Colin prodded her on with a pointed look. What did any of it matter anymore? She wasn't about to pretend Deacon was her husband for another minute, so none of this mattered anymore.

Five minutes later, she'd retold the entire story about how she forged the marriage certificate and why.

"Seems even more foolish now"—she sniffed—

"given what I've learned about my parents and how they deceived all of us."

The judge's face remained stern. "Regardless of what your parents may have done, or didn't do," he said, "the one thing you have to believe, Rhea, is that they loved you and your brother more than anything else."

Colin rolled his eyes and snorted loudly, but the judge ignored him.

"Why do you think they tried so hard to keep this from you? They didn't want to hurt you."

"Well, they did."

"Yes," he agreed over a frown. "They did. I did. And I'm more sorry about that than anything else I've ever done, as I'm sure they both are."

"What happens now?" She shook her head and brushed away the last of her tears. "If I'd known the truth about my parents and what went on in that store, I would have gladly sold it and never gotten in this mess in the first place."

For the first time since she'd walked in, the judge actually smiled at her, then turned an angry frown on Colin.

"If memory serves," he said, "the store was willed to both of you in equal shares, is that right?"

Rhea nodded, but Colin didn't even seem to be breathing.

"As such," the judge continued, "neither one of you can sell the store without the consent of the other."

"But that means . . ." She blinked up at him, then at Colin. "Colin couldn't have sold it to the Dietrichs unless I agreed."

"That's correct."

Rhea shot out of her chair and stood toe to toe with her brother. "Did you know this?"

He didn't answer, nor did he look at her.

"You knew!" She reached up and slapped his face so

hard the sound repeated through the room for long seconds afterward. Colin didn't move, but he did finally look at her.

"I was trying to protect you," he said quietly. "I thought you'd be better off somewhere else, somewhere far away from the gossip."

The urge to slap him again was almost overwhelming. "I've made some horrible mistakes this past year," she forced out. "And I'm not proud of them. But they were my mistakes, Colin. My life, my mistakes."

"But I—"

"I know." She closed her eyes, breathed in slowly and then opened them. "But I'm not a child, and you have to stop treating me like one."

Her own words echoed through her brain until she saw the truth in them. "And I, likewise, will stop treating you like one."

The corner of Colin's mouth tightened, but he didn't respond.

"If I need your help, I'll ask. If I need your protection, I'll ask. Otherwise, my mistakes are mine to fix. Deal?"

Grudgingly, Colin finally managed a short nod.

A small wave of relief coursed through her, but it was short-lived. She still had one other thing to sort out.

She turned back to Judge Hicks. "What about the marriage certificate?"

"Well, that depends." Judge Hicks shrugged casually.

"On what?"

"On how much value your 'husband' puts on that piece of paper."

Deacon.

"It's over between us," Rhea said. "So that won't be an issue."

"I wouldn't be so sure," Colin muttered, nodding toward the window.

She followed his gaze to find Deacon peering through the window, cupping his hands on either side of his face to block the glare. The glass was too grimy to see him clearly, but there was no question it was him.

"What the—"

"Who's that?" The judge stood up and stared out the window, too.

Deacon continued to look in until his gaze locked on Rhea's. Then he dropped his hands and turned away.

"That," Colin answered, "would be the 'husband.'"

"Doesn't look like it's over for him," the judge said, his gray eyes worried. "Are you sure he won't want to press charges?"

"Yes." Rhea nodded for emphasis. "He'll be just as happy as I am to find out he's free of this so-called marriage."

"Seems odd that someone who doesn't care would be pacing outside the way he is." The judge cocked a small grin at Colin.

Before Rhea could open her mouth, the judge was out the door and ushering Deacon inside.

His bottom lip was split open, his nose had obviously been bleeding and a huge bruise had started to develop around his left eye.

She started to go to him, then stopped. His injuries were physical; he'd recover as he had so many other times. But her wounds were on the inside, and this time, her shattered heart would never heal.

"What the hell happened to you?" Colin asked, squinting at Deacon's injuries as though he'd suffered them himself.

"Ernest happened to me." Deacon walked straight

past the judge and Colin and stopped in front of Rhea. "Are you all right?"

She folded her arms over her stomach and lifted her chin. "I'm fine," she said. "And you'll be glad to know you are free of me now, unless you want to press charges against me for forging the marriage certificate."

He started to turn to the judge, but decided against it, and turned back to Rhea instead. "What about . . . how will you explain . . ."

"You?" she asked. "I won't. If anyone asks, I'll tell them what I did. If they choose not to shop in my store anymore, there's nothing I can do about that."

It was shocking to hear the confidence in her own voice, because every inch of her was trembling inside, especially as she forced out her next words.

"I don't need you anymore."

The only way to describe Deacon's expression was devastated. Her hands itched to reach for him; her heart begged her to say something, to do something to ease his torment. But her head flat out refused.

"Thank you for your help," she said quietly, stepping around him. "Given what's happened this week, I believe you've exacted enough payment from me, so we should be square now."

She pushed past Colin, who tried to slow her escape, and ran outside. Where was she going? She didn't want to go to the store, and she wouldn't go to either of the rooms she'd shared with Deacon. As usual, that left Colin's.

Step by hurried step, she found herself in the barn, sitting in the stall next to the cow's. She had no tears left. In fact, she'd never felt so completely empty in her entire life.

"I was beginning to think you'd never give up on him."

Rhea didn't need to look up to know it was Kit. The woman's voice was unlike any other, and her denim trousers scratched together as she moved around Rhea in a wide circle. One quick glance at the cow explained why it wasn't balking at Kit's presence. It seemed to be locked in its position, unable to move or blink.

"It's fine," Kit said. "I just didn't want to listen to it carry on while I'm here."

"What do you want, Kit?"

"Not a thing," she said. "I'm just here to help."

"I don't need your help," Rhea snorted, finally looking up at the other woman. "You and your brother have done quite enough, thank you very much."

"Ah, yes," she said. "My brother." She dragged the stool over and plunked down on it as though she were going to do the milking. "I'm afraid you've made him soft. He's nothing like what he used to be."

Kit wasn't the least bit put off by Rhea's silence. "There was a time, not so long ago, when he'd do whatever was asked of him, but now . . ." She shook her head and sighed. "Now he'd rather dance around the truth than just spit it out like I do."

Without even looking at Kit, Rhea could feel the other woman's gaze on her.

"Come on, Rhea," she said after a pause. "You must have questions about all of this, and knowing how Deacon feels about you, I'd wager he's too busy trying to save you from the truth, isn't he? So go ahead—ask me anything."

Kit was Deacon's sister; she could only be there for one reason, and that was to make everyone around her miserable, including, or probably especially, her brother.

And the best way to make him miserable would be to spill the secrets he'd been keeping.

Heavy footsteps sounded outside. How did he get here so fast?

"When did he get his powers back?"

"The day after Kit stood and watched me take twenty lashes in the old feed store." Deacon stepped between Rhea and Kit and stood with his feet slightly apart, his arms over his chest. If he had any hope of this going well, he needed Rhea to see him, to listen to him, not Kit.

"It could have been a lot sooner," Kit said from behind him, "if he'd just asked."

Rhea's eyes widened. "He didn't want them back?"

"No," Kit snorted. "Can you believe that?"

Wide brown eyes stared up at him in silent question. He chewed his lip for a long moment, his gaze flicking between Rhea and Kit. Telling Rhea the truth was one thing; admitting these things in front of his sister was another thing entirely.

"I wanted you to see *me*," he said. "Not the devil's son—just me. I wanted to prove to you I didn't need any of that."

"But then you took them back anyway?"

"I didn't take them." He kept his eyes focused directly on hers, willing her to believe him. "They were pushed back on me to try and tempt me to return."

Rhea's mouth opened and closed twice. Deep lines creased her forehead. "What did you do with them once he gave them back?"

"Nothing!" Kit threw her arms in the air and pushed up from her stool. "Can you believe he went through all that and then didn't even use them?"

"Why not?"

Kit tipped her head up to listen for Deacon's answer, but he didn't dare look at her. If he did, he couldn't be sure he wouldn't use his powers and send her back to Hell with one swift blow.

"I didn't need them," he said.

"I beg to differ," Kit scoffed. "One quick twist and you could have avoided the lump that boy gave you."

Rhea forced herself to blink. "You *let* Ernest do that to you?"

"I didn't *let him* do it," Deacon sighed. "But he seemed to think I had it coming, and I couldn't honestly say he was wrong."

"See what I mean?" Kit scoffed. "He never would have let anyone—especially a human—do something like that to him before."

Rhea's frown deepened. "Why did you make me believe you and Salma . . ."

"Had sex." Kit tipped her head so she could see Rhea. "Sorry—would you prefer 'had relations'?"

If she'd have given him a minute, he would have found the right words to explain, but instead, she shoved him aside and reached for the damned pitchfork. Could the woman not stand still for two minutes?

"Deacon has this . . . thing . . . for you," Kit said, trailing behind Rhea. "Always has. Our father's tried more than once to beat it out of him, but nothing's worked."

Rhea jabbed the fork into a pile of fresh straw, then leaned against it. "The scars."

"Mm-hmm." Kit nodded. "Didn't have a mark on him before he met you."

"Kit!" Deacon turned and lunged for her, but she vanished, then reappeared a few feet away.

Rhea looked as though she was going to be sick again. She gripped the fork with both hands and bent over at the waist, taking in great gulps of air.

It took Deacon a long time to find the words, and even when he did, he had difficulty getting them out.

"The first time I met you," he began, "something changed inside me. I don't know how or why, but whatever it was, it's what made me tell you the truth about who I am."

"The first of several mistakes," Kit muttered.

"Wrong," Deacon said. "It was the first right thing I'd ever done."

For less than a heartbeat, the anger and confusion vanished from Rhea's face, but it didn't stay away long.

"When I came back last summer," he said, "I knew I wouldn't be staying. I didn't know how long I had, but even so, I shouldn't have let things go as far as they did."

"Selfish beast," Kit muttered, shaking her head.

"Yes." Deacon nodded freely. "I was selfish. I wanted what I wanted, and that was all that mattered."

"You should have told me." She lifted the pitchfork and jabbed it into a spot higher up.

He nodded again.

"Why didn't you? You'd already told me who you were; did you really think I'd find it so shocking to hear you were going back to H-hell?"

Kit snorted again but they ignored her.

Deacon looked at his boots for a long time before lifting his gaze back to hers. This was it. He could take the easy route, accept his powers and run, or he could tell her everything.

"I wasn't just going back to Hell," he said. "I was being sent to do a job."

Rhea lifted a scoop full of hay, but dropped it back in the exact same spot. "What kind of job?"

"Yes, Deacon," Kit smirked. "What kind of job? Were you selling harnesses and bolts of fabrics to nosy humans?"

"Rhea." He stepped toward her, but she lifted the pitchfork and pointed it toward him.

"What job?" she repeated.

He gripped the top of the nearest stall with one hand

and rubbed his face with the other. Given what she knew about him already, nothing else should have been this difficult to tell her, yet the longer it took him to tell her, the worse he felt.

His hands fisted, relaxed, fisted again, and then suddenly the words were spilling out of him faster than he could think them.

"To help my sister steal a soul."

"Oh my . . . no. No."

"That's why I couldn't tell you I was leaving. I didn't want you to know what I was doing, or where I was going."

She shook her head and shoved out of the stall, leaving Deacon and Kit to chase after her. She ran into the chicken coop and closed the gate behind her. Instantly, the chickens went crazy, flapping and squawking and running in every different direction.

Rhea moved into the henhouse, and Deacon followed. The noise was unbearable, but before it even registered in his brain that he could have done it, Kit froze the whole flock with a flick of her hand. The sudden silence caught him off guard.

"Rhea." He took a tentative step toward her as she lifted eggs from each nest. The urge to grab her, make her stand still, was almost too much. But that was what Rhea did. Taking care of these animals was the only way she knew to think through everything else.

"No matter what happened with Lucille," he said, "I didn't think I'd ever make it back here. If I succeeded with her, I knew I could never face you again. And if I failed . . ."

Her hand paused under a hen frozen in mid-squawk. "What?" she asked.

He gripped the door frame for support as he forced each word from his tongue. "If I failed," he repeated, "I had no reason to think I'd ever see the light of another day."

"You almost didn't." Kit suddenly appeared inside the henhouse, her eyes dramatically wide.

"Either way," Deacon went on, "I was never going to see you again."

"But you're here," she murmured. "So does that mean . . ."

"I failed. Lucille fell in love, and I couldn't stop her."

"More like he gave up," Kit grunted. "But we're getting ahead of ourselves."

The shame of what he'd tried to do to his sister continued to gnaw at him. "I knew how you felt, Rhea. I knew what you expected from me, and what you hoped for, and I knew I couldn't give it to you."

Rhea's hand closed around the egg, but didn't lift it. "Did you want to?"

His throat squeezed tight, and much as it pained him, he couldn't look away from her. "More than I've ever wanted anything else."

"But then why—?"

"I couldn't tell you where I was going—" he started.

"Because he was scared," Kit finished.

"And I couldn't tell you I wasn't coming back—"

"Because he was even more scared."

"You were scared of me?" Rhea released the egg and moved closer, but not too close. "Is that true?"

Damn Kit. The last thing he wanted was Rhea finding out he was scared, but now that it was out there, he couldn't deny it.

"You were right, Rhea." He shrugged softly. "I'm a coward."

Shame splashed across her face until she couldn't look him in the eye anymore.

"It was easier for me to end it fast," he said. "I didn't want you thinking there was any hope for us, and I knew the only way to do that was to make you hate me."

"Oh, Deacon." Tears cut a crooked trail down her right cheek, but she didn't wipe them away. "How could hating you make anything easier?"

Kit cleared her throat. "Perhaps you should meet our father," she said. "A couple minutes with him and you'd understand—"

"Kit!"

"Just trying to help," she grumbled.

Deacon's shoulder lifted in a weary shrug. "The only way you can ever have the life you want is if you are free of me, and of everything you feel for me, good or bad. You said yourself you wouldn't marry a man you don't love, and as long as you had any feelings for me, your heart wouldn't be open to love anyone else." He dragged his gaze away from her and stared at the ground. "I thought if I hurt you badly enough, you'd have to hate me and that would be enough to break this . . . thing . . . between us."

"And did it?"

Kit snorted, but it took Deacon a long time before he finally shook his head.

"So, what . . . you came back to finish the job?" she choked. "You came back to hurt me more?"

"No."

"Then what?"

"I came back," he sighed, "to try to ease the pain you have in your heart." Satan's teeth, it sounded stupid now.

"And in his own," Kit added. "You've made him so weak that he feels your pain as if it were his, and in case you hadn't noticed, he's got enough pain without having to carry yours as well."

Rhea looked as though she'd been slapped. Her face blanched, her hand pressed against her chest and she slumped back against the wall.

"You feel the same pain I do?" she whispered.

"Yes."

It hurt too much to look at her. Humiliation he could deal with, but this . . . admitting his weakness to her, and knowing full well there was nothing to be done about it, was more than he could take.

He spun around and walked to the far side of the pen. Gripping the rail in both hands, he tucked his head between his forearms and sighed.

"Is there anything else?" Rhea had come out of the henhouse and now stood about halfway between it and him.

With a hard exhale, he shoved away from the fence. "No."

"Are you sure?"

"Look, Rhea." He could feel the vein pulsing in his neck. "I didn't tell you these things because I wanted to protect you."

"Protect me from what?" she cried. "From the truth?"

"Yes!" He gripped her upper arms between his hands. "You keep insisting that the truth is so great, but what's so great about it?"

He released her in a rush, shoved his hands through his hair and bent over at the waist. If it was truth she wanted, truth she'd get. And it would be her own fault if it caused her more pain.

"Here's the truth." He straightened up and began to pace in front of her, trying his best to ignore Kit, who continued to hover in the narrow doorway. "No amount of pain my father has been able to inflict on me has broken this . . . thing . . . I have for you inside."

"Stop calling it a 'thing.'"

"What else should I call it?" His mouth twisted against each word. "Love? Is this what love feels like? All this frustration and anger . . ."

Rhea sucked in a sharp gasp.

"I did what I thought was best for you, even when it meant I had to leave." He jammed his fingers through his hair as he walked. "And even when it hurt more than the whippings."

A deep frown creased against Kit's forehead. "Deacon . . ."

He ignored her and reached for Rhea. "I thought if I came back, I could make you see that I felt this . . . thing . . . for you, too. This affection. Then I could make you trust me enough to see past the lie I told you."

The strain of each word he spoke etched itself across Rhea's face.

"If I could do that, maybe I could make your heart hurt a little less. But as you've pointed out so many times this past week, I can't make you do anything, can I?"

She slammed her fists against his chest and pounded until he staggered back. "Why didn't you tell me this at the beginning?"

He sucked in a sharp breath but didn't try to stop her.

"If you'll recall," Kit cut in, sliding down the fence post until she sat in a crouch, "he tried to explain right up front, but you were too busy shooting at him to listen."

"Kit!" Rhea and Deacon's voiced blended as one.

Aside from the hammering on his chest, this was the longest he'd ever seen Rhea stand still, and the sudden realization unsettled him. When she spoke, her voice was low, quivering and weary.

"What happens now?"

"Nothing's changed." He didn't dare move closer to her in case she hit him again. "I have to go back."

"Why?" A low moan started deep in her lungs and by the time it broke loose, she was sitting in a heap with Deacon crouched in front of her.

"I'm the son of Satan," he said quietly. "I'll never be anything more than that, just as you'll never be anything less than who you are."

"But you didn't do it," she mumbled. "You didn't make my heart hurt less."

"I know, and I'm sorry." He tucked her hair back from her face and smiled, pathetic as it was. "And that's why I have to go back."

"Honestly," Kit grumped. "If Father had any idea of how many times you've . . . ugh . . . apologized to her since you arrived—"

"That's it!" Rhea fisted her hands in Deacon's shirt and struggled to stand. "You *are* sorry, aren't you?"

"More than you'll ever know."

"Then stay with me," she cried, yanking on his shirt until he staggered to his feet beside her.

"I can't."

"Yes, you can! You feel anger and pain and regret— I've seen it."

"That doesn't mean anything," Kit snorted.

"Yes, it does!" Rhea cried. "If he can feel those emotions, he can feel everything else, too." She spoke to Kit, but kept her eyes focused on Deacon's. There was a fire inside her, burning with a renewed hope. "The pain you feel isn't mine—it's yours! This 'thing' inside you is more than just affection, Deacon. It's love."

She pressed her hand over his heart and nodded. "It's inside you, and there's nothing you can do about it."

Very slowly, the clouds in Deacon's mind cleared. The pain that had wrapped itself so tightly around his heart began to loosen, and this new idea of hope he'd so recently discovered sparked to life.

He had the power now. And it was greater than anything his father had ever given him.

"Yes," he said quietly. "There is something I can do about it."

"It's too late." Kit's voice tightened. "He's coming back with me."

"But—" When her voice broke over a sob, Rhea tightened her fists around his shirt and shook him as hard as she could. "Listen to me, Deacon. You can do this."

"It's pointless to even try." Kit's voice wasn't near as steady as usual, nor was it as calm or even.

Deacon gazed down into Rhea's beautiful brown eyes and smiled. She still loved him. Despite everything he'd done, despite everything he hadn't done, she still loved him.

He could only hope she loved him enough.

"I . . . I . . ." Rhea watched the emotions float through Deacon's eyes as he looked down at her. In that moment, she saw everything she needed to see, everything she should have seen all along. He loved her, and despite his twisted ideas of what that meant, he really had tried to protect her. He'd only been doing what he thought was . . .

Wait. What was happening? Where was he going?

Without touching him, Kit was somehow forcing Deacon to move, and he didn't seem to be putting up much of a fight.

"Use your powers," Rhea cried. "Fight back."

"I'm sorry." He shook his head slowly, his mouth tipped into a tiny smile. "I have to do this."

Rhea leapt up, grasping for his shirt again, his jacket or anything she could wrap her fingers around.

"Come back," she cried. "Stay with me!"

"There'll be no coming back after this," Kit said, her

voice tinged with something—regret? Awe? Rhea couldn't say for sure.

"Rhea." Deacon's voice faded into the afternoon air. "I'll be ba—"

But he was already gone.

CHAPTER SIXTEEN

Six months later

"A re you out of your mind?" Colin came out of his chair like a shot. "It's the only way."

"No, it's not." Rhea stood on the other side of his desk, her hands fisted at her waist.

"But Ernest and Polly are moving to Houston next week," he ground out. "You'll have no one to help you—it's the perfect time to sell the store and move on with your life."

"We're not selling."

Colin pressed the heels of his hands into his eye sockets and growled like a wounded dog. "Doesn't it bother you to hear everyone whispering about you? Aren't you tired of it?"

"No," she said. "There's nothing they can say about me that hasn't already been said."

"That's the point!"

"Colin." She took her brother's hands in hers and squeezed them gently. "I know I brought it all on myself, and I'm sorry for that, but only because it's caused you embarrassment." She forced a bright smile and nodded. "You just wait. Deacon will come back, and that'll shut them all up once and for all."

"For God's sake," Colin groaned, "he's not coming back. When are you going to get that through your head?"

Tears prickled the backs of her eyes until it felt as though they were burning holes in the back of her sockets.

"It's only been six months," she said quietly. "He'll be back."

"You don't even know where he went."

Oh, she knew all right. And it ate at her day and night. She couldn't keep busy enough to stop thinking about it. In fact, Colin's animals had never been so well tended.

"It's different now," she murmured.

"No, it's not." Colin lowered his voice. "He's still not your husband."

"Deacon is my husband in every way that matters to me," she said. "If the world thinks a piece of paper signed by a judge makes him more of a husband, that's their concern, not mine."

"Can you even hear yourself?" He crossed his arms and leaned back against his desk. "A year ago, your biggest concern was saving your reputation and the family name. Now you're as much as throwing them both away."

"No, I'm not. I'm just not letting the rest of the town decide who I should be or how I should act." She waved her hands down the front of her and shrugged. "This is who I am."

Colin exhaled a loud breath and shook his head. The last few months had seen so many changes in him, she almost didn't recognize him anymore. And they had Donnelda to thank for each one of them.

After a long moment of silence, he pushed away from the desk and looked down at her with eyes full of regret.

"I think you should be prepared for the possibility that he's not coming back."

If there was a way to prepare herself for something like that, she couldn't begin to guess what it might be.

"Thank you for your concern, but I'll be fine." She hugged him tight, kissed his cheek and headed for the door. "People will find someone else to talk about sooner or later," she said. "Just pray it isn't you!"

She stepped out onto the boardwalk and took a moment to catch her breath. The street was oddly quiet, considering the number of people milling about.

They stood in various groups, talking quietly and glancing around as though expecting something to pop out of the air.

Rhea kept her head down, putting one foot in front of the other and silently praying the odd distraction would be enough to keep their attention away from her.

She was halfway across the street when she felt it: a disturbing shift in the air that made her stop and look around. Nothing. The quiet vibrated against her nerves, pushing her back into motion.

A few more steps and it came again, not so much a breeze as a definite shift.

"Rhea."

Her heart stuttered up into her throat; her brain screamed at her feet to keep moving, to move faster, but they wouldn't listen. Instead, she stood in the middle of the street, frozen in a cloud of disbelief.

The lingering crowd seemed to move as one, closing in around her like predators circling their prey.

Her name came again, carrying above the constant buzzing of whispers. "Rhea."

She turned slowly, half afraid she'd imagined it, half afraid she hadn't.

And there he was, stumbling through the crowd,

barely keeping upright and grimacing with each new step. His eyes were fixed on her, his stride determined and looking like he'd been dragged behind a wagon for the last ten miles.

Rhea clutched her hands to her stomach and forced breath into her lungs. She made no move toward him, nor did she speak. If she did either, surely she'd wake up and he'd be gone.

He kept moving toward her, stopping only when he was an arm's reach away. If she did reach out, would she touch him, or would he turn out to be nothing more than a mirage?

His clothes all but hung from his body, and if she wasn't mistaken, his shirt wasn't silk, but—could it be?— Kit's blue chambray shirt! His hair hadn't been combed in too long to tell, whiskers covered his cheeks and chin and the toe of his left boot was ripped open, leaving his sock to push out the end.

Even his eyes were different. Still as blue as the sky above, but there was something more, a look of solid determination she'd never seen in him before.

He tipped his head to the right and smiled that crooked little smile of his. "Hello, Rhea."

She forced her heart back down into her chest and laced her fingers so tight, her knuckles ached.

"Well," she answered slowly. "Look what the wind blew in. And me without my rifle."

A glint of laughter sparkled in his eyes as the crowd closed in around them, buzzing like the bloodsucking insects they were. Rhea didn't care anymore; let them buzz.

"I was beginning to think you weren't coming back," she said, fighting for control of her voice.

"Ah, sweetheart," he said, taking a small step closer. "I always come back—you know that."

Not only was he back, but he was standing there in front of the whole town, looking as if he had, in fact, died and come back to life this time.

Rhea thought she'd die right then and there if he didn't kiss her.

"But what about . . ." She lowered her voice. "Kit said you wouldn't . . . you couldn't . . ."

"Who do you think dragged my sorry hide back here?" His head barely moved, but it was enough to make Rhea look around him, back to where he'd come from. A flash of red hair was all she saw before it disappeared like the wind.

"But how—?"

"You loved me," he said. "Even when you shouldn't have, you did. And you made me realize I could . . ." He hesitated, glanced around at the crowd and then smiled down at her again. "You made me realize that *the thing* I felt for you was more than just a *thing*."

"Is that right?" She let herself smile back at him, even if it was small and quivery.

"That's right. I love you."

The oddest feeling spread through her veins. Hope mixed with anxiety, worry and confusion.

"You . . . ?"

"I do."

From somewhere behind Rhea, a woman sighed.

"You said you couldn't," she murmured.

"Ah, but you said I could." He reached to tuck her hair back, and Rhea found herself leaning into his touch. "It's what got me through every . . ."

He didn't finish, but he didn't have to. Rhea knew what he meant, and that was all that mattered. His father had tried repeatedly to beat the love out of Deacon, but he couldn't do it.

"It must have been horrible," she choked out, feeling the bile creep up her throat. "We should get you to Doc Jamieson."

Deacon pressed his fingers against her mouth and smiled. "I'll go see Kwan later. There's something else we need to straighten out first."

Deacon dropped to one knee, right there in the dirt, and grinned up at her with the most ridiculously painful smile she'd ever seen.

"I love you, Rhea. Marry me."

The buzzing crowd hummed louder, one voice carrying above all the rest. "Thought they already was married."

Rhea ground her teeth together and tried to pretend the entire town wasn't hanging on every word she and Deacon said. Mrs. Foster would no doubt chew on this new impropriety for years to come.

"People are staring," Rhea whispered hoarsely.

"I don't care."

And he truly looked as though he didn't care; he'd hardly given the crowd a single glance the whole time he stood there.

She grabbed the sleeve of his shirt and dragged him to his feet, but before she could release him, his other hand closed around her wrist.

"Marry me," he repeated softly, his voice barely above a desperate whisper. "Marry me, and let me be your husband for real."

The crowd seemed to be leaning in, waiting for her answer. She searched their faces for Colin, needing someone to help her, someone who would keep her thinking straight. Her brother was leaning against the post outside the jail, his mouth set in a wry smile and his arm resting around Donnelda's shoulders.

All these years he'd kept his secret, allowing Rhea to

live in her fantasy world of husbands and wives who loved each other enough to honor their vows. He'd only done it to protect her, she understood that now, even if she still didn't agree with it.

And Deacon had done the same thing.

Finally she turned back to him, gazing into those amazing blue eyes, eyes that had suddenly taken on a shade of desperation.

"You don't have to marry me," she said. "It would seem you caused quite a stir coming back the first time, so the whole town's been waiting for you to come back again."

"And no doubt gossiping like magpies," he muttered.

"True," she laughed, "but it keeps them coming into the store to see if there's been any news. And since they now see me as the poor lonely wife, they can't very well come into the store without buying something, can they? Sales are up!"

"I don't give a hot damn about sales, Rhea." A slow and easy grin lifted the corners of his mouth. "I never have."

He brushed his knuckles across her cheek in a slow and agonizing trail down to her lips. It took every bit of resolve she had left not to lean into the touch, not to kiss those fingers as they lingered against her mouth.

"I know you don't need a husband, especially a sorry excuse like me, who'll never be able to give you the children you want. Let's get married anyway."

"Deacon, please." She kept her voice low. "Can we do this somewhere a little less public?"

"No." He cupped her face in his palms and eased her chin up until their eyes met. His eyes sparkled with mirth, even as a challenge. "I'm going to make you stand right here until you agree to be my wife."

"You're going to *make* me?" She laughed lightly and twisted out of his hands, giving him a bit of a shove. The second she did it, she remembered what he'd just suffered through and made to grab for his shirt. He tripped over his own boot, staggered backward several feet and would have hit the dirt if three men hadn't raced forward and caught him under the arms.

"Don't be lettin' a skirt take that tone with you, man."

"A skirt?" she fumed, charging toward the offensive man.

Deacon straightened his shirt, grinned stupidly and tried to get between them.

"Out of my way, Deacon," she warned. "I shot you once, and I'll do it again."

Mrs. Foster gasped sharply and crumpled to the sidewalk in a heap of green satin. When no one so much as glanced her way, Colin clicked his tongue and marched over to help.

"For God's sake, Rhea."

Neither Rhea nor Deacon paid him or Mrs. Foster any mind.

"You don't have a gun," Deacon said, taking another step.

She opened her mouth, slammed it shut and wagged her finger at him instead. "You . . . you . . . ugh."

Deacon kept his gaze fixed directly on Rhea. "I don't care what any man says. You can talk to me in any tone you like, sweetheart."

"And I will!"

"I know." He laughed softly and took her hands in his. "It's one of the things I love about you."

Her anger melted with his touch. Her heart expanded with his smile. "You love me," she said.

"I do." He was suddenly too close, too overwhelming. She pulled her hands away and pressed them against his chest, but he kept coming until she was forced to back up.

"How do I know you won't leave me again?" The strength was beginning to seep out of her body, her fears threatening to swallow everything else.

"You're just going to have to trust me." Another step forward, another step backward. "I love you. You love me. And I'm not going anywhere without you."

"Deacon, I . . ." She stumbled on her next step, but he steadied her.

"Say it."

"I do. I trust you."

"And what else?" His voice was like a silky caress against her weary soul.

Flames raced over her skin. How much more humiliating could things get? Had she not embarrassed herself enough in front of all these people?

"Say it." His smile didn't tease; it didn't taunt and it didn't dare her. It just asked for the one thing he wanted most to hear, and the one thing she wanted most to say.

Every woman still standing moved closer; a few pressed their hands over their hearts, Mrs. Hale openly wept and Polly stood beside Ernest, their hands clasped together, both grinning like fools.

It was the same grin Deacon wore when Rhea first told him she loved him. It was the same grin she ached to see again.

"I love you." Hardly a whisper, her voice barely reached her own ears. She let her tears burn matching trails down her cheeks, choked out a sob and said it again, louder. "I love you."

"Say you'll marry me."

"Deacon—"

"Rhea." His eyes danced, his lips twitched, but he didn't smile. Not yet. "Say yes."

"I . . ." It was as if her heart had grown too large for her chest and was now threatening to break wide open. Deacon was there with her; nothing else mattered. Not her parents, not the store and certainly not the dozens of people standing around watching her make a complete fool of herself again.

All that mattered was him, right here, right now.

"Yes."

And just like that, the grin was back. He swung her up into his arms and kissed her full on the lips, right there in front of everyone.

Rhea melted into him, wrapped her arms around his neck and kissed him back with everything she had.

All around them, havoc ensued. Men coughed, shook their heads and spat wads of tobacco. Women wept, sighed and hugged whoever was standing next to them.

Mrs. Dietrich did nothing of the sort. She lifted her beaded reticule and brought it down on the back of her husband's head. "Why don't you ever do anything romantic anymore?"

Mr. Dietrich flushed clear up over his bald head and chased after her down the road, with Annabelle and Suzanne hurrying behind.

Deacon laughed, watching the family scurry away. "Maybe he'll keep his nosy wife at home from now on."

"I doubt it." Rhea turned his face back to her. "Say it again."

"I love you."

"And you won't ever leave me again."

"Never." He nuzzled her neck just below her ear.

"And you'll bring me breakfast every Sunday morning."

"Every Sunday morning," he repeated, nipping at her earlobe.

"And you'll help me sort the button bowl whenever I ask."

Deacon's lips froze against her skin. "The button bowl?"

"Mm-hmm." She tilted her head a little, willing his lips back to her neck.

With a wicked grin, he kissed her throat and then stared into her face again. "The button bowl's gonna cost you."

"That's okay," she chuckled. "I've got lots of money."

"Good," he growled between kisses, "because I really need some new clothes."

EPILOGUE

1885

"Mail from Houston." Deacon held the missive above his head as he walked through the door.

Rhea ran over from the stove and grabbed for it, but he dangled it higher.

"First things first." He wrapped his other arm around her waist and dragged her up against him. "Say it."

"I love you," she laughed, struggling against him to get to the letter.

"Oh no." He shook his head at her and held her tighter. Damn, but she felt good there. "Say it like you mean it."

Rhea stopped wiggling and looked right at him. She slid both hands around his neck and leaned up until they were nose to nose.

"I love you." She breathed a kiss against his jaw, and then one more against his mouth, tempting him to take more.

He sought out her lips with his own and feasted on everything she offered. But the second his arm came down, she snatched the letter and spun away from him.

She was quick, but not quick enough to escape his arms. Laughing as she ripped the letter open, Deacon wrapped his arms around her belly, pulling her back up against his chest.

Three years of marriage, and he still couldn't stop touching her. How pathetic was he?

"It's from Ernest and Polly." She skimmed the letter quickly and leaned her head back against him. "Another girl," she sighed. "Louisa Mae."

He kissed the top of her head and held her a little bit tighter. "How's Polly?"

"Everyone's doing well," she said, continuing to skim the letter for more details. "Mr. and Mrs. Hale are there to mind little Katie for a while. Sounds like Mr. Hale is enjoying Houston more than any of them . . . oh!" Her fingers flew to her lips. "Ernest has finished their new house. Isn't that wonderful?"

She twisted in his arms and looked up at him, her face awash with joy.

"Yes," he said, sweeping his thumb over her cheek. He couldn't look her in the eye, so he focused on her lips. "If I could give you a child—"

"Shh." She pressed her fingers over his mouth and smiled up at him with even more joy than she had a moment ago. "You're what I want, Deacon. You give me more than I ever dreamed of having."

"Everything but a child."

"Deacon." It wasn't sorrow he heard in her voice, and it wasn't regret. It was love, plain and simple. "I'd be lying if I said I didn't want children. I did. I do. But it's not a case of you not being able to give me one. It's a case of *us* not being able to give *each other* one."

The pain in his heart eased a little, but it didn't disappear completely. Every time news came of someone's impending arrival, that pain was sure to surface again.

"Besides"—Rhea wiggled her eyebrows as she pressed

herself against him—"If we had children, we wouldn't be able to do this right in the middle of the kitchen."

"Do what?" he asked with all the innocence he could muster, even as she reached for the buttons of his trousers.

"A little of this." She pulled his shirt out of his waistband and pressed a soft kiss against his belly. Deacon sucked in a breath but didn't move. He quite enjoyed her little bits of this.

"And a little of that." She unbuttoned his trousers, pushed them down his legs and brushed her fingers up the entire length of him.

Oh, he liked her little bits of that even more.

"Right here in the kitchen?" he rasped. "Really?"

"Really." She popped half a dozen buttons off his shirt in her haste to get it opened. "And then the sitting room, maybe in the hall . . ."

He made short work of her dress and left it pooled at her feet. "What about the bedroom?" he murmured against her breast.

"Oh yes." She pressed up into his touch and sighed. "Most definitely the bedroom."

"Good," he moaned, sliding his fingers beneath the waistband of her drawers. " 'Cuz I'm going to want a whole lot of this and that."

"Deacon?" Her fingers were in his hair, her lips on his throat.

"Mm-hmm?"

"Say it again."

"I love you, Rhea." He slipped her drawers down with one hand while he ripped her chemise off with the other.

"Swear you'll love me for the rest of time."

He pressed a kiss against her belly. "Didn't we already do that in front of the judge?"

She moved against him, slipping up on her toes, then slowly back down. "Swear it again."

"Hmm. Do that again."

Her fingers moved lower, seeking him out. "Deacon."

He swallowed a long growl, lifted her off the ground and slid deep inside her.

"I swear it by all that is holy." He waggled his brow and kissed her waiting lips. "Or not."

PAMELA CLARE

MacKinnon's Rangers: They were a band of brothers, their loyalty to one another forged by hardship and battle, the bond between these Highland warriors, rugged colonials, and fierce Native Americans stronger even than blood ties.

UNTAMED

Though forced to fight for the hated British, Morgan MacKinnon would no more betray the men he leads than slit his own throat—not even when he was captured by the French and threatened with an agonizing death by fire at the hands of their Abenaki allies. Only the look of innocent longing in the eyes of a convent-bred French lass could make him question his vow to escape and return to the Rangers. And soon the sweet passion he awoke in Amalie had him cursing the war that forced him to choose between upholding his honor and pledging himself to the woman he loves.

ISBN 13: 978-0-8439-5489-0

JANE CANDIA COLEMAN
Award-winning Author of *Tumbleweed*

He was a self-made king who couldn't survive without

THE SILVER QUEEN

RAGS TO RICHES

Augusta Tabor may have been the first woman in the Colorado silver-mining camps, but she never dreamed of making the big strike. She labored hard to support her family, while her husband went out prospecting for months at a time and gave away their store credit to just about anyone who asked. And then one of his schemes finally worked out. Suddenly they were the richest folk in Colorado Territory and Haw Tabor was elected lieutenant governor. But untold wealth and power led them to a scandal that shocked the country—a scandal that would push Augusta's strength to its limits....

Jane Candia Coleman is a six-time Pulitzer Prize nominee, three-time winner of the Western Heritage Award, and two-time winner of the Spur Award. *The Silver Queen*, based on the actual memoirs of Augusta Tabor, was a finalist for the Willa Award, named in honor of *O Pioneers!* author Willa Cather.

ISBN 13: 978-0-8439-6105-8

Bobbi SMITH

New York Times bestselling author

WANTED: The Texan

Even the most successful bounty hunter has to settle down sometime, so when a run-in with a pair of killers leaves him wounded, Josh Grady decides to make a fresh start at the Rocking R Ranch. Compared to his last job, wrangling cattle and repairing fences seem downright relaxing. But that's before he meets the boss's daughter from back East. Emmie Ryan's highfalutin manners make him testier than a rattlesnake, but he's convinced that her oh-so-proper exterior conceals the wild nature of a true Texan. All Josh needs to do is help her to forget that she's a lady...and remember that she's a woman.

"Nobody does a Western better than Bobbi Smith."
—*Romantic Times BOOKreviews*

ISBN 13: 978-0-8439-5851-5

☐ **YES!**

Sign me up for the Historical Romance Book Club and send my FREE BOOKS! If I choose to stay in the club, I will pay only $8.50* each month, a savings of $6.48!

NAME: _____

ADDRESS: _____

TELEPHONE: _____ _____

EMAIL: _____

☐ I want to pay by credit card.

☐ **VISA**   ☐ **MasterCard**   ☐ **DISCOVER**

ACCOUNT #: _____

EXPIRATION DATE: _____

SIGNATURE: _____

Mail this page along with $2.00 shipping and handling to:
Historical Romance Book Club
PO Box 6640
Wayne, PA 19087
Or fax (must include credit card information) to:
610-995-9274
You can also sign up online at **www.dorchesterpub.com**.
*Plus $2.00 for shipping. Offer open to residents of the U.S. and Canada only.
Canadian residents please call 1-800-481-9191 for pricing information.
If under 18, a parent or guardian must sign. Terms, prices and conditions subject to
change. Subscription subject to acceptance. Dorchester Publishing reserves the right
to reject any order or cancel any subscription.